THE
PRIZE

ALSO BY JILL BIALOSKY

FICTION

The Life Room
House Under Snow

POETRY

The Players
Intruder
Subterranean
The End of Desire

NONFICTION

History of a Suicide: My Sister's Unfinished Life

ANTHOLOGY

Wanting a Child, edited, with Helen Schulman

THE PRIZE

A NOVEL

JILL BIALOSKY

COUNTERPOINT
BERKELEY

Library of Congress Cataloging-in-Publication Data

Bialosky, Jill.
 The prize : a novel / Jill Bialosky.
    pages ; cm
  ISBN 978-1-61902-570-7 (hardcover)
1. Artists--Fiction. 2. Avarice--Fiction. 3. Ethical problems--Fiction. I. Title.
PS3552.I19P75 2015
813'.54--dc23
2015023052

Cover design by Michael Fusco
Interior design by Megan Jones Design

COUNTERPOINT
2560 Ninth Street, Suite 318
Berkeley, CA 94710
www.counterpointpress.com

Printed in the United States of America
Distributed by Publishers Group West

10 9 8 7 6 5 4 3 2 1

For Milton Abraham Bialosky

"For ever panting, and for ever young"

—John Keats, "Ode on a Grecian Urn"

"Our doubt is our passion and our passion is our task.
The rest is the madness of art."

—Henry James, "The Middle Years"

"Art is the window to the interior."

—Harold Darby, "The Unrealized Self"

PROLOGUE

E DWARD DARBY KNEW that an artist's work had the power to change the way in which art was perceived, for every successful artist must recreate the medium, but he did not know, each time he went to a new artist's studio, if he'd ever find it. *When you see a work of art, it will be as if everything else in relationship to it has faded. Art should transport the seer from the ordinary to the sublime.* His father, a scholar of Romantic poetry, told him this when he was a boy. But it was more than that. It was the myths artists created about their art that gave the work authority, and as an art dealer, he was part of that creation. He thought about all this as he looked for Agnes Murray's name on the directory in the vestibule of a crumbling old warehouse in Bushwick. It was a cold and gray morning in April. He hoped he wasn't wasting his time.

He climbed four staircases to her studio. Out of breath, he saw her leaning against the battered door at the end of a dim hall in paint-spattered stretch pants and a moth-eaten cardigan pulled across her chest. She clutched the ends of her sweater. She was pale. Dark circles lined her eyes. She looked as if she hadn't seen another person in months. She thanked him for coming, held out her hand, and brightened, remarking that she liked the work he showed. "I heard you can see into an artist's soul," she said.

1

He took her hand, red and chapped, with scratches and cuts, surprisingly tiny for a painter. Something about her earnestness touched him. A slant of light came through her window, and in the brightness she looked different than when she'd greeted him: an Irish beauty with corkscrew curls of red hair held back with a folded bandanna, pea-green eyes, and light freckles peppered on the slope of her nose and upper cheekbones. She was petite but emanated stature.

He traversed the studio, stiff in his blue suit and embarrassed by the squeaking of his new Italian leather shoes. Paintings leaned against the walls and others were stacked on the floor. Paint pots, brushes, and open art books cluttered a worktable. At the farthest end of the studio stood an unmade cot, and on the windowsill, a creaky hotpot and boxes of cereal. A mini-fridge hummed. Unwashed mugs with dried tea bags strung around their handles stood on top. The room smelled of paint, turpentine, and the slight whiff of her odor. Clearly she lived in the studio.

Agnes was a painter with one show under her belt. Leonard Horowitz, her manager who'd arranged this studio visit, warned Edward that at her first solo show at a small gallery on the Bowery, unable to stomach the superficial chatter of the guests who she believed had come for the party rather than for the work, and the tastemakers who, in her words, had their swords out, Agnes spent the opening in the back room nervously chipping her blue fingernail polish. She was high-strung and high-maintenance, an explosive combination.

The first painting she revealed was *Two Boys Holding Hands*. She threw off a white sheet and beamed. It depicted two boys searching in the rubble of 9/11, the eerie ghost remains of the towers behind them. Wearing pantaloons and ruffled shirts, the boys looked as if they had stepped out of another century. There was, of course, a sense of irony to their dress, to Agnes's clear reference to the great Dutch portrait artists of the seventeenth century, but there was also a solemnity to their expression that cut through that irony, transcended it. Their beautiful and tender faces reminded him of Vermeer's portraits. Though Agnes had painted a vast, sprawling scene, a history painting more in the vein of Rembrandt's *Night Watch*, the faces themselves had an intimacy and quietude that reminded him of Vermeer's portraits of women. Since his student days Edward had been drawn to the old master. He liked that Vermeer didn't try to impose on the world by painting grand scenes. He tried to describe the world as it was in moments of solitude and quiet domesticity.

It was rare that he saw a contemporary artist whose work invited comparisons to the old masters. The art world was insular, and so much of the time no one was looking back more than fifty years. Agnes clearly was.

She walked to the back of the studio where some canvases were stacked and put up a miniature, a study of a girl from the painting. Her head was slightly turned so that her gaze stared back at him. Her hair was pulled back behind a scarf. He looked at it again. The girl, with her tender and wanting eyes, reminded him of his first love, Tess. He hadn't thought of her in years.

The paintings were beautiful with an edge of something darker and deeper. In the juxtaposition of creation and destruction, Agnes brought to life in a personal way the agony of the lives that had been lost when the towers collapsed. He thought it would have been something impossible to catch and yet she had. He was convinced that this work would define a particular moment in history. No contemporary painter that he knew of had captured it yet.

He stepped closer to the canvas. "It's gorgeous. And so much feeling."

"I'm too close to the work, I can't always see it. I view the studio as a room of visual problems to be solved," she said, with a sigh. She worked until she was depleted, afraid to stop, as if there were an emptiness inside her that needed to be continually filled to validate her self-worth. He'd seen it in other artists and knew it in the vulnerability in her eyes.

She slowly revealed the other finished canvases, at first shyly, as if exposing parts of herself. Seeing how each of the fifteen paintings reflected off the others, magnifying the whole series like the prisms in a diamond, he was more convinced of her talent. He had to be the one to show it. It was the most original and daring work he'd seen in years. He asked about her process. She worked from drawings, hundreds of them. She lifted her hand to push back a spring of curls that had come loose from her bandanna and explained that from the drawings to a finished painting might take two to three years. She touched the layered paint and then leaned in to smell it. "My work is focused on 9/11 now but really I'm interested in it as one piece—our piece—of the history of human anguish. And how painting bears witness to it. I know it sounds rather grand."

She motioned him toward an old fold-up wooden chair, then scooted another chair across from him, sat down, opened her fridge, took out two small plastic bottles of Evian, and offered him one. A man's gold Rolex wristwatch slid along her willowy wrist when she raised her arm. Maybe her boyfriend's. She wound her slender legs around the leg of the chair, opened her water, and took a swig. She studied him as if she were drinking him. It made him uncomfortable. He stretched his neck awkwardly.

Realizing she'd embarrassed him, she took a breath and sighed. "I'm exhausted. I haven't left the studio in weeks. It's amazing how much isolation goes into each painting. All the doubts and second-guessing. And then voilà, something happens and it paints itself." She half smiled and cocked her head, pleased with herself.

To indulge her, or maybe because it was true, he said that the paintings felt as if she'd dug deep to make them. She turned her head up and laughed. She asked if he knew the painter Nate Fisher. Of course he did. Edward couldn't open an art journal or walk into a gallery without hearing about or seeing Nate Fisher. He was one of the most visible contemporary painters on the scene. She explained that he was still teaching at Columbia when she did her MFA and she'd been his student. He'd introduced her to Leonard, who had a knack for discovering young talent. "I was doing a lot of portraits of strangers. I was sort of lost. My first studio visit with Nate, he told me he could tell I didn't care about them. He told me to start over, to only paint what I couldn't forget." She explained that she started working from images that she was personally close to and that she'd been accused of exploiting her family's tragedy in a piece in *ArtForum*. Her grandparents emigrated from Ireland with only the clothes on their backs and her father was the firstborn American in her family. She worked from a specific visual memory of her grandparents' homeland where she saw beauty embedded with a sense of loss and regret as if from beyond the grave. She explained her interest in the idea of inheritance—of what she could give back, through her work. She had been riding her bike across the Brooklyn Bridge into the city when she saw the first tower come crashing down. She quieted, looked down, and then raised her eyes. "I'll never forget it. We have no control over what haunts us. We're helpless to it." It completely changed her life. She was afraid to ride the subway, cross bridges. "Art must capture what we're afraid of most," she said.

"Fisher again?" He smiled, not to patronize, but with affection. He'd seen artists who listened to their mentors this way before.

She nodded and smiled back. Then she tipped out of her chair and crouched in front of the painting. Again she touched the layered paint with her finger, carefully scraping off a piece of dust. "If you take me on," she said, her earlier insecurity fading, "would you make them see that my interest in anguish and destruction isn't overwrought or sentimental?"

"I wouldn't have to. It's all there on the canvas. All that complexity. Between that and your process, the references you're making . . . It's brilliant. We'll position you as a new Old Master." He stood up and returned to view the first painting again. "What makes this successful is its timelessness, the way it slips free of any attempt to nail down its meaning or objective."

She put her head in her hands and he wondered if he'd said something to upset her. She took her hands away, trembling, and explained that she hadn't slept in days. She'd been frightened to let anyone in the studio, and his reaction to the work moved her. For a moment he looked into her grainy eyes and soft prettiness and thought that if she weren't so young and childlike, he'd fall in love with her.

The next morning, Agnes Murray sent him a bouquet of white roses. *I'm so glad we found each other*, the note said. *When do we begin?*

PART ONE

1 CONNECTICUT

I T WAS A gray, overcast late Sunday in September. The windows were open in his third-floor study and a light breeze rustled the papers on his desk. He looked at the tray next to him with his pens and his water glass and the two or three books and catalogues he referred to every now and then. Each word and sentence he'd put to paper he worried over. Chosen to present at the international fair in Berlin, he was reviewing the talk he'd written about the work of Agnes Murray and several other lesser known contemporary artists. He reflected that four years had passed since he'd first met Agnes in her dusty studio in Bushwick. A lot had happened to both of them since then.

"New Movements in American Art: A Desire for Authenticity." Christ. He hoped he didn't come across as high-minded. An unsettling cry from outside disturbed him. Probably a lost cat or dog from the neighborhood. He looked at his watch to discover two hours had passed. He went back to the talk. *A new vanguard emerged in New York after 9/11 . . .* That cry again; it now sounded like a baby's whimper. He remembered how Annabel used to cry in her crib sometimes in the middle of the night. He and Holly hadn't the constitution to let her cry herself back to sleep. He'd get up, go to her, and bring her into their bed, and she'd fall asleep between the two of them, sandwiched by their warmth. The summer was over and another school year had begun. Annabel was almost sixteen. It seemed incredible.

He heard the sound again. He crossed the room to look out the front window facing the street. By the side of the road lay a dead deer, stiff, with its legs tucked back, middle gutted with dried blood. The cry was coming from the other side of the house near the woods. From the back window, he saw Holly in a plaid flannel shirt and high rubber boots rush out the kitchen door and his daughter Annabel behind her. The door slammed shut. He climbed down the three flights of stairs from his study and followed them. A spotted baby fawn lay camouflaged in a patch of leaves and thistle just at the outskirts of their garden. The fawn stretched its neck and unsuccessfully attempted to lift itself. Fear was in its eyes and the fawn was shaking. Holly peered over the fawn. She volunteered at an animal refuge, was sometimes called out in the middle of dinner or early in the morning to help rescue a fledgling or a jackrabbit or a stray dog. The fawn couldn't move.

"Maybe she's waiting for her mother?" Annabel wondered.

"If a doe hears her fawn in distress she'll come. She won't forage far. I bet the doe's been hurt too," Holly said.

"Killed," Edward added, making the connection. He mentioned the dead deer he saw from his study window on the other side of the house.

"Poor orphaned baby," Holly said. The fawn cried out again, thrusting her head in another attempt to get up. Holly asked Annabel to go into the trunk of her car where she kept a pair of gardening gloves, blanket, and injection kit. She explained that she'd sedate the fawn and take her to the refuge. The fawn trembled. "It's scared," Holly said, and stepped away to give the fawn room. An excited look was in her eyes. Holly read about animals and birds and had shelves full of journals and guides in their library. She owned copies of *Animal Behavior Desk Reference* and Sibley's and Peterson's guidebooks about birds. She subscribed to *National Geographic* and obscure animal and horse journals. She was interested in animal and bird anatomy and sixth sense, as she called it. She remarked once when she'd been called to rescue a pigeon with a torn wing that pigeons have an ability to detect the earth's magnetic field, a sense they use like a compass to navigate distance. She said a horse can pick up a rider's fear in its heart rate. She'd read her books and journals at night or in the breakfast nook, glasses perched at the end of her nose. He liked to watch her this way when she didn't know he was watching. She was a woman who knew a great deal but often said little. God only knows why she had a temple inside her where she alone could rest and restore when others of us did not. You have your art, and I have this, she said once when he caught her looking at the *Journal of Animal Science.*

Annabel returned with the items Holly had requested. Holly put on her gloves and draped the blanket over the fawn's head to calm her. Edward looked on with admiration. He'd never before witnessed his wife at work. Underneath the blanket the fawn curled her head and quieted. Holly filled the injection needle and pressed it into the fawn's side. She lifted the fawn in her arms as if she were cradling a hurt child and brought it toward her SUV. Annabel and Edward trailed behind. He opened the back hatch and laid out another wool blanket for the fawn to lie on.

"I'll go with you, Mom," Annabel offered, caught up in the drama. Edward asked if Holly wanted him to come too.

"No, stay home and finish your talk," she said, closing the hatch.

"The talk," he said, dread filling him.

"What's wrong? It will be brilliant," Holly said. "You'll be brilliant."

"Doubtful," he remarked. She had no idea what it was like to put himself out there in front of everyone who mattered in his world. It was a part of him she could never understand. Nothing frightened her.

"Look at Dad," Annabel said, laughing. "Daddy, it's just a hurt fawn." Annabel sprang onto her tiptoes to kiss him on the cheek. "I don't know what you'd do if something happened to me." Annabel was right. The thought of his wife and daughter hurt or upset caused him to stir with agitation. It would be like a tree coming up from its roots. If Holly went before him he'd be one of those lost men who padded around the house still talking to her.

Holly started to laugh and then looked at her husband and stopped. "Edward, you look peaked. Annabel, stop making fun of your father." She touched his arm. "The fawn will be okay. It's probably broken one of its back legs."

"It's not that," Edward said.

"Then what is it?"

"It's you. You're amazing." He watched his wife and daughter get into the car, and suddenly he didn't want them to leave. The light shifted and shadows fell into the grass, and silence entered him, cool and severe. He thought about getting up in the morning and traveling across the ocean to Berlin to speak in front of hundreds and the thought of it and separating from his wife and daughter filled him for a moment with panic. An owl screeched. He lifted his head to the purple sky careening into the sudden fall of evening.

E DWARD WATCHED OUT of the corner of his eye as Julia Rosenthal, an American sculptor, chatted with Charlotte Moss while they waited for cabs outside the hotel. Julia's latest work was an installation set in a darkened room with hay strewn on the floor and barbed wire lining the walls, with photographs of crematoria behind the wire. He'd seen it at the Jewish Museum.

He stood apart from the group. Though he kept to himself, he was not unfriendly. He'd spent much of his boyhood alone, an only child of a complicated marriage, and though he'd been in the business for years, he'd never acquired the talent for superficial conversation. He preferred to read art books or an absorbing biography or work of history at home with his family, rather than to dine out on chatter. But here he was at the fair in Berlin, along with a group of Americans. It wasn't as though he could skip the lecture and go back to his hotel room—though part of him wanted to. He looked at Charlotte Moss hovering over Julia. Charlotte was an up-and-comer at Matthew Marks. He wondered what they were talking about.

He thought about Holly at home. She was different from his art colleagues. Unpretentious. Earthy. Self-contained. He did not know why when he was tense it was this image he conjured up, but it was always in the garden that he pictured his wife, kneeling over her flowering plants, hair in front of her face, trowel in her gloved hand, intent, pulling out weeds or planting. She could spend all of Saturday morning running between the garden and the kitchen where she went for a glass of cold water and then out again, sometimes stopping to give him a quick kiss, the whip and heat of her hair against his neck. There was something in Holly's face, in her smile, in the way she looked at him and fussed over him, the promise of her and him together, and the children they would have that from the moment he met her had made him feel as if the first half of his life was only preparation for the bliss that would come.

Julia Rosenthal lifted her head away from Charlotte and they exchanged a quick glance. He studied her face. She wore large black-framed professor glasses that overtook her small features. From a distance she looked studious and prim but up close the look was softer. Tiny worry lines fanned from the outskirts of her eyes. She gestured with her hands as she spoke, glancing up at him with brightness in her face. He remembered meeting her twenty years ago at a reception after she won the Rome Prize, and being drawn to her then, too. Funny how one person could strike you as someone you'd like to know, and years later you felt the same tug. He watched as she tucked herself into a cab with Charlotte. So much had happened since then. For a second he thought about scooting into the seat next to her but waited for another cab with the others. Once he'd checked into his hotel and called home, the anxiety of separating from his family dissipated. In the cab, the warm breeze against his face, anticipating the morning ahead, he felt as if he'd suddenly come alive.

He entered the gallery space and found an aisle seat in one of the uncomfortable folding chairs arranged in rows. In New York there were contracts to review and budgets to approve and clients to keep in touch with. He loved what he did but as of late it was beginning to feel stale. He wanted to discover someone new whose work would excite him again and make an indelible mark. More of his work was about profits and making margins and less about the inventiveness of art and putting his stamp on it, but here he was, far away from all that.

He'd been chosen to speak in Berlin at one of the fair's select events based on the gallery's recent flurry of successful shows, including Agnes Murray's, but he wasn't sure he should have accepted the invitation. He looked down at the schedule in his lap. The seven days ahead were filled with trips to prominent museums and galleries, lectures, luncheons, and dinners. Thinking about it was exhausting.

He watched as Julia wandered in, wearing a cranberry dress and a silk scarf with a Matisse-like pattern draped around her neck. It occurred to him, watching her, that another man might find her to be ordinary, but there was something about the way she held herself that to him was sexy. She looked for an empty seat and found one in his row. Her hips brushed against him when he stood to let her scoot past. She wasn't exactly beautiful—you had to feel it to be beautiful—but there was a freshness to her look that he found compelling.

Gerhardt Strauss of Strauss and Keipen stood before the podium and everyone quieted. Thinking of his own presentation later in the week, he wondered how Strauss would command an audience.

Tall, with a crop of spiky white hair, Strauss began an informal overview of contemporary German art in the overheated gallery space. Edward's BlackBerry vibrated in his pocket; he missed another call from Holly. When their daughter was little, Holly packed her days while Annabel was at preschool with her volunteer work at the animal refuge and weekends riding at the barn. She was involved in numerous committees for animal rights. She hadn't minded his traveling. Or maybe it was that he hadn't traveled quite so much then.

His BlackBerry buzzed again. It was Georgia, his assistant at the gallery. He turned it off. Lately, when he woke in the middle of the night, his hand went for his BlackBerry. He told himself to enjoy Berlin, to take in the art and the city, to try to relax. Holly and Annabel were fine.

When he came out of his thoughts, he'd lost the flow of the lecture. "Exactly a century after the first stirrings of German Expressionism, Germany's young artists are gaining traction and creating some of the most assured art to be found anywhere. Outstanding artists abound in all areas, but it is the boldness of current German painting that is generating waves of excitement in the art world." Strauss mentioned the American painter Nate Fisher, by way of comparing his work with that of Strauss and Keipen's renowned artist Edgar Schlinder.

Alex Savan interrupted to ask a question. "Is Schlinder as popular as Nate Fisher? In America Fisher revitalized the art world after 9/11. He's become a trailblazer for other artists."

In New York, Savan was at every significant function and opening. He wore slick loafers with silly tassels without socks, pink shirts and gold cufflinks, and walked briskly into a room, gravitating to the power circle, with an air of self-importance. His wavy blond hair—a color so unnaturally yellow and shiny it looked dyed—was pushed back from his large forehead. With a dimpled, thick chin and sallow eyes, he was unpleasant to look at. Edward shook his head and sighed. Poor Savan. After he'd come to know him, he learned that Savan's parents were from a small, impoverished town in West Virginia. He'd gotten a scholarship at Princeton—he never let you forget it—and was an art handler at Christie's before he landed his entry-level position at Reinstein and climbed through the ranks. All his grandiosity was a cover. It made Edward have a soft spot for him, but he feared that Savan's compulsive need to make himself known was going to ruin Berlin. He gazed at Julia, totally engaged by Strauss's lecture, occasionally making a note in the little black Moleskine book she carried in her bag, and she gave him a knowing nod. Her fingers were slim and petite, fingernails clean and manicured with a sheer polish. His eye caught hers—he saw dark sapphires through her glasses—and she smiled at him, a half smile that freed her face of its seriousness. He wondered if she remembered that time at the Academy. It was twenty years ago. He returned her smile.

"NATE FISHER IS huge in New York. His work is brilliant." Alex held court among a group of German collectors at the reception afterward. Charlotte leaned in to listen, not one to miss out on gossip. Julia and Gerhardt, and a few others, trailed over and joined the conversation.

"I met Nate when I invited him to give a talk at Princeton," Savan boasted, never forgetting to pepper his Princeton pedigree into the conversation. The brilliant and masterful artists on his roster were, in his words, utterly devoted to him; he crowed about famous dinners he had attended and the luminaries who also had been invited; he alluded to how much money he secured for a painting, believing the higher the amount, the better the work of art. With Savan, it was impossible to tell what was true and what was fiction. Unlike Savan, Edward didn't prize money above all else, as long as his artists were happy, the gallery turned a profit, and he was able to take care of his family. And, on occasion, able to purchase an object or piece of art that lit him, on which he could gaze and dream and be transported—that was the real luxury, to be carried away.

"Nate is revolutionizing American art. No one else comes close to his self-awareness, his sense of the performative nature of it all. Don't you agree he's extraordinary, Edward?"

"Reproductions about banality. I'm not so sure." The last person he wanted to talk about in Berlin was Fisher. Since Agnes married him four years ago, the same year Edward had taken her on, she couldn't drink a cup of coffee without his approval. Having come to the party late and making up for lost time, Fisher was known as much for his work's provocation as for his partying. Once the fashionable work took off, he was quoted in the *Observer* as saying that all he could remember of the excitement was "drinking the minibar dry." In press photographs there was always an entourage of pretty women by his side. Though there was something about Nate's confidence and swagger that intrigued him, maybe even made him jealous, Edward wasn't impressed. The work was derivative and empty. Irony works only if there is genuine pain underneath it, and he didn't feel it.

Savan looked rattled, but soldiered on. "Whether you buy into it or not, Fisher is at Koons's level. And Agnes Murray—her work is totally different, but she's neck and neck with him, in terms of visibility. She's everywhere. She deserves to be; her work is totally brilliant. Edward represents her."

"Agnes Murray is good," Edward agreed, hoping his clipped answer would cut Savan off. He didn't want to encourage Savan. There was an untrustworthy air about him that made Edward not want to get too close. The last time they had drinks in the austere lobby of the Gansevoort Hotel, Savan had ordered a dirty martini, Edward was convinced, because of its sexy connotations. He smiled after he said it, stroked his chin, and salaciously popped the olive in his mouth. Edward wondered if Savan was coming on to him. Savan usually had an attractive woman on his arm, an affair that lasted for about fifteen minutes before a new girl was on the horizon, but Edward thought his heterosexuality was questionable. It wasn't that, though. Edward believed that Savan wanted to use him to gain the approval of others. At the end of the day, he knew that Savan had only his own interests at heart. Edward had to tread carefully. The art world was too insular and small for enemies.

"Gerhardt, one of yours is Colin Henning? I like his work," Edward said, steering the conversation away from Agnes.

"If you follow me I'll show you some recent paintings."

Edward walked beside Gerhardt, glad to escape. Since Murray's show Savan had been making himself known at Mayweather and Darby, Edward's gallery, whose star had risen along with Agnes's, where Edward was the managing partner of their small shop. As her dealer, he should have been glad when others—including Savan—recognized Agnes's brilliance. But when he thought about her, a wave of inexplicable anxiety followed. It wasn't that he didn't have other prominent artists in his stable, but Agnes was their crown jewel, and he felt he had to protect the relationship for the sake of the gallery.

Right before Edward had left for Europe, Agnes's new manager, Ryan Reynolds, called to tell him that she was weeks away from letting him see her work for the new show. Reynolds put him on edge. The lead-up Edward had mounted for her had been tense. She was disciplined and exacting, which meant that every detail had to be thought through and obsessed over and tweaked to perfection.

Both Nate's and Agnes's art explored the legacy of 9/11. After 9/11 many artists questioned how they could make the same work they had made before. Some were consciously aware of wanting to capture or commemorate a cataclysmic event that shaped the nation's collective consciousness. Others were more aware of their own fragility and mortality. Nate was the first New York artist to show work that reflected the attacks. Blending methods of pop and conceptual art, the paintings were representative of youthful swagger and energy—that Nate was fifty seemed to make no difference. They opened a new door for artists to approach dark subject matter. Hordes flocked to his exhibition. Every young painter wanted to emulate his style. It was slightly unfortunate for Agnes, when they met again in Rome years after she'd finished her MFA, that she was also at work on paintings—hers more classical and poetic than Nate's, but no less convincing, some thought more so—influenced by the attacks.

At Columbia she'd modeled some early work after Nate's and as her mentor he'd been an early influence. Nate was quoted in the trades after her first show saying he felt that Agnes had been his most gifted student in twenty-five years of teaching. They joked that they'd fallen in love, or lust, however you chose to categorize it, over art, but if you sorted that sentence it meant they were attracted because of their admiration for each other's work. The narcissism hadn't escaped Edward. Agnes's early work had received some recognition, but it wasn't until she'd become romantically involved with Fisher—both separating from their respective partners immediately after they returned from Rome—that her career had taken a turn. Edward suspected that each secretly competed against the other (for Nate there must have been nothing more infuriating than recognizing that his own student, twenty years younger, might be more naturally gifted), and their striving for creative excellence, power, and fame had had a positive effect on their canvases.

After taking her on, Edward attended a party in a loft on Spring Street where joints were being passed and saw the two of them, Agnes in Nate's lap, making out like teenagers on a couch the shape and color of a banana, as if acting in their own performance piece. Edward imagined them in private wrapped up in each other's thoughts, feelings, emotions all at once and it sort of thrilled him— but flaunting their attraction seemed purposely provocative. Nate broke free to chat up the new director of a posh shop in Chelsea, a stylish, lanky Brit with a fringe of dark hair around her face and the fake eyelashes of a doe, leaving Agnes alone on the couch. A look of anxious adoration lit her face when she looked at Nate. In it was an unconscious desire to want from Nate something she could never fully obtain. And it would be this suffering, Edward was convinced later, that fueled her work and gave it an aching beauty and eroticism.

Gerhardt showed Edward some of Henning's early paintings and after led him to his back office to ask in private about Agnes Murray's new work. He was interested in making an investment for a lucrative client. "Murray's historical value will depend on whether she'll be able to sustain it. What motivates her?"

Edward thought for a moment. "She says it's her father, a hotel financier with a dark past. There's a hall at Lincoln Center he underwrote. But I wonder if her ambition arises now out of a compulsion to surpass the husband."

Gerhardt stroked his chin and nodded.

WHEN THEY RETURNED, Savan was still holding court, this time talking about million-dollar deals he'd scored.

"Have you noticed that money is so much easier to talk about than art?" Gerhardt scoffed. "Some of my top collectors are prepared to buy unseen what they think will be highly competitive paintings. Not that I'm complaining."

"Murray's work? Is that what the two of you were huddled over? That should make Nate happy," Alex interjected.

"Why Nate?" Gerhardt wondered.

"He credits himself for her success."

"Instead of her gallery?" Gerhardt groaned.

Edward glanced at Julia. Her face broke into a grin, and they locked eyes. She slipped out of the gallery. Edward excused himself and quickly followed.

"Smoke?" Edward met her on the sidewalk and offered her one from his pack.

"Sure. Why not?"

He tugged at his collar. "Don't they believe in air-conditioning?"

"We *are* in Europe," she said, fanning herself with the handout and rolling her eyes. She nodded toward the gallery. "Such pretentiousness."

"The Germans take themselves seriously."

She nodded in agreement. "Is Alex Savan a friend of yours? He looks to you for approval."

"Everyone knows Savan. He makes it a point, you know."

"He's very successful, isn't he?" she said, rather wistfully.

"If you call it success."

"What would you call it, then?"

"I'm not sure there's exactly a word for it." He paused. "Horse's ass," he said, and they both laughed. "Really, though. Once you get to know him, he's not that bad."

"All that nonsense about Nate Fisher? The art world whore. He'll do anything for attention," Julia moaned. She leaned against a lamppost on the sidewalk beside them and stretched her arms, revealing her soft curves. He looked around and thought to himself that in that moment he was in love with the city, with the old-world architecture, the steins of dark beer and sausages and little turnips and white beans he'd eaten the night before. With the ornate black railings in front of townhouses and the harsh, guttural sounds of the German language he heard from passersby on the street. With the utter foreignness of it all.

"Alex Savan. I don't know," Julia continued. "He's a little too slick for my taste." She shook her head, as if she took it personally. "How does he do it? He enters a room as if he owns it."

"He listens carefully. That's his gift."

"You're more brilliant than you appear," Julia said, with a slight grin.

"Is that a compliment?" Edward lifted his chin, uncertain.

"Of course it is. You sound glum. Or jaded. I'm not sure."

"I'm not. That's my problem. I still hope to be moved." The pavement darkened and then the sun came out from behind a cloud. "We met once. Do you remember? After you got the Rome Prize."

She raised her eyes and nodded. Then she put her cigarette out in the planter. Edward noticed the understated gold wedding band on her finger.

"Why did you come?" she looked up to ask.

He put his hands in his pocket and stared at her. "To the fair? I suppose I wanted to escape for a while."

"What are you running away from?"

"It's good to have a break from the gallery. I realized on the flight over that I'm not sure I've ever known how to enjoy myself. I only serve," he said, and heat rose to his cheeks and he laughed awkwardly.

"We'll have to make sure you do. I mean, enjoy yourself. Why shouldn't you?"

He looked at her and smiled. Maybe Berlin would be okay after all.

"I suppose we should get back." She looked at her watch. "They'll be starting lunch soon."

They pushed through the revolving door, Savan, lingering, watching. Edward excused himself for the men's, and Savan swooped in and escorted Julia toward the group awaiting them. Her value had gone up once he saw that Edward had taken an interest in her. He'd probably woo her over to Reinstein before the seven days were over, Edward thought, shaking his head.

Returning a few minutes later, he canvassed the room for Julia. Savan had left her side to chat up Gerhardt. Julia strolled toward the garden behind the gallery. He threaded briskly through the crowded hall to catch up with her.

"Has Savan won you over? I saw the two of you talking."

Julia smiled. "It's amazing what flattery will do. What's more amazing is how desperate we are for it. I doubt he knows my work."

"I'm sure he does. He knows a great artist when he sees one."

"Or when someone else deems her so. I think he's lonely."

"Savan? Maybe. His clients are his best friends. Or at least he'll tell you so. And not really friends, if you ask me, since there's a contract between them."

Julia nodded. "Before. Back there. What did you mean by 'serve'?"

"I didn't mean it the way it sounded. At the gallery I'm either serving the artists I represent or the clients we're selling to. I'm not complaining about it. It's what I do best."

"You need someone to serve you."

"I don't know why I'm telling you this."

"I have that effect on people," she sighed. She thrust out her chin and shook her head, as if uncertain of whether or not she liked being a person others confided in.

They walked through the gallery doors into the courtyard. Julia's cell phone rang. She excused herself to take it and walked toward the rosebushes.

Berlin was the largest city in Germany, home of the Kingdom of Prussia, the German Empire, and the atrocities of the Third Reich. He felt its power, its magnanimity, its horrors and destruction as he looked up at the stone façade of the building and at the sharp angles and strong heights throughout the city. He thought about the birth of the German Expressionist movement before the First World War as a reaction against industrialization and about how history influenced art and that somehow he was a part of it all, or wanted to be. For years he had been waiting to lay his claim on it and thought that perhaps with the stable of artists he had invested in, artists like Agnes Murray, he was at the edge of achieving it. It was a grandiose thought, but you couldn't be good in the business without a bit of ego, and it was a rare moment when he gave himself credit for his accomplishments. He gazed at Julia huddled into her phone and smiled to himself.

He lit up another cigarette, and waited for her while the others strolled toward the garden for lunch. She was a breath of fresh air among the megalomaniacs, the seekers, wishers, and climbers.

When she returned she looked shaken. He asked if everything was okay. Her eyes filled.

"I'm fine, really," she said. "We should go."

He held out his arm and escorted her to the beer garden where Gerhardt was hosting lunch. He sat across from her at the long table, draped with a white cloth and enlivened by a centerpiece of freshly cut flowers. Once seated, Julia's mood brightened. A debate had begun about whether artists like Koons and Hirst were responding to the media-saturated culture or simply creating sensational work that would please the public. Julia mentioned that she thought it was too easy. After the plates of tender bratwurst and sauerkraut had been served, Edward watched her become intensely swept up in the conversation. Her cheeks turned pink and she talked excitedly, gesturing with her hands.

She said she'd read that Koons had hired a consultant to create an image for him. She wondered whether Fisher had, too.

"Koons has stated that there is no meaning behind his work," Gerhardt said. "Is that the case for Nate Fisher as well?"

"I'm not sure," Julia pondered. "His work strives for meaning. But it's unclear whether he's aware that the meaning is . . . well, Edward said it earlier. It's banal. You might admire it if you like kitsch."

He looked at Julia again. Her sincerity moved him. He breathed in the sharp scent of pollen and fragrant roses, sipped his wine, and leaned back in his chair. His eyes drew toward her again.

The waiter poured the coffee, and Julia stood up and excused herself. When she returned, her red lipstick was restored and her face again seemed composed. There was no sign she'd been upset earlier. She sat next to Gerhardt, instead of across from Edward, and though there was no particular reason why she would return to sit across from him, he was disappointed.

3 BERLIN

AFTER GERHARDT'S LECTURE and lunch, the Americans had a few unscheduled hours. Edward slowly walked to the Neue Nationalgalerie. Under the glow of the September sun, the air was warm and pleasant and the violet and blue pansies in the window-boxes shimmered. He admired the elaborate cornices and lead-glass windows of the prewar architecture, and as he took in the pleasing sensations he told himself it was okay to enjoy himself. Away from home, flying overseas, taking solitary walks, he had to remind himself that he was lucky to have a full life at home: a career he enjoyed, and a beautiful wife and daughter.

As he walked he thought about his father, who had spent many summers in Europe doing research. He was approaching the age at which his father died, forty-two, and it left him unsettled. Sometimes when he thought of his father tears sprang to his eyes. He had dreams in which his father was handsome and youthful, unlike the last years of his life, when his illness destroyed his mind. The medications made him lethargic and withdrawn. He couldn't work anymore. He'd studied painting in college and had put it aside and when he couldn't work he'd taken it up again. He painted the same landscape over and over again from the window in his study. He said that when he looked at his hands he didn't think they belonged to him. Eventually he left the house only for psychiatric appointments. That first winter he was ill, Edward was seventeen. He promised himself he'd do well on his final exams and be nicer to his mother if his father would return to the way he'd been before he got sick. Ice coated the windows of his bedroom, the steps to the house. The wooden floors were cold. The faint odor of sickness filled the chilly air. He refrained from putting on heavy sweaters to keep warm, and stopped hanging out with his friends, unable to find joy while his father was suffering, but none of the bargaining worked. When he was twenty-one his father died from an overdose of lithium. He could never quite put it all together.

Years before he'd gotten sick, his father took him on a trip to New York to view a collection of Keats's letters in an exhibition at the New York Public Library. He'd been working on a book about the Romantic poets, and after three years of research and writing was frustrated by his lack of progress and his inability to articulate his thoughts with the precision and clarity that had once come easily. After a long morning at the library, they took a cab to the Metropolitan Museum of Art. His father's dark hair was unkempt, and wire-rim glasses shadowed his eyes. He was an elegant, sensitive man with a thoughtful expression and delicate hands. He ranted about his department and not having enough time to work on his book but once he was taken out of himself, coming upon a painted urn in one of the Greek galleries, he brightened. He believed that there were those who sought freedom through wealth and attainment, and those who sought it in art and literature, and he hoped Edward would be in the latter camp. The urn reminded him of Keats's "Ode on a Grecian Urn." His father had been obsessed with Keats. He quoted from one of the letters he'd read at the library earlier that day. "'The

excellence of every Art is its intensity, capable of making all dis-
agreeables evaporate, from their being in close relationship with
Beauty & Truth.' This, my son, is the reason for my living," he'd
said. Edward knew, as children of brilliant parents do, that his
father was not ordinary. He was an enigma; he wondered if all
parents were to their children.

His father's ideals became Edward's benchmark for judging
a work of art. In college he studied art history and painting. He
wanted to immerse himself in art. But the solitude required was
oppressive. After a few hours of painting he couldn't wait to burst
out of the studio and take a walk in the fresh air, or see a friend.
During critiques he was more excited by his classmates' work than
his own. Artists and the inspiration behind their subjects, their
choice of medium and material, fascinated him. By his senior year
he came to realize he didn't have the constitution and talent necessary to make a livelihood as an artist, and that it wasn't so much
the making of art that moved and excited him, anyhow, but being
in the presence of it. When he first began working at the gallery he
couldn't believe he was being paid, pitiful as the salary was, to be
around art that thrilled him and to work with artists who believed
he could help them.

He walked the wide streets dotted with maples and lindens,
thinking about his father's passion for poetry and art, the ability
of writers and artists to express the inner life and elements of life
itself, and wondered what his father would think of the work he
was doing. He stopped to check the map he'd picked up at the
hotel and soon reached the Neue Nationalgalerie, where, inspired
by Gerhardt's lecture, he hoped to view some holdings of Munch,
Picasso, and Klee.

He stood on the steps before entering the museum and checked his phone. Georgia, his assistant, had sent him a message that Agnes Murray had called. He punched in the gallery number.

"She said she hoped you'd be back soon. She was feeling anxious and needed to speak to you."

Georgia filled him in on a few other business matters before they hung up. He debated whether to phone Agnes or wait until he returned to New York. He knew he held more power if he kept her at a slight distance but did not want to take any chances of alienating her. They were expecting her new work not only to boost the bottom line but to revive their cachet. It had been four years since she'd last shown. She was elusive and mysterious about the work in progress. The longer she waited to show it to Edward, the more she upped the ante. He didn't want to pressure her, but he knew that an artist in her position needed to show new work every few years to maintain her star power. The last time he'd gone to her studio she was working on one of her mural-like paintings and was dissatisfied with her figures. She said that Rembrandt together with his students produced thousands of drawings and was convinced they improved his paintings. She asked if Edward would sit for her. She made three or four quick sketches using charcoal until she was pleased with one. When the sketch was done, they looked at it together. It was different from the face he saw in the mirror. It wasn't unattractive or ugly, but it was far from handsome. It had been sketched quickly, with fierce strokes. He could make out the faint dimple of his chin and the slope of his slender nose, but it was the eyes that struck him. They were serious, dark, with formidable circles—piercing and sad. She had captured something, and as he gazed at the drawing it reminded him of the way he'd felt when he lost his father. Or when he thought too hard about himself. Or when his heart was broken.

Before going into the museum he sent May, the widow of the founder of the gallery, a message to let her know about Henning's work and that he intended to secure a group of paintings to sell at the gallery. Before his success with Agnes Murray, every time he wanted to take on a new artist's work, he had presented an analysis of numbers and market value, drawing comparisons with other successful artists working in the same vein, even though at the end of the day it was all speculative. A dealer placed a price on a piece of art, and since the market was unregulated, anything was possible. He was glad he no longer had to go through that song and dance.

The last quarter, they'd been down, and he'd had a few sleepless nights. He'd been particularly anxious about not being able to get a clear timeline from Agnes. She was dragging her goddamn feet and in the meantime they were losing money. Selling some of Henning's work would help them through the next quarter. He was in the process of selecting a new gallery to mount a show for Agnes in Berlin, and that morning, after a couple of calls before the lecture, he'd made some inroads. Now that he had decided to take on some of Henning's work and was close to closing a deal for Agnes, his time wouldn't be wasted, and he felt he could attempt to enjoy himself.

He hated having to think this way. He wanted to be able to let Agnes take her time, not to feel that his fate hinged on hers.

He tucked his phone in his pocket and walked into the museum. There was a small exhibition of Bonnard he wanted to see and he followed the signs to the gallery. Bonnard was one of his favorites. The paintings evoked a world secure and safe in its privilege and taste—a cultivated bourgeoisie in which, money, security, art, talent, and new ideas exist in peaceful harmony, a world insulated from catastrophe.

He stood before *Le petit déjeuner*. It was such a peaceful, romantic painting, full of light and mystery. He admired the exuberance in the colors and the afternoon glow from the window. He felt his shoulders loosen. He hadn't realized he'd been tense. The colors reminded him of the warm tones of red and yellow that Julia wore. He thought of her and pictured her inside the painting. She, too, seemed of another world, or in Berlin, away from his own life, she appeared so. He sat down on the bench across from the painting and then imagined himself in it with her.

4 NEW YORK

After a successful studio visit, the thing to do was to invite the artist to the gallery and begin the seduction. Relaxed in turtleneck and navy jacket, Leonard took the seat next to Agnes around a large glass table. Edward sat across from them. Leonard was a small man with soft eyes, a knowing smile, and a reputation for excellent taste. His expertise was not only in spotting young talent but in putting a particular artist with the right dealer. He and Edward had worked together before and were close friends. It was two weeks after Edward's first visit to Agnes's studio in Bushwick, when he had seen her paintings for the first time.

Agnes glanced at Leonard and he nodded for her to proceed. With a sweep of her eyes she scanned the open conference room with views into the gallery, and then, as if pleased, relaxed in her chair. She'd cleaned up for the meeting as if to set in her couture what she demanded for her work, looking more like a starving model than an artist, hair in a twist, draped in an expensive-looking peasant blouse, black slacks, and high short boots, a gloss of blackberry stain on her lips, large apricot-gold hoops in her ears, Prada bag slung over her shoulder. She asserted that her former dealer never understood her work. She didn't like the crowded way he hung her paintings and that in the catalogue he misrepresented her intentions.

"I'm quite frankly hurt by his callousness. I think there were like two reviews."

"Let's just say Morgenstein doesn't engage in the details," Leonard conceded. "He's a broad-strokes guy. We're looking for the opposite."

"You've been painting since you were a child, haven't you?" Edward pointedly asked.

She nodded. "How did you know?"

"It's all there."

"That means a lot. I never felt that Morgenstein understood me."

"How can we make the experience different for you?"

She twisted a lock of hair that had come loose behind her ear, glanced at the catalogues and printouts of excellent reviews arranged on the table to impress her, and quickly hid her smile. "I suppose if the work is as brilliant as you say, I should have all of it," she said, nodding toward the reviews. She pulled at another sprig of hair. "Exploit what you need to, that's Nate's motto," she said. "But it has to be genuine. And I don't want just anyone buying my paintings. It's hard to part from them. I'd like to approve the buyers."

"Our clients are serious art collectors."

"It isn't that *I* alone deserve to be taken seriously. It's what every serious artist deserves. Otherwise, what is the point to it all?" She pulled back her shoulders and sat tall.

"Of course it is. Tell me, where does it come from? If we're going to exploit, er, rather, authenticate you, let's begin there." Edward grinned.

She pulled down her blouse, which had crept up, and shook back her hair, content that he'd taken it upon himself to want to make her known. She explained that many of her ancestors had died in the Irish Famine or on the immigrant ships. Her father's parents had nothing when they arrived. He had started out as a doorman in a fancy building and now owned a fleet of hotels. Like many children of immigrants, she suffered from survivor's guilt and proving her self-worth through her art was the source of her bottomless ambition.

"That's interesting. My father was a scholar of Romantic poetry. That might have something to do with what I became," Edward added, more to establish a connection.

"You're Harold Darby's son?" She twirled her swivel chair toward him, impressed. "He was a genius. I read his book on the Romantic period. My father has the soul of a poet too. Our name, Murray, it's Gaelic. It means 'of the sea.' Sea master. Everything I paint is in a way for him. He's my rudder."

He crossed his arms over his chest and leaned back, pleased with himself. The meeting had gone like clockwork.

AFTER THE MEETING, Edward invited Agnes and Leonard to an expensive lunch at the Gramercy Park Café. Leonard bowed out, saying he had another meeting across town. Astor Mayweather, known as May, was the widow of an automobile heir who founded the gallery. After her husband died, she became the principal of the gallery, taking over the business side, and hired Edward to be, in her words, her eyes. Before departing for lunch, she told Edward to order the most expensive wine on the list. "You might not think these young bohemians care about expensive things. But believe me, they're voracious. Narcissism and ambition are not a good combination." She grinned. Nothing got past her.

At the restaurant, with its wood-beamed ceilings and elegant understatement, Edward heeded May's advice and ordered a penetrating cabernet from the South of France. Agnes stopped the waiter attempting to fill her glass, holding her hand over her goblet and saying she rarely drank at lunch, and then conceded, asking for a little bit. She was shapely in all the right places, but thin, almost anorexic. Food did not interest or excite her. She ordered a salad of macrobiotic greens and a side of asparagus and barely finished either dish. Her sense of pleasure derived solely from her work, as if she experienced the world only to see what elements would go into her canvas. She exuded an atmosphere of unattainability and otherworldly glow. She touched Edward. It was all so genuinely important to her.

"You're sort of a Renaissance man, aren't you? One can always tell. Nate's more of a . . . well, I don't know how to describe him. He's not an intellectual. He's more muscular. Physical. He paints with his body." She sipped her wine and blinked up at him from the rim of her glass. "If we are going to work together, then I have to be able to tell you everything. I'm worried that I'll always be seen in Nate's shadow. You're the only one I've ever said that to. I feel guilty for saying it. We're very much in love."

"When I saw your work for the first time, at your studio, I had no idea you were engaged to Fisher. The work was completely your own."

"You didn't know we were a couple? Really?"

He shook his head. It was true. He hardly read the gossip columns.

"Jesus. You're like . . . How can I say it without offending you? You're a gentleman. There aren't many like you anymore."

He didn't know whether she meant it as a compliment, but fortunately she wasn't waiting for a response. Once she started talking about her work it was hard for her to stop. Her mania manifested or resulted from her unabashed desire to be known as a complex and singular artist. She explained that her art was nothing like Nate's. She conceded that they both explored 9/11 as subject matter, but that his work was bold and colorful while hers was muted and subdued. She'd been his student, yes, but that didn't mean his work influenced her. The best teachers, she said, encouraged their students to find their own way. She looked at the lit candle sconces on the wall and then back, the flicker of the flame casting light onto her excited face. She strained her neck, flung back her hair, and looked at him carefully to be sure he understood.

"Nate has a son, Liam, from his former marriage. He's my age. I'll be his stepmother." She laughed nervously, bringing a sprig of macrobiotic greens to her lips. "Be honest. Am I committing career suicide by marrying him?" She leaned in and in her breath he smelled the wine from her stained lips. "I mean, I love Nate. But I can't risk my work for him."

"Marriage is personal," he said, because it was the right thing to say. "Your talent speaks for itself."

She flitted from Nate to give a brief lecture on the difficulty of being a woman painter. She believed it was perfectly natural for women to be the subject of paintings but to have their own work exhibited and taken seriously was another story. She mentioned Frederick Jackson. He'd been Nate's student too, a few years ahead of her at Columbia. "Do you know his work? It's like he's fucking his models with his brush. And he wins a major prize for idealizing women." She was referring to the Tanning Prize, one of the most prestigious in the art world, awarded every five years to an American artist under the age of forty. Earlier that week it had gone to Jackson. "Only winning a major prize can change the way women artists are perceived. It's why I stay away from domesticity as a subject. Did you think it was worthy of the prize—Frederick's work?"

"I can see what the judges saw in it. He has a convincing brush."

"My work is driven by compulsive and neurotic jealousy. It's terrible to admit it, but there you go. You can't imagine how many dinners I've endured with Nate and Frederick going on about this or that European dealer or museum. I need this show to work." She stroked her pale cheek with her hand and timidly licked her lips. "You understand, don't you?"

Edward eyed her assertively and nodded. "It will work."

He knew from the minute he met her that she was difficult. But she was worth it. So much of what Edward saw in the art world was good, but little seemed brilliant. Agnes's art was different. He could look at her paintings for long periods of time, continually finding new things in them, the way he liked to plant a beach chair near the waves and stare out to the horizon.

"What inspires you?" he inquired, genuinely interested, after he'd ordered a chocolate dessert for them to share. It was plated meticulously, almost too beautiful to eat, decorated with a mint leaf and carefully arranged dots of raspberry sauce.

"Inspiration?" she said, lurching her shoulders backward with disdain. "I don't paint from inspiration. I paint from necessity." She speared a tiny bite of the chocolate tart with her fork. "I'm filled with Catholic guilt. For Lent I gave up painting—it was the hardest thing to part from. I am a good Catholic. But honestly, if I can't paint I don't know who I am."

The waiter topped off their wineglasses. Later, over espresso, Agnes asked Edward a few obligatory questions about himself, inquired about his wife and his daughter, and though she barely waited to hear his reply before she turned the conversation back to herself, he didn't mind. He didn't like talking about himself and he found it interesting the way she meticulously steered the conversation so as to make sure he understood what he was getting into. She had mastered the art of passive aggression.

He asked her what other contemporary painters she admired, since it helped him to know a painter's influences and taste. She explained that she didn't go to many shows and that seeing contemporary work made her anxious. She was a little tipsy by then, having gone from "just a little" wine to half a bottle. She said she wasn't interested in hanging out with other artists and by nature she was an introvert. It was why she didn't attend art openings. She didn't have much use for friends. Her parents were her best friends growing up. She stabbed another bite of tart with her fork, paused, and put her fork down.

"Nate was my first best friend." She looked at her watch. "I need to go," she said. "He'll be waiting for me. You know, to find out what we discussed."

"Is he concerned?"

"That I've made the right decision by coming to you?"

"That's not exactly what I meant." Edward fondled his espresso cup. "Have you?" he said. He was good at this too.

"Of course I have," she laughed. "Nate's as invested in my work as I am." She shook her head and grinned. "Sometimes it's like he thinks it's his."

She excused herself to the ladies' room. He thought of something his father had once told him—*true art is born from an almost animalistic urge in the artist*. His father insisted on absolute quiet when he worked, as if their home were a sanctuary solely dedicated to the pursuit of his intellect. He walked through the world with blinders on, prizing literature and art above all else, and he believed Agnes was the same.

Agnes returned, crossed her hands, and rested them on the white-clothed table decorated with a silver saucer of sugar and spoon and a single flower in a clear vase. "There's one more thing, before we go." She gazed into the cavernous bowl of the restaurant. "It's about timing. We have to make sure that my show is mounted before Nate's next show. I want a wide berth."

"Absolutely." He asked for the check and tried to be optimistic so as not to be concerned. Her expectations were high. He hoped they wouldn't disappoint her. In the end, he could only control how they mounted the show, the marketing they'd throw behind it, and their private exchanges with collectors and dealers. The rest of it—how the work was perceived, talked about in the press, and the word of mouth that might or might not travel—was about timing and luck.

AFTER THAT FIRST lunch Edward and Agnes were in touch almost daily. They agreed on how each painting should be mounted, considered the way in which viewers would enter the room and the first painting they would see. And before he knew it, the day disappeared. The whole day was lost in Agnes's art. They chose frames together. Wrote and rewrote copy. Agnes was enthralled by the close collaboration. She loved all the attention he gave her. "What we're doing here. You have the ability to bring to life what's in my head." She had a way of sentimentalizing experience and including him in the fiction, and though Edward knew it was a fiction, it pleased him nevertheless. Like many men, he found it a thrill to make a woman happy. And to make Agnes Murray happy, well, that was something.

There was one piece she had wanted to include in the show that was gratuitous and evoked easy emotions, and Edward cautioned her against it. She became defensive, eventually acquiesced, and later acknowledged he'd saved her from embarrassment. A week later he heard her say to an assistant, who was wrapping the rejected painting for storage, that she was her own harshest critic. It was interesting to him how quickly artists forgot the curator's hand, but he let it go. Part of being a successful dealer was to be self-effacing and to allow oneself to be a mirror for the artist.

Months before the infamous show was to open—and by then they were so familiar they were finishing each other's sentences— Edward sent over the catalogue. Agnes objected to the choice of cover painting and demanded the catalogue be redone. Edward explained that the title painting wasn't necessarily the most inviting of her work and that the purpose of the catalogue was for collectors and the press. After reviewing other options, and a morning of agonizing (they'd already printed ten thousand copies), he finally persuaded her. He rang Leonard once it was sorted.

"Let me tell you something about Agnes," Leonard began. "It's the key to her psyche. She has no one but her family and Nate. *No one.* She doesn't need anyone else. When I first met her she invited me out to Spring Lake on the New Jersey shore to see her parents' house on the water. It was the most magnificent house I'd ever seen. Art filled the walls, sculptures decorated the garden. But it wasn't lived-in. Her parents have built a mausoleum for themselves. What I'm saying, man, is that she cares about no one but them. She has to control someone. And that person is you."

Though the comment disturbed him, he wasn't so sure. Yes, she was a handful, but it was his job to figure out how to handle her. The difference between Agnes and Nate was that she wanted people to genuinely admire her paintings, while Nate wanted to provoke. Edward learned to present things to her in such a way that she felt as if she'd come up with the idea. Not only was the cover an issue, she wanted to approve every sentence he wrote about her work, including the typeface and layout of the catalogue. He was used to control freaks, but Agnes was extreme.

The day before the show was to open, she came into the gallery to do a final run-through. After hours of rearranging and deciding on lighting, Nate, rough peppery stubble on his face, entered the gallery, decked in black jeans, jacket, and cashmere scarf around his neck. It was ninety degrees with one hundred percent humidity. He acknowledged Edward with a nod and looped his arm around Agnes's waist, then gave her an openmouthed kiss, as if he planned to fuck her on the gallery floor. Agnes flushed.

"I'm having lunch with Frederick around the corner. I'm late," Nate said, breaking away. "I couldn't go another minute without seeing you, baby. Come here." He brought her close again, drinking in her neck.

She laughed. "I've missed you, too," she said. "If you wait a few minutes, I'll join you."

"Can't. Frederick needs me for something. I'll call you later."

"Will you?" she said with a pout. She was disappointed.

"Of course I will. How's it going, Edward?" Nate gave him a handshake. Before Edward answered, he swaggered down the hallway toward the doors. "Hey, man," he called back. "I saw how skillfully you hung Jean Faber's last show." He must have seen the framed poster in the gallery entrance. "You took him from a solid B to an A. I didn't know he was yours." There was something in his voice, Edward couldn't exactly make it out, but he thought that maybe Nate seemed a little thrown.

After he left, Agnes smiled uncomfortably and shook her head to hide her awkwardness. "I know he's a little much. But he loves me." She paused, stepped back, and looked at her paintings mounted on the wall. "He thinks the show is going to be brilliant. Do you think he's just saying that? Being my husband. I don't know if I should trust him."

"It will," Edward said.

A few minutes later they heard again the sound of Nate's boots clicking on the gallery's wooden floors.

"Baby, come here." He beckoned with his hand for her. She excused herself and as they looked at each other the effect was as if they'd stepped onto a lofty precipice above where the rest of humanity lived. Nate took Agnes's face between his two hands and kissed the top of her forehead. He held her in his half-opened, sleepy eyes. Agnes returned his look.

"I'm sorry, baby, of course you can come to lunch." He looked at her as if she were the only person that mattered. "I'll wait for you." Nate's impression was one of stature without elegance. Every interaction was a seduction. His gift was to make you feel as if you alone existed and when his spotlight was pointed on you it made all his other shortcomings fade.

After they'd left the gallery, a wind of loneliness blew in. Edward had been so engaged with Agnes, everything suddenly felt too quiet. He thought about Agnes and Nate and wondered, as he had many times, if their interaction was genuine or curated to elicit a response.

A few days before the opening, in an interview in the *Times*, Agnes was quoted saying she had chosen Mayweather because of how moved Edward had been by the work and the way in which he had put the meaning of her work into words. "I feel like Matisse must have felt when Gertrude Stein first discovered his work."

5 HAMBURG

THE AMERICAN GROUP had flown to Hamburg to see two renowned galleries, before returning to Berlin for their last dinner. Once they landed and were congregating in the terminal waiting for the rest of the group before hailing cabs, Julia dug in her purse, taking out various items: makeup bag, brush with gum wrappers stuck in its bristles, wallet, a wad of rubber-banded envelopes, Kleenex. "I can't find my passport. I used it when we checked in and may have left it on the plane. I have to go back to the gate. How will I get home without it?" She searched her bag again.

"If we wait for you we'll be late for our first meeting in Hamburg," Tina, their escort from the German council, asserted. Tina wore the same uniform each day: plain cotton shift, in a new color, black pumps, and a string of pearls. Throughout the trip she had kept them on a tight schedule. Tina handed Julia her itinerary. "After you get your passport sorted, take a cab directly to the gallery. We'll meet you there."

Julia looked upset.

"I'll stay with you," Edward volunteered.

"Are you sure?" Julia questioned, relieved.

He nodded.

"We'd better hurry, then. What if I'm stuck in this godforsaken country?"

They walked briskly, almost running, through the overly lit airport. After taking a quick turn, Edward slipped and fell on the waxed floor and his bag tumbled. He quickly recovered and stood up. His face colored with embarrassment.

"Are you okay?" Julia said.

He picked up his bag and dusted off his pants. "I'm fine."

"Are you sure?"

"I'm fine. Really. Jesus, these floors are slick."

"I'm sorry. It's my fault, making you run like that." She brushed off the back of his jacket with her hand in an intimate gesture, and as if realizing it together they stopped and then awkwardly fumbled with their bags and continued to the gate.

When they arrived the plane doors were already shut and Julia wasn't going to be let into the cabin to check. She sat down, distraught, and fumbled in her large bag again. "I found it," she said. A huge smile lit up her face. "I'm an idiot. I've made us late for nothing." Her cheeks turned pink. "I'm not a good traveler. I'm sorry."

Edward smiled. "Well, you might want to consider another bag? It looks like you have your entire life in there."

"Thank you," she said again. "For staying." She looked around her at the unfamiliar airport filled with German signage and foreign travelers.

"I should be thanking you. I've had enough meetings with German collectors. If I hear about one more brilliant German artist . . ."

For the last five days they'd traveled in a posse, going to gallery meetings, restaurants, parties, attending lectures and receptions, where he often found himself in the back of a room, overheated, trying not to draw too much attention to himself and grateful for the cocktail hour.

Julia laughed. "I'm glad to hear you say that. After this trip, being around dealers and the business of art . . . I don't mean to sound naive, but it wasn't why I wanted to become an artist. I'm glad the council selected me for the fellowship. I'm thrilled to have my work shown here. I don't have a German gallery. But still, I'm uneasy about it."

"Your work stood out at the exhibition yesterday. You should be pleased."

"Really?" They walked swiftly with their roll-on cases behind them toward the taxi line. "When you see your work finally hung, you see the good and the bad. All the time in the studio and you miss it completely. All you can see is a succession of failures."

"People were impressed."

"I'm glad to hear that. It's hard to know." She looked at her watch. "I have to admit it's nice to be away from the group and not think about any of it. We've missed our morning appointments."

"Then how about we bow out and wander around Hamburg? We can meet up with the crew for dinner."

"Yes. Let's."

"We'll take a cab straight to the Elbe, to one of the little restaurants there, and we can pretend we're in Venice."

"WE ARE IN Venice!" Julia declared as they strolled along the riverbank after dropping off their luggage at a café where later they planned to lunch. A warm wind blew over the embankment. "Hamburg and Berlin are beautiful cities, but beneath all the beauty, Germany leaves me cold. I can't forget what happened. It wasn't that long ago, when you think about it. Sixty years."

"I understand. It must be strange. I feel it too. And I'm not Jewish."

"When I speak to a German, Gerhardt or Tina, I see guilt in their eyes. Sometimes it feels like hate. You know, the way we come to dislike those who make us feel ashamed? Or maybe I'm being paranoid. It's just that when I thought I might be stuck in Germany without my passport . . ."

"I trust your instincts. I saw it in your work yesterday. That flash of disquiet and brilliance."

"Disquiet?"

"Your work can be uncomfortable to look at. It makes us feel things we don't want to acknowledge."

She smiled. "You mean not profitable." She flung back a lock of hair. "I'm kidding. I wasn't fishing for a compliment. Or intending to turn the conversation to my work."

"Of course you weren't." Edward looked at her carefully. She was self-conscious and it touched him. They stopped to admire the water.

The sky grew cloudy and a dark shadow cast its long arm over the river. In the distance they heard the faint laughter of children. Julia looked out into the water and her face filled with momentary sadness, as if she were thinking of something that hurt her. For a second Edward thought about reaching for her hand, but he held back. Julia raised her head to push past it and, as if reading his mind, said, "It's nice to have this time with you. I thought you were upset with me."

"Upset with you? Why?"

"I thought I must have said something wrong. At Strauss's gallery. At lunch. We were getting along so well and then, well, you didn't say anything. This is the first time we've really talked since then."

"That's not it." He stumbled to explain himself. He hadn't spoken to her because he'd been intimidated. Or was protecting himself. Or was shy. He wasn't sure. "I didn't want to encroach upon your time."

"That's silly. I thought we connected."

"We did." He turned his face for a moment to the water and followed the sound of it and then sat on a bench and she followed. He remembered when he'd met her twenty years ago at the Academy of Arts and Letters. It was funny how memory took its time, had a life of its own. She had been one of the newly minted Rome fellows. He'd been in the business only a year or two and went to the ceremony and reception afterward to network. His friend Charlie, one of the young Turks at the gallery, was at the reception too. He introduced Julia to Edward, along with the other five fellows. How Charlie had memorized their names from the program and put name to face was impressive. It was clear then that he was on the verge of becoming a major player. Edward didn't have that instinct. Instead he was seduced by a kind of inexplicable magic, not the flashy, fashionable sense but the subtler kind, the kind that slips under the door and takes you by surprise. He knew it when he saw it and when he felt it, but he did not know how often it would come around or whether he'd be able to make a career out of it.

After he'd congratulated Julia on the Rome fellowship, she remarked that she hadn't deserved it. "I'm still too influenced by my predecessors. I haven't found my own voice yet. What's true to my core. That no one else can do." She was a few years younger than Edward, a strange creature who seemed to him then part decorative bird and part, well, he didn't know. At the time she was a little too curated for his taste. He offered his card and said he wanted to come see her studio one day, "that is, once you've found your voice," he'd said, recognizing that he might have something to offer her.

"Maybe when I'm back from Rome. If I've made any art by then."

"You've made no art yet?"

"None at all."

"The fellowship committee endowed nothing?"

"Not really. It was only the idea that captured them."

"So do you hope to be remarkable, then?"

"Yes, don't you?"

Did he? Of course he did—he was Harold Darby's son—only he'd never thought of it that way before.

Edward offered her a glass of champagne from the tray of a passing waiter but she refused, saying her fiancé was waiting by the door. A man with an open face, looking impatient, leaned against a pillar by the doorway.

"What does he do?"

"He makes money," she responded, and they both laughed.

From time to time after their short encounter he saw her name and work mentioned in trade magazines or gallery catalogues, and once even went to the trouble of finding out the name of her gallery, but for a reason he couldn't put his finger on he'd never contacted her.

"Your fiancé you were with? You know, when we met each other all those years ago . . ." he said as they stood up again and continued to stroll along the river. "Did you end up marrying him?"

She smiled. "Yes."

"Are you still married to him?"

"Yes," she said.

AT AN OUTDOOR café he ordered an expensive bottle of Gewürz-traminer with lunch. He watched Julia's eyes turn soft after she finished her first glass and allowed him to refill it. They had traveled together for many days and he had watched her a lot, listening carefully and trying to intuit her gestures, but one couldn't really know someone else, even some of the time. The sun revealed itself from behind a sheath of dark clouds and pushed forth making everything, their plates, glasses, the surrounding trees and shrubs, shimmer, and everything that had come before faded for a moment into the distance. He looked across the table. With her white ruffled blouse underneath a trim black velvet blazer, long neck, pale skin, and clear eyes that shone a more liquid blue in the sun, she resembled a woman of a different era. It was a vacation just to look at her.

"What have been your impressions? You know, about the scene?" Edward asked.

"Have you noticed that it's bad-boy week? All those overbearing, obstreperous works."

He looked up from his glass.

"The galleries we've visited mostly show work by male artists. It's all about bold images and conspicuous display. And there's this tendency to glamorize sloppiness. Have you noticed the penchant for extra-large and sinister phallic objects?" She stopped and looked down at her plate. "It's just something I've noticed. How men command attention." She took another sip from her wine. "You're laughing at me."

"I'm not laughing."

"But you were smiling."

"I guess I was. Affectionately," he said.

"You were brilliant yesterday. Your talk," she offered.

"I didn't make a fool of myself?"

"Oh, no. I haven't stopped thinking about it. The way in which you spoke about bringing inventiveness into preconceived and tired ideas. How art has the power to suggest that the most ordinary spaces of human life can be made special."

The sun came out in full force. The river was sparkling. A parade of small toy sailboats sailed in the current. Children were playing in a little garden park. "We're in a painting," Edward said. It was a game he used to play with his father. "What painting is it?"

"*Sunday in the Park*, of course," she said.

He threw back his head and laughed.

"I love the sky here," she said, closing her eyes as if the sight slightly pained her.

THEY ARRIVED AT the hotel in time to shower, dress, and meet the others for drinks before the dinner gala. In the morning they were headed back to Berlin. "Edward and Julia have turned up," Savan announced to the group when they walked in. He detailed the galleries and museums the group had visited. "Shame you had to miss. I know you would have enjoyed it. Myers put on a great show. It was called *The Disobedients*."

Edward escaped to the bar. He wasn't in the mood. Savan's desperation to please stemmed from inner hollowness, or loneliness, as Julia had perceived—or both. A person didn't try that hard otherwise.

Julia caught up with Charlotte, who was known for her special gift for organizing dinners, painstakingly inviting just the right
combination of high-profile celebs to ensure the evening was a success. Edward had been to two or three of her parties. When Julia
entered the room Charlotte embraced her and they spoke eagerly
and with warm affection, and in the moment he regretted he wasn't
part of their intimacy.

He needed another drink. He started on vodka and wished he
hadn't. He should switch to beer, but it was too late. The vodka
had run through his system, making everything a little easier.

Savan wandered over and clapped Edward on the back. He felt
himself recoil. He wanted to have his drink alone and reflect upon
the day with Julia. It had been a relief to be with someone for whom
he didn't have to be on guard or put on a show.

"When I spoke with Nate the other day, he said Agnes is happy."
Savan raised his eyebrows.

"Happy?" Edward said.

"With you. And the gallery."

"Why shouldn't she be?" He was relieved when Julia and
Charlotte wandered into the mahogany-paneled bar for a drink and
broke into their conversation. Julia mentioned that she'd learned
that Cabot White had taken on Christopher Landis. Julia said she'd
gone to school with him at RISD.

"It's been fascinating to watch his career. Every time he takes a
new wife, his work changes direction."

Edward laughed.

"No, I'm serious. He reinvents himself with each woman."

"I suppose that's one way of doing it," Edward said. "Of course,
that means I'll always be a bore."

"It's terrible, isn't it? To be always left out of the party," Julia said, a solemn look on her face.

"Jimmy Oldman is a reinventer too. Do you know Jimmy? He's got that new shop in L.A."

"Is he monogamous?"

"Jimmy?" Edward laughed. "Jimmy's the least monogamous person I know."

"Too bad he isn't here to spice up the group."

Edward leaned over the bar to address Julia. "What about you? Are you monogamous?"

"Hopelessly so," Julia sighed.

"Kids?"

Julia shook her head and her face darkened. "Long story."

Savan and Charlotte divided the bill. Edward moved closer to Julia.

"I suppose we could too," Julia said. Her cheeks were flushed after several glasses of wine.

"You mean reinvent ourselves?"

"Yes, why not," Julia said, reveling for a moment in her liberation, and then slinking back into herself.

Tina entered the room and with a clap of her hands motioned for the Americans to follow her to the dining room.

Charlotte possessively took Julia's arm and escorted her out of the bar. The women spoke in whispers. Julia looked back at Edward and then allowed Charlotte to pull her away. He held back and watched her from across the room. She stopped and looked over her shoulder, noticing that he hadn't followed, and motioned with a nod for him to come.

6 HAMBURG

WHEN HE RETURNED to his hotel room he was too wound up to sleep. He'd had too much to drink. The minute he undressed and lay down he thought about unfinished business at the gallery, calls he needed to make, e-mails that required an answer. He'd wanted to be a dealer because he revered art, but not necessarily the business of it. The constant jockeying for position. The bravado and showmanship. He thought about calling Holly to say good night but couldn't bring himself to do it. He felt far away from her.

The hotel room was stuffy, even with the ceiling fan swirling above him, churning warm air. He watched it spin around and pulled at the neck of his T-shirt and closed his eyes. He was dizzy, the room now spinning in the blackness behind his eyes, even as he lay flat on his back. He thought about Julia, and how she hid her understated beauty behind those oversized glasses. Something was disturbing her. Something at home. Maybe there was trouble with her marriage, trouble with her work. He didn't know. But there was something else about her. He smiled thinking about her, and felt a stirring in his groin. He switched on the light and got out of bed. He poured himself a scotch from the bottle he'd bought for his room, moved a chair near the window, and sipped it, lost in thought.

His phone rang. It was Holly. For a moment he considered whether he should answer, not quite wanting to break his mood.

"Edward," she said. "You didn't call me? Why didn't you pick up? I called like a hundred times."

"I haven't had a free moment."

"Not one moment?"

Here we go, he thought, the wilderness of their marriage blowing in. He took in a breath and braced himself.

"You sound a million miles away," he said. "I think we have a bad connection."

"I'm in Connecticut and you're in Germany. Of course we do. Is everything okay? You sound funny."

"Just tired. Everything's fine, Hol. I'll see you in a few days."

"I miss you," Holly said.

"I miss you, too."

"I wish you didn't have to travel so much."

"I know. But I can't help the travel. It's what I do."

She yawned into the phone. "Are you sure everything is okay?"

"Everything's fine. I'm sorry I didn't call earlier."

"Daddy lost his balance again and almost fainted at the Nelsons' christening. Mom's been driving me crazy with worry. It's been a terrible day."

"I'm sorry. I should have called. How's your father?"

"He's going in for more tests tomorrow. You don't sound like yourself. I hear it in your voice."

"It's being around these people. I don't know. I always feel like there's more I should be doing."

"Doing? All you do is work."

"That's not it." Or maybe it was. He didn't know exactly what was wrong but there was no reason to worry Holly. "You know how I get. It's because I'm away from you. Go. Get some sleep. I'll call you tomorrow."

After he hung up he rose from the bed and went to the window to light up a cigarette. He told himself everything was fine at the gallery and at home and he needed to slow down and stop putting pressure on himself. Once he returned, he'd ease back into their rhythm and all would be fine again. He inhaled his cigarette and blew the smoke out the window, watching the traffic on the street slowly loll by. Below at the hotel entrance he saw a couple, a young man and a woman, saying good-bye, the man tucking the woman into a cab and then reaching in and kissing her. For a few moments he thought about the couple, maybe lovers who met once or even twice a year, and imagined what they might say to each other, and how their lives would resume after they had parted.

AT BREAKFAST IN the hotel café before their flight back to Berlin, Julia waltzed toward him fresh from a morning walk and gave him a beaming smile. "Shall we have a drink together tonight?" she said, taking him out of himself. "It's our last night."

"I would like that," Edward said, leaning over his plate of two weakly scrambled eggs and whole wheat toast. His mood lifted. He finished his breakfast hungrily.

It was a free afternoon once they arrived back in Berlin. He spent it alone wandering through a few museums and galleries, stopping at the Museum Berggruen to see the Picassos and at fountains to watch children tossing in coins. He looked at couples walking arm in arm, and at a group of gregarious foreign students taking photographs. The intimacy and activity around him left him feeling that the most exciting moments of his life were past, and regret and emptiness filled him. Dark thoughts about the passing of time and aging consumed him. By the fountain he watched a girl slip her hand into her boyfriend's jacket pocket and then suddenly throw out her arms, jump up, and climb on top of him. When had he ever been that free and spontaneous?

On the way back to the hotel he bumped into Savan.

"How about a beer?" Savan said, and Edward agreed, glad for any company and to be taken out of his mood.

They wandered into the hotel bar and sat on stools near the end and talked about some of the galleries and artists they had seen. "Do you ever wonder how we do it? Make a living out of what we do?" Savan shook his head. "It's a fucking circus. You know Lyle Lewis, the artist who makes those metallic sculptures of superheroes? He was a stockbroker in his first life. Can you imagine what he puts me through? Sometimes I think I'm the luckiest guy on the planet and other times I think it will all disappear."

"Agreed," Edward said, staring into his stein of dark beer.

"At Reinstein, I feel closed in. I can't make a decision without Reinstein breathing down my neck. I'm too old to answer to anyone. It's his turf and he knows it. He wants me to be successful, but not too successful. Then I'm stepping on his toes."

"You'll know when it's time to make a move. You're still young in this business."

"He's a descendant of a banking dynasty in Vienna. He wears a hanky from Harrod's in his breast pocket. Around him I freeze up. It's like when you want to give it to a girl and then suddenly you can't let your mind go."

"Well, I don't exactly know," Edward said.

"Tell me. What do you think of Nate, really?"

Edward decided to be discreet. His relationship with Agnes was too precious to breach her trust. "Nate's great," Edward said.

"He's a fucking egomaniac," Savan said. They ordered another round, and to his surprise, Edward found himself having a good time. "You know, Savan, you have to tone it down sometimes. Be yourself. Don't try so hard."

"I know," Savan said. "My mother told me that when I was a kid."

"You don't have to anymore. You've got a reputation now."

"You think so?"

Edward nodded, though he thought to himself that it wasn't quite the reputation he would want for himself.

HE WAS IN a better mood when he returned to his room to prepare for the last dinner in Berlin. The group dined at the hotel restaurant and then Edward and Julia excused themselves, sliding out of the long booth, first one and then the other, saying they were tired and calling it a night. They went down the street to a bar in another hotel to have a drink.

The hotel was opulent, with crystal chandeliers and gold trim on the ceilings and wall. Edward had spotted it on one of his walks alone. In the lounge a woman in a short cocktail dress with bleached hair wrapped on top of her head sat alone at a table. Another woman at a table in the corner, with thin, painted-on eyebrows, sipped a glass of champagne.

"The women dress here," Julia observed. She looked down at her simple light blue cashmere sweater, black skirt and heels, then excused herself and went to the women's lounge. When she returned, she'd combed her hair and applied fresh lipstick.

"They're prostitutes," he said to her, once she sat down.

"Are you trying to make me uncomfortable?"

"No."

She ran her hand through her hair several times. "Yes, you were," she said and smiled.

They had a drink and then another and the conversation began to flow more easily. After they exhausted several topics, Julia rearranged herself in her chair and looked at him carefully. "So we haven't told our stories. Did you have a normal family with a mother and a father?"

"Normal? I don't know. My father was an English professor. He had a breakdown. He overdosed on lithium when I was away at college." He looked down at his hands.

"Oh, I'm sorry. That must have broken your heart." She looked at him with enveloping eyes and leaned closer. "Have you ever been in therapy?"

"No." He looked at her uncomfortably and, suddenly exposed, or threatened, he sat taller in his chair.

"I don't know how you go through something like that and not need therapy. It's the things we don't like to think about that destroy us. I think everyone should be in therapy. It should be required, as part of one's education, like having to take Western civilization or composition."

Was she serious?

Then she broke out into laughter and he laughed too.

"No, really," she said, tenderly. "Sometimes you seem adrift. Almost as if you are not quite there."

"Adrift from what?" He took a sip from his glass and then another. He was suddenly interested in what she'd made of him.

"From yourself, silly," she said, and then laughed again so warmly that he did not consider whether he should be offended.

"But what would I gain from it?"

"Brilliance."

"You mean happiness?"

"No." She looked at her folded hands, took off her glasses, and placed them on the table. Her eyes looked naked and vulnerable without them. "Only those who live in the dark are happy." They listened to the faint sound of music coming from the ceiling speakers; it was an opera he couldn't quite place.

"I don't know. Do you think one person can make us happy? Roy and I both work all the time. I wish sometimes we'd cultivated more friends."

"You know what C.S. Lewis said about friendship. He said it was unnecessary, like philosophy and art. That it had no survival value but rather it 'is one of those things which add value to survival.' My father had that quote pinned up in his study." He stopped to take a sip of his drink. "He was sick when I was in high school. His medication made him lethargic. He couldn't read or write anymore. For him it was like a prison sentence. Sometimes he asked me to come into his study and read to him. It was hard to look at him. His fingers were stained with nicotine. He stopped shaving. It was awful."

"Poor man. What did you read him?"

"Keats. Before he got sick he was working on a new book about the Romantics and ideas of immortality and selfhood. He was obsessed with Keats. I've been thinking about it. I think he related to his idealism. It was as if he was still longing for something." He stopped and stared into Julia's eyes. "It did break my heart," he said.

"I'm so sorry." Julia leaned over and touched his arm.

"Your turn," Edward said.

"My parents divorced when I was three. I never knew my father as a child. He moved to Los Angeles and got married again. And had two other children. They were more his than I was."

"I'm sorry."

"Don't be. He's a son of a bitch."

"When you got that phone call at Strauss's gallery, our first day here. Something happened. Do you want to talk about it?"

Her face darkened. "Not now."

"You're a mystery, you know that, right?"

She smiled into her wineglass.

"I'm glad you were on this trip," he said.

THEY SIPPED FROM their drinks, occasionally looking at the people at the tables around them and then back at each other. It was a luxury to be quiet with another person.

"Since we're telling our stories, there's something else," he said. "But first I need another drink." He called the waiter over and asked for another round.

"What is it?" she said, when the waiter had returned with their drinks.

He took a long swallow. "I was married before I met Holly. I was twenty-two." He'd never told anyone about his former wife, but telling a woman with no connection to his private life made him feel safe, as if by revealing it he were somehow letting himself off the hook, or exonerating himself. It was strange to think of his past, as if it belonged to another man.

"Did you leave your first wife for Holly?"

"It wasn't like that." He swirled his drink, knocking the ice against the glass. "Tess was my girlfriend in college. We moved to New York after we graduated. She wanted to get married and I guess I didn't want to disappoint her. It was right after my father died. I wasn't in a great place."

"Do you always do things that you don't want to do just so you don't disappoint others?"

"I don't know." He thought for a moment. "No. That's not it. I loved her. She was my first love." A lump formed in his throat. "She was killed in an accident. It was almost twenty years ago."

"That's so tragic."

"I don't know why I wanted to tell you. I feel like I can tell you anything."

"You're not happy? Is that it?" She folded her arms on the marble table and looked at him carefully.

"Are you?" He pressed his back against the booth.

"It depends what kind of happiness we're talking about. For some, pain and pleasure are intertwined. I had that kind of relationship once. The kind where the intensity feels as if you're going to burn out. You crave it and then you can't take it."

"You're not really answering my question."

"What's the question? I've forgotten."

"Your husband. Does he make you happy?"

She lifted her hand from her lap and reached for her wineglass. "I'm not sure we know each other well enough to tell those secrets," she said.

"I feel as if I know you."

"Do you?" Her face relaxed. "We should read Keats together. When we get back to New York. Then we can discuss the odes. That's something I could never do with my husband."

He looked into her eyes and nodded his head and smiled. "I never told Holly about Tess. I don't know why."

"You really do need to see a shrink," she said.

A man in a business suit approached the woman with the thin eyebrows at her table. He sat down, ordered a cocktail and another for her, and after their drink they both rose and climbed the winding, golden brocade staircase to the upper lobby of the hotel. Edward's eyes met Julia's. He paid the bill and they left.

The cool air summoned both of them out of their interiors, and as they walked, their bodies occasionally brushing against each other, he felt remarkably unburdened. They strolled slowly, staring up at the buildings, stopping at a fountain, looking into shop windows, as if to prolong the evening.

At the hotel desk they procured their individual keys and rode the elevator without speaking. Edward walked Julia to her room and they lingered in the dim doorway a minute and discussed the coming morning, the airport, returning home. He wasn't quite ready to leave. He placed his hand against the doorframe next to her. He moved close and then stopped and looked into her eyes deeply and she returned the look. "I guess it's time," Julia said, to fill the awkwardness. She reached up and kissed him on the cheek. He felt for her hand and took it in his and he was glad she didn't mind that he held it. "Well, I guess it's time," she said again. She slipped the key in the lock, turned to say good night, and before she went into her room, she stopped and turned back. "I like what you said about friendship. You know, C.S. Lewis. About it adding value to survival."

"Does that mean I'll see you in New York?" Edward asked.

She nodded.

"Safe flight," he said, before she closed the door.

HE TURNED ON the light in his hotel room, walked past the mirror on the wall toward the bathroom, and stopped. He saw his own image and smiled at himself, first with pleasure, but then unease filled him and heat traveled up his neck. In all the years he'd been with Holly he'd never felt drawn to another woman. He kept thinking of Julia's vulnerable eyes behind her glasses, and the way she scrunched up her eyebrows when something troubled her, her soft lips. He listened to the fan churning the air above him and the squeak of the metal frame of the bed when he turned on the mattress. He tried to put Julia out of his mind but bits and pieces of their conversation came to him. Even when he tried not to think of her, her scent and sound were with him. He awoke once in the middle of the night, unsure where he was, and panic filled him until he remembered.

H IS FATHER HAD arranged an interview with a trustee of Amherst, an old friend from graduate school, to whom, because he hadn't done well on the SATs, Edward attributed his college acceptance and the lingering sense that he was a fraud and with it the feeling that forever followed him—that he wasn't deserving and intellectually equal to his peers. All summer before his freshman year, his father in and out of hospitals, he didn't think he'd talked to anyone other than his parents. The last few days in August, his mother packed up his trunk and duffel while he sat on the bed in denial that he was leaving. He told her he'd defer for a year and help take care of his father, but she insisted he go. On the Greyhound bus, nauseated from the smell of gasoline fumes, he pressed his face against the window and watched New Haven fade into the distance. A gray bird soared skyward and a weight lifted off his chest, and for a few moments he experienced a flicker of happiness until guilt took hold.

His first few weeks at Amherst, he couldn't remember how to make conversation. His roommate, a stubby kicker from Minnesota, was either at practice or at the frat. They had nothing in common. When his roommate was out, Edward spent painful hours propped against the cement wall on his narrow bed feeling unsure of himself, afraid to come out of the dorm room for fear of bumping into another student and having nothing to say. To calm himself, he sometimes thought of his sexy English professor and jerked off. Alone in his room, an image came to him of his father lying lifeless on his bed miles away in New Haven, the glare from the light turning him into his pillow. The man who quoted lines from Keats and Wordsworth, threw a football with him in the backyard, read his English papers zealously correcting his grammar, had all but vanished. Edward went to the gym and kicked soccer balls against the wall.

He met Tess in his art history class the second semester of his junior year. Occasionally he turned to look at her seated at the end of the row, wearing a snug Amherst T-shirt over her small chest, her hair in a high ponytail, and she returned his stare. He was impressed by how poised she looked in the lecture hall, while many of the other students were slumped in their seats, falling asleep. Sometimes he saw her in the library in one of the carrels by the window. Once she caught his eye, looked up, and smiled. Nothing was ever said between them, but he found himself remembering her when he was walking home from the library at night or after soccer practice or right before he fell asleep. In his memory he could make out the darkness of her brown eyes and her very white skin, and the way she moved her head up and down taking notes, and knew that she was extraordinary. But more profound was her voice, warm and alive and stirring with emotion when she raised her hand in class and spoke about the hues in Vermeer's work or Rembrandt's empathy. He mentioned her name to his buddy Chris Blake, trying to find out something about her. He'd heard that Chris and Tess had gone to the same high school in Michigan. "Her mom died from breast cancer when she was a kid. You didn't know?" Edward didn't, and knowing it moved him. He tried to find her in the library during study hall the next day, but once he saw her in the wooden carrel, underlining passages in a book, stroking her finger back and forth across her lips in concentration, he walked away. He spent his days going from class to the cafeteria to soccer practice, and his evenings shut in his dorm room getting stoned, listening to music, locked in a deeper interior fog of her. And then one day, when they were looking at slides in the auditorium, Tess leaned over in the darkness and asked his name. After class he walked her back to the house she shared with four roommates, and on Saturdays they met in the library to study and that became their routine. Afraid to make a move out of fear of being rebuffed, he resigned himself to their becoming close friends.

Shortly after he received the phone call from his mother about his father's death, dividing his life into before and after—she told him the details softly ... *when I came down in the morning the pill-box for the week was empty*—he went to find Tess and she hugged him and said she'd drive him to New Haven for the funeral. In the front seat with his fists clenched, he stared out the windshield smudged with bird droppings watching cars race past, aware his future had remarkably changed. *His father gone? His mother a widow?* Anxious thoughts paralyzed him. Tess popped in a cassette; she'd been listening to *War and Peace* for her lit class. "Pierre was right when he said that one must believe in the possibility of happiness in order to be happy, and I now believe in it. Let the dead bury the dead, but while I'm alive, I must live and be happy." Anthony Hopkins narrating Tolstoy resounded from the speaker of her Honda Civic as they traveled the highway.

Once home, he went to his parents' bedroom. On the nightstand beside his father's side of the bed sat a half-empty glass of water and his father's reading glasses. His father had always put a glass of water beside his bed before he went to sleep. The sight of it made him break down.

At the funeral service, the dean of his father's department gave a eulogy praising Harold Darby's dedication, precision, and intellect, quoting from his books and reviews. One of his students, a heroin addict in recovery, approached the podium and talked about how Professor Darby had saved his life by turning him on to literature and offering him a window into the dark and contradictory nature of the soul. John Kincaid, his father's closest colleague, took the podium and read from his father's book on Keats and immortality. His parents were close with the Kincaids. Their daughter, Violet, with a wild head of frizzy hair she tried unsuccessfully to tame into a braid down her back, was a year younger than Edward and growing up the families had shared dinners and vacations together. Kincaid spoke about how all of Harold's work was an attempt to understand existence and how he believed that art was the threshold of truth, offering the possibility of transcendence.

"He could not accept that the most trivial, transient of infatuations and associations lack any real cause. Through veils and layers he tried to document every thought, every action as if we human beings understand what we do and every action has a cause, and that the same is true of feelings that go deeper. Through literature and poetry he attempted to understand the contradictory nature of the human soul. He believed there had to be an underlying cause or reason for two people to be drawn together and that this union offered the possibility for self-knowledge, even transcendence.

Writing at once tortured and compelled him—he could not live with uncertainty and embrace the mysteries he couldn't fully grasp."

Kincaid choked up and then continued. "Harold couldn't live in the same world as the rest of us, because he could not succumb to the beliefs to which the rest of us conform. In that sense Harold Darby was an aesthete of the highest order." He concluded by quoting lines from Keats's "Ode on a Grecian Urn," saying that Harry had lived by these words, "Beauty is truth, truth beauty," choking up again before taking his seat.

Another colleague, Margery Greer, spoke about how Harold believed, like Keats, that the only way to attain immortality, to lead a life that held meaning, was to create something lasting, and that indeed Darby's work would last. She closed by saying that it was unfortunate that he had gotten ill before being able to finish his current project, that she'd read drafts of it and believed it to be his most brilliant and compelling.

Edward sat stiffly in the church pew, a crick in his neck, rubbing his stinging eyes with his sleeve, Tess on one side of him stroking his arm, his mother on the other, regretting as he listened to his father being eulogized that he had not fully acknowledged the great man's accomplishments. Why hadn't he taken the time to read his father's books? To talk more about his ideas when they took walks together? His father's early death signaled to him that he, too, must find meaning in his life and seek divine truth outside the here and now.

On the ride back to Amherst Tess said, "I'm here for you," and took his hand.

"I don't know how I'm supposed to feel," he shared.

"Why would you," Tess said, and he felt his throat close up. His mother put the house on the market and moved to New Horizons, a retirement community where Bev, her old friend from college, lived. She boxed up his father's study, including his books and papers, and they resided in a storage bin in a remote area of New Haven until, years later, Edward obtained them.

Edward felt like one of the alabaster statues of *The Mourners*, as if he were wrapped in one of their dark hoods. Rembrandt's *Sheet of Studies with a Woman Lying Ill in Bed*, Munch's *Death in the Sickroom*, Picasso's *The Weeping Woman*, paintings he had studied in art history, he saw with a new and personal meaning. "Beauty is truth, truth beauty," Edward said to himself, unable to quite penetrate the phrase's meaning but repeating it anyway.

He spent his waking hours outside class in the art studio, where he attempted to make dark and mercurial (and not completely successful) paintings to express his sadness, and strange collages made out of found objects, and afterward he'd find Tess at the library. He pulled a chair next to her, bleary-eyed from the studio, until she finished, not wanting to return to the house without her. Tess rented foreign films for them to watch at night, and together they witnessed complex and historic moments played out in small domestic scenes and made popcorn in the microwave, listening to the pop, pop, pop of the kernels until it was done. Her presence calmed him. One night they got stoned together, fell into a tranquil, narcotic-laden sleep in her bed, and, as if bringing to life unconscious wishes, upon awakening they moved toward each other, and Edward reached over and kissed her, and then slowly moved on top of her, relieved she did not push him away. They made love two or three times that morning and throughout the day, only getting out of bed to get a glass of water, and later he went in the kitchen and made them orange juice from a frozen container. From that day forward they never slept apart. All of a sudden it hit him, how much he was in love with her.

He grew to depend on the smell of her hair and the outline of her cheek resting against his nose when he awoke in the morning. He was suddenly drawn to her, wanting her constantly. She was all he could think about. After class they met in dark, unused lecture halls to study and wound up having sex behind the podium or met at the football stadium where they planned to eat a picnic lunch and had sex behind the bleachers. Why? When they could go back to her room at her house, or to his dorm room that looked like a prison cell? Because somehow the urge overtook them the minute they met. Maybe Kincaid was right: there was no apparent cause for one's attraction or feelings for another person, no knowing when they might be unleashed. When the housemates were gone, Tess rhapsodically traipsed through the living room wearing T-shirts and bikini underwear that revealed curls of her pubic hair, humming to Phoebe Snow on the stereo. Sometimes he grabbed her thigh when she walked by and she came over and sat on his lap. He liked the sounds she made when he made her come, and the way she stroked her fingers underneath the hairline on his neck when she held him. He liked how sure she was of herself. How damn sure.

He broke into crying jags when he was in the shower, or driving, sometimes remembering his father nearly sleepwalking through the house in his flannel slippers and matching robe. Death had not offered relief. Tess said it wasn't supposed to. Zen-like, she encouraged him to embrace his pain, when what he really wanted to do was to embrace her, and he did, as often as she would let him.

His mother settled into life at New Horizons. She had bridge afternoons with Bev and her new friends Pat and John, and shared the same seating with the threesome for dinner. In the evenings they played bingo or Scrabble. Edward took the train up to see her for a day. At Scrabble she quibbled with John over whether *jack* was a common noun or not (it was). They complained about the food and the saccharine and often neglectful staff. Bev mentioned she was on blood thinners, and his mother patted her hand. He was glad for her until he realized that when he graduated he would have no home to return to. On the train ride back to Amherst he felt alone and adrift.

New York City was Tess's idea. He couldn't have cracked the city on his own. It was loud and overpopulated; opening a bank account took all morning. If you found an apartment you not only had to pay a management fee to get it, but there were ten or more other would-be renters in competition. After losing two or three places the size of broom closets, and tired of eating greasy takeout on the moldy carpet floor of their room at the Y, Tess figured it would be easier for them to get a lease if they got married. He wondered for a moment whether they ought to and then looked into her practical and hopeful eyes and agreed. They exchanged vows at City Hall and celebrated by renting a boat at the boathouse in Central Park and getting sloshed on cheap champagne. They knew that each remaining parent wouldn't approve of the elopement and decided not to tell them, rationalizing that they were like Tess and Angel in *Tess of the D'Urbervilles*, a novel they'd both read in a lit class— Tess's idea, since she shared the protagonist's name, and they were bound together by spiritual bliss, a connection that could never be undone. Once they got settled they would gently break the news.

Tess got a job waitressing at Café Luxembourg on the Upper West Side and studied for her LSATs during the day. One of Edward's father's friends set him up with an interview with Gertrude Silverman, who owned a gallery in SoHo. Slim, pale-faced, with fierce black eyes and severely cut black hair, Gertrude lectured him on the appropriate relationship between assistant and artist. When asked why he wanted to work at her gallery, he said that after his father's death art was the only thing that held meaning. When he was in the presence of art that moved him goose bumps traveled along his arms and he felt closer to a divine truth. There had to be more than the here and now, otherwise his father's suffering and early death was without meaning. He mentioned that he'd read a biography of Jackson Pollock and that Pollock's father had abandoned the family when he was nine. "Those spills and swirls of color in his paintings are expressions of his rage," Edward remarked. Gertrude offered him eleven thousand dollars a year and two weeks' vacation. "Take it," Tess said. "At least we'll be able to pay the utilities."

Along with picking up her dry cleaning, sorting her mail, and handling her correspondence, Gertrude de Vil (as the gallery underlings had dubbed her) sent him prowling for talent to art studios in Brooklyn and the Lower East Side. He scurried in and out of drab and dusty spaces, looking for art that, as his father said, made all else fade in its presence. He wasn't interested in the blockbuster crowd-pleaser, or the weird-for-the-sake-of-weird. He found a young abstract painter whose work he liked and an installation artist from Bulgaria who created intricate figures out of car parts. Gertrude instructed him that a relationship with an artist was about trust. She explained that all their deals were concluded with a handshake. If an artist wanted a letter of intent, she'd give him one, and if he preferred a contract, they could do that too, but what was paramount was making sure the artist knew that what mattered most was that the gallery believed in the work. Sometimes the artist leaves the gallery if the work isn't selling and sometimes they come back. What an artist wants most from a gallerist is to know that he or she understood the work and believed in it enough to put a price tag on it and find it a home.

After work he went gallery-hopping or for drinks with the other assistants; Tess waited tables in the evenings, putting her tips in an empty mayonnaise jar in the kitchen and counting it at the end of the week. His salary per week was less than Tess made serving tables in a night. She had it all worked out. Two years of law school, then she'd get a job and by then he'd be promoted and in four years they could buy an apartment and start a family.

Among his gallery friends, he didn't mention he was married; no one else was, and then later it seemed awkward to bring it up. Tess thought Edward's friends from the gallery, with multiple ear pierces, draped in vintage clothes that didn't match, were pretentious. She was possessive, wanting him home when she got back from work, and if he was still out, she pouted in the bedroom and refused to speak to him when he came home. Once he invited her to come to an opening on her night off and she spent the greater part of the evening talking to the bartender, who was from Detroit. Edward spent most of the reception chatting with Noreen and Bill Witherspoon, a couple who made environmental art. They were planning to create a bridge across a canyon in Sedona that would take a decade to complete using a particular kind of copper wire that had to do with the earth's energy grid system. They cornered Edward to ask about grants and whether he knew any investors.

"Your friends are narcissists," Tess said when they were walking home. "All they talk about is their work. I don't think they asked me one question about myself." He pondered what she'd said. He thought Noreen and Bill, in their mid-thirties, were kind of cool. They weren't married, but they called themselves life partners. He was impressed by their bohemian lifestyle and their dedication to art. Tess thought the art world was filled with phonies and that most contemporary art looked like it had been painted by a first-grader. "You're different around them. I don't know. What you do—it seems fake or something," she said.

Charlie Baker was another assistant director. They were rivals but friends too. The gallery's underlings lunched at the Blue Flame diner around the corner, where over greasy omelets they gossiped about their colleagues, ragged on Gertrude, bitched about certain entitled artists and revered others, and as a result had become close. Tess didn't get it. No one spoke about art, because that was beside the point. He liked going to artists' studios and attempting to access an artist's intentions. *All art must have a conceptual component,* one of his art teachers had said during crit. He liked hanging out with his friends from the gallery and being a part of this new world of abstract ideas. Valuing art was something he'd grown up on. His father had recited poetry to him when he tucked him in to sleep at night. He took him to museum shows when he was a boy, purchasing the headsets so that he could hear the museum director lecturing on the paintings. Art and literature were his father's religion. He was slowly learning how to file things in his mind as he went along, making connections between techniques or motifs he had picked up in works by the masters and contemporary work, and learning to access their value in intellectual and economic terms.

And after a long day and evening immersed in it all, so much that sometimes he felt his head was spinning, he liked nothing more than to come home to the cozy apartment Tess had decorated with odds and ends from Pottery Barn. In bed he listened, half asleep, for her to come in, dump her change from her apron pocket into the half-filled mayonnaise jar in the kitchen, and slip into bed smelling like French fries, and once she was in his arms, all the stimulus faded away.

Nearly a year in, the glamour of the city had worn off and they were barely making the rent. On Sunday, their only day together, over a too-expensive brunch at a trendy diner, Tess asked him one question after another about the gallery and, slightly hungover and not into talking about work, he glumly stared into his eggs Benedict, giving her one-word answers like he gave to his mother when he was a kid. For months she had complained that she thought he ought to get commission or a raise and was pressing him to talk to Gertrude.

"Are you sure this is the life you want?" she started in. "Don't you think you'd make more money, like, if you . . . I don't know. Did you see all those bar tabs you put on the Visa?"

"What, like go to law school or get an MBA? You don't think I'll cut it, do you?"

"We can't live in a three-hundred-square-foot apartment forever," she said, tightening her ponytail. "You've changed."

He liked being around artists who wore all black and smoked European cigarettes, and going to parties in fancy apartments in the city with views of Central Park and paintings by Balthus on the wall. Art existed beyond the fray of ordinary life, though its intent was often to capture it. He admired artists who worked rigorously and near poverty simply because they could do nothing else. At first he was surprised by the incongruity between the bohemian artists he knew living in flats in Brooklyn or the Lower East Side, earning a living by bartending or waiting tables or temping, and the wealthy art buyers they were dependent upon in one way or another if they were to be successful. There was something marvelous about the way in which a painting, for instance, could soften the social divide and bring diverse people together. He once saw a man and a woman, strangers, flirting over a painting by Magritte at the Met and then walk off together. When he saw an object or piece of art he liked it was like a shot of adrenaline went through his veins. He couldn't imagine anything he'd want to do more than be a part of it.

Art was a way of controlling the chaos of the mind that had entrapped his father. Color, line, composition ordered the universe of the canvas or installation in timeless stasis. It was extraordinary. At Gertrude's shop he was exposed to the geography of the art world, a network of associates in New York and various cities around the world who did business together, especially those who were interested in the same kind of art and showed similar artists. They were colleagues, some close friends and others rivals, at the end of the day competing for the same work and sometimes, with an international gallery, sharing a particular artist. He watched how the senior dealers at the gallery flitted off to European cities, scoring deals and putting more money in their pockets. Hanging a show, drumming up press, finding an artist whose work he admired, hoping he might be able to help get the work known, building a roster, energized him.

After they paid the bill, they walked home from brunch through Central Park. "What do you mean, I've changed?" he finally asked, kicking some leaves in their path.

"You treat me like one of your buddies. I never got a wedding ring. I don't feel special around you."

"I don't feel special with you either." They walked back to their apartment in silence. Tess said she was going to her study group, and Edward spent the rest of the afternoon sitting in front of the TV filled with self-loathing. He hated disappointing her.

He stayed out late pursuing collectors, or going to parties to network. Tess had to study anyway. One of her study buddies was a guy named Adam Weinberg. When Adam called, he noticed that Tess did this little stretch with her neck and stood on her tiptoes as if she were performing. It made him jealous and he stayed out all night with Charlie getting trashed. Tess called him the next morning at the gallery and asked if he planned to send in the rent check. It was two weeks overdue. Touché. "You're the kindest person I know," she said, "except when you're being a jerk."

Maybe Tess was right. He needed to buckle down and get serious. He remembered when they had first crossed the bridge into Manhattan with their futures spread out before them. *Which building do you want to live in,* Tess said, her face fresh and eyes shiny as the skyline came into focus. He liked the fact that she wasn't a part of his world—keeping it private was like a secret that if revealed would lose its poignancy. He liked having something that was all his own, separate. He decided he would hate to be like Bill and Noreen Witherspoon, always together, obsessed by the same things. He took a break and walked to a jewelry shop on Forty-Seventh Street and bargained with a jeweler for a ring with a small starter diamond and bought it with the credit on his Visa card. He would give the ring to Tess that night.

When he arrived home the apartment looked eerily different. He found an envelope with his name on it propped against the ketchup bottle on the kitchen table. It contained a letter a few pages long, meticulously composed in her perfect cursive. She was heading back to Michigan for a while to live with her dad and study for the LSATs. *You don't have the guts to admit you want your freedom*, she'd written. *You have an uncanny brilliance for not picking up on what you don't want to pick up on.* He read the letter twice, heat rising to his face. He looked around the apartment and noticed it was empty of her things. He called her in Michigan and spoke to her dad but she refused to come to the phone. He called her the next day, and the next, hoping she'd finally pick up. *No, she was wrong. He didn't want his freedom. He wanted her.* If he didn't hear from her by the weekend he'd fly to Michigan and show up at her door. He missed the sound of her banging pots in the kitchen when she was cooking and little things like the way she forgot to turn the faucet all the way off in the bathroom and he awoke in the mornings to the sound of dripping water. He didn't know what to do if she never came back. Who would fold his socks into little balls in his drawers? But it wasn't just those little things. She gave him a reason to wake up in the morning.

Days later, recognizing the Michigan area code on the caller ID at the gallery, he answered the phone in a quick rush of excitement and relief. It was her father. Tess had been out jogging and got sideswiped by a truck and was instantly killed. After he got off the phone he stood up and then sat back down. He was trembling. For minutes his mind spun. He left the gallery and went back to their apartment with the strange expectation that she'd be there waiting for him, and upon seeing in the kitchen the two empty café chairs they'd bought at an antique fair, he vomited in the sink. He found a clump of her long hair still in the shower drain. He planned to go to her funeral, but at the airport he couldn't bring himself to get on the flight. He called Mr. Thompson and told him that he'd come out and spend a few days with him once he got his feet back on the ground but he couldn't face the funeral. He took long subway rides to parts of the city he'd never been to before. There was something about the motion and anonymity of the train that seemed to settle him, or allow his thoughts to wander. He ended up in Queens or somewhere in the Bronx and then got back on a train and went home. He found their wedding license in the utensil drawer in an envelope and stared at it. At twenty-three he was technically a widower. He put the ring in its neat velvet box alongside it in the drawer. He kept making plane reservations for a trip to Michigan to see Mr. Thompson and then at the last minute canceled them. He began work on an intricate collage from bits and pieces of Tess's possessions—letters and little notes she'd written to him, photos of the two of them, materials like buttons and trim from some of her clothes. He made one collage after the other, the smell of the shellac made him a little high and while he worked it was as if Tess was with him. He sent one of the collages to Mr. Thompson as a gift along with the boxes he had packed of Tess's things.

Weekends alone on the couch in front of the TV for hours, he popped sleeves of Fig Newtons. Monday mornings he found it challenging to get out of bed. Once he called in sick for a week. What difference did it make? He lay in bed and conjured her, not wanting to get up, or let her go. He thought about days they spent together, and if he closed his eyes and shut the blinds it was as if she were still in bed next to him. Days passed, weeks during which he seemed to be sleepwalking. Everything in life seemed random and without meaning. His life had been reordered in a way he didn't understand. Outside it was so hot he could barely breathe. August in New York. Everything was suffocating. Things she'd said—*he didn't make her feel special*—haunted him. He replayed their last few arguments wishing he could change the outcome. On the street he thought he saw her from a distance, the way we do when someone is on our minds, her ponytail bouncing when she walked, and his heart quickened before he realized it wasn't her. In a lull at work he thought of calling her, forgetting. Memories of her twisted inside him like a strange root, sprouting their own inexorable branches and fibers. He missed her so much his lungs hurt. Her memory, along with the force of his longing, became a dark icy lake in his consciousness where he submerged his emotions, frozen and safe.

ON THE PLANE Berlin was fading behind him, but still he carried the wide, beautiful streets and buildings, the walk by the river in Hamburg, the opulent hotels. He thought of the fragrance that came off Julia's clothes, her heavily lashed blue eyes, and the way she took off her glasses once they sat down for drinks, as if she needed him to see her more closely.

After landing, clearing immigration, and collecting his luggage, he found himself in the backseat of a town car with yet another stranger, this one a very friendly and elegant man wearing a business suit. His anxieties rushed him. He thought about Holly and Annabel at home.

It was after five by then, dark when the driver pulled up his driveway. The sun had tucked itself away so that all he could make out was wet piles of leaves and the skeletal shape of branches in the headlights. It was still cool, not quite cold, and, though it wasn't winter yet, the autumn left him with a sensation of sadness and regret. There were no lights on in the house. Why? He was sure he'd told Holly what time he was getting in. He signed the voucher and waited for the driver to deposit his roll-on luggage on the wet drive.

"I'll take it from here," Edward said to the driver. Twenty years of taking the train back and forth from Manhattan to Westport, so he could own the white farmhouse for which he still paid monthly

mortgage payments, meaning that in reality the house was only par-
tially his. The house and a few thousand dollars in the stock market, and the shares he owned in the gallery, and whatever was in
his 401(k)—this was what the last twenty years had amounted to?
As he inserted his key, still groggy from the flight, everything
felt strangely foreign. He had loved coming home to Annabel in her
playpen when she was little, lying on her back, her feet in the air,
enchanted by her toes, and Holly in another room talking on the
phone to one of the volunteers at the refuge or out in the garden
returning to him with dirt underneath her fingernails and smudged
on her face. He liked coming home to the smell of baked chicken or
a hearty sauce cooking, and the anticipation of making a fire in the
living room, where he and Holly ended the evening with another
glass of wine. He liked to check in on Annabel in her room with
the pink-and-white polka dot wallpaper that Holly had carefully
picked out once she discovered she was having a girl, to make sure
she was asleep on her back, because they'd heard that you should
never let a baby sleep on her stomach. Annabel's childhood could
be mapped out and charted in every room in the house. The rug
they'd bought for the living room when she was just an infant,
learning to crawl, because Edward was worried she'd topple over
and hit her head on the wood floor. Or the coffee table, purchased
for its height, so that their daughter could learn to pull herself up
by it. Or that little china figurine, a ballet dancer, on the bookshelf
in the den, which they'd given to her for her fourth birthday, when
she'd just started taking ballet.

In those early years when Edward opened the door after a long
day in the city he thought only of making love to his wife, this person who seemed so sure of herself, who had been born into privilege

and felt guilty for it, who possessed a love and gentleness and sixth sense for creatures great and small, marveling that this woman, who loved taking a long walk with the dogs at her heels and found sustenance in the shades of color in a sky, had chosen him. Getting remarried had thrust him back into life. They'd been happy in those early years. He liked how she pressed against him when they stood together at cocktail parties, or the way she slipped her hand into his arm, or the look of her as she entered a room. Or the way she had of describing the tenderness of a sheepdog she'd rescued off the road. He liked the wildness in her eyes.

When Annabel was born his devotion to Holly deepened. He could never get over how she had carried his child inside her, and given birth to someone for whom he felt the deepest love. It seemed to him that he had little to do with her accomplishment and he felt profoundly obligated to her for giving him a prize he didn't feel he deserved.

He liked taking long walks with her and the dogs and Annabel in her stroller on a Sunday, and then later in the afternoon making love on their bed with the cool breeze coming through the window. He wanted Holly to know how she grounded him and gave him a reason for living, but he never knew how to tell her. The years passed and he grew to accept that she wasn't going to leave or tire of him. She wasn't the kind of woman who needed him to articulate in words what she meant to him, she did not expect him to be a poet; it would undermine what they had. But in the last few years something had shifted. After dinner Holly withdrew to the den to read one of her obscure magazines or journals—the latest was called *Horse Husbandry*—and he wandered upstairs to work. They moved around the house as if on their own private vessels.

On the evening he returned home from Berlin, things felt different. The key no longer turned with ease, he had to jiggle it, just a little, and then turn it again before the door swung open, and this time there was no smell of a home-cooked meal to overpower him. It was completely dark inside and the only beings that greeted him were Simon and Trudy, their dogs.

He climbed the stairs with his suitcase, the creak on the wooden steps breaking the quiet, dumped his dirty clothes from his suitcase into the hamper, let out of the luggage bag the suit he'd worn his last night in Berlin—he smelled the lingering scent of Julia's perfume in the fabric and for a moment thought of her. There was something about her; he couldn't quite name it, exactly. He stamped the suit into the bottom of the dry cleaner bag along with his shirts and pulled the drawstring. He'd drop it off on his way to work in the morning. He showered, changed into a pair of weekend khakis and a sweatshirt, and went downstairs, slowly readjusting to the nuances of being home. Everything around him looked a little dull and colorless without Holly and Annabel.

He'd gotten in late on Saturday afternoon. Holly had left him a note pinned to the refrigerator saying they'd gone to the coffee shop for dinner and then to the barn to see the new pony that had been born a few days ago.

"YOU'RE HOME," HOLLY said when she opened the door a few hours later and entered the kitchen with Annabel.

"Hi, Daddy." Annabel stood on her tiptoes and kissed him on the cheek. "How was Berlin? You were in Berlin, right?"

"Yes, Bell. Berlin."

"Did you get dinner?" Holly said, kissing him quickly on the lips. He smelled the pungent and familiar odor of horsehair.

A tightness passed across his face. Now that they'd returned, he found it difficult to get past the fact that they had not been at home waiting for him.

"What is it? What's wrong?"

"I thought we'd have dinner together. I was looking forward to it."

"I'm sorry. I didn't know what time your flight got in. I've been preoccupied with Daddy. And Annabel wanted to see the new pony." Immediately he was sorry. He had forgotten about Holly's father.

"How's your father?" Edward asked.

"The same," Holly said.

"Why don't we go into the city tomorrow and see them," Edward said.

"We'll see. Bell and I went in to see them yesterday." It hadn't occurred to him until they walked through the door that Holly and Annabel might prefer his absence. They had their own routine. When they weren't at the barn, they liked splurging on manicures or going for tea at one of the fancy Manhattan hotels. He remembered how the air in his house would clear when his mother left for her bridge group. He and his father watched a James Bond film together—his father had a passion for what he called Bond's "magisterial elegance"—or they'd toss a football in the backyard. Sometimes he wondered what he and Annabel would have to talk about a year or two from now. Annabel liked getting dessert at the cafeteria after a tour around a well-chosen gallery, so he could still

persuade her to join him. Every now and then he had wished they'd
tried harder to have another child.

"It's fine about dinner. I made a sandwich."

After Annabel hung up her coat she had gone racing upstairs to
her room.

"I can barely keep my eyes open," Holly said, and started for
the staircase. "Are you coming to bed?"

"I'll be up soon. You holding up okay, Hol? You look tired."

"I have to be." Holly yawned. His eyes moved to the tender
skin above her throat. He reached toward her but she continued
climbing the stairs. "We'll catch up tomorrow," she said, covering
another yawn with her hand. "I'm glad you're home."

He lolled into the kitchen, poured himself a glass of scotch, and
climbed the stairs to his third-floor study. They had procured an
antique walnut desk and a Victorian velvet couch at an estate sale
to furnish it after they bought the house. Edward took his father's
library out of storage, alphabetized his books, and shelved them
in the study. He hung his father's paintings on the wall. The attic
room with its low ceiling and wood-paneled walls reminded him
that his father was metaphysically present. He'd been working on
an essay for a catalogue raisonné for one of the gallery's artists and
he thought he'd try to polish it, but couldn't concentrate. He looked
for the copy of Keats's poetry his father had given him, remembering Julia's wish to read the odes. He thought about what John
Kincaid had said at his father's funeral: his father believed that in
union with a kindred spirit one might find the divine. Keats wrote
the odes in a sort of winter of eternal youth (he died at age twenty-
five). He opened the dusty pages that smelled like mothballs and
dust, and, enveloped in unexpected sorrow, put the book down.

He uncapped a bottle of scotch from his desk drawer and poured another inch into his glass. He liked how his body relaxed and his mind drifted when he drank it. He settled into his chair and turned on the desk lamp. Next to the desk, on the sill, two or three dead flies were curled in the corner, and another, nearly half-dead, buzzed limply against the glass. It raged and then quieted and then resumed buzzing and flinging itself against the window. A strange feeling of deadness engulfed him. He swatted the fly with his hand and it fell to the sill with the others. He swirled the dark liquid in his glass, took a sip, and winced from the whiskey's hot burn in his throat. He turned on his computer and logged into his e-mail account. There were ninety-two unread messages awaiting him. He took from his wallet the stack of business cards he'd accumulated in Germany and went through them. On one he'd scribbled Julia's e-mail address. He held the card in his hand. The air in the warm room felt confining. He cracked open the window, letting in the cold, damp air. His mind drifted to her lovely smile and warm eyes.

How are you? How was your flight? He hit the Send button without recognizing that in writing to her he was taking a step back from his life as he knew it and into the unknown future, for one cannot embark upon the new without giving up something in return.

NEARLY TWO DECADES earlier, when he'd first started out, Edward ordered a cocktail from a young artist slumming as a bartender. Having heard he was an up-and-coming gallerist at Gertrude Silverman, the bartender asked if Edward would visit his studio. Edward liked the guy, Josh Swartzman, shaggy hair and muscular arms underneath a black tee, from a Jewish background in Queens, son of a worker at a failing button factory. Though Edward rarely made commitments on a first viewing, he was knocked out. Bold and expressive, the work revolutionized a technique in which Swartzman used different-sized buttons from his dad's factory and applied them in patterns to form an image, the way Seurat's work was made from dots. It celebrated the integrity of the working class and confirmed Edward's conviction that it was possible to turn materials into something as transparent as life itself. In the faces of the workers he saw there was illumination behind death, that memory could be objectified. Edward snapped him up immediately. It was his first major find.

Swartzman's unusual working-class background got him a big feature in the *Times* and the work flew off the walls. If a painting sold, or he scored an institutional sale, he felt weirdly as if he were still doing it for Tess. He had dreams where she was sitting at their kitchen table waiting for him. In the dream her cheeks were rosy and wisps of hair came loose from her ponytail, the way she looked after she came back from a run around the reservoir. There were strange moments in the dream when he was trying to enter the room to see her, but somehow couldn't move closer, like he was out at sea and the waves kept pushing him back. When he awoke it was as if she was there beside him.

After she died he walked through his days as if living behind a veil, and then, unable to stand himself, he threw himself into his work. It was the only time he felt free of his sadness. He told himself that Tess would want him to make something of himself—she was always in his thoughts, a second consciousness. He conversed, mused, read, wrote, thought, obsessed, and fantasized about art—breakfast, lunch, dinner with collectors, artists, gallerists—evenings pounding back shots at their favorite corner bar on Cornelia Street with pals from the gallery, so that he felt like his life was one long arduous effort to prove there was a reason to go on living. After Tess died he was attracted to work that spoke to the fragility of the human condition and grew obsessed with the randomness of existence. He began to get a reputation at the gallery for being way too serious.

EACH MORNING HOLLY Moore, the gallery's full-time reception-ist, greeted him with a wide and buoyant smile and cheery wel-come. It annoyed him to see happiness incarnate at nine thirty every morning. Pretty and always dressed in a crisp white blouse and slim black skirt or pants, hers was the perfect face for the gallery. Once walking in after a somber weekend, he heard her laughing on the phone—a clear, effervescent laugh unencumbered, almost like a trill. He felt a sudden pang. *Why is she so happy?* Walking home, he noticed that little grass blades had come up in the park, and stubborn shoots of daffodils sprang forth as if thrusting themselves up from the darkness of the earth. He thought about her laugh. Another time when he walked into the gallery, thinking about an unpleasant conversation he'd had with a collector, she traced her lips with her index fingers in the shape of a smile. "Life can't be that bad," she said. "Is your girlfriend giving you trouble?"

Edward froze. It had been almost a year since Tess died. "It's over," he said, and tears welled in his eyes. He hadn't confided to his friends and colleagues at the gallery much about his private life. No one did. There was an unspoken etiquette that once you entered the gallery nothing mattered but the work.

"I'm sorry," Holly said, tenderly. He nodded and, afraid he'd break, ducked into the men's room. He couldn't look himself in the mirror. When he came out, he avoided her. His darkness felt contagious.

On Monday mornings by the water cooler Holly mentioned her volunteer work at the wildlife refuge in Connecticut. Once she'd wrested a jackrabbit's leg from a trap; another time she mentioned puppies she was looking after at the sanctuary who were waiting for a home. She'd taken lessons at the stables in Central Park when she was young, and boarded her own horse at a barn near her parents' country house in Connecticut. The best part of her week was volunteering for a program at the barn where as a form of therapy autistic kids interacted with the horses. Tom Drury, a childhood friend, owned the horse farm and had started the program. Pictures of the children riding at the barn were tacked up on the bulletin board above her desk.

She took pleasure in the simplest things—a cappuccino and croissant for breakfast, for instance, delighted and sustained her throughout a dull morning of answering phones. It hadn't occurred to him that some people considered pleasure to be a worthy ambition. He observed Holly like she was a foreign species, marveling at a life untouched, or so it seemed, by any need to prove herself. Every now and then a memory of Holly would pop into his head when he was drifting off to sleep. He didn't know why. He pictured her leaning against the reception desk, teasing him for kissing up to Gertrude when he came in with her dry cleaning. She showed him photos of her favorite horse at the barn where she rode. Once she called him over with the curl of her finger when she caught him staring at her from behind his computer screen. "Let me give you some advice," she said. "Stop trying so hard. Gertrude thinks the world of you," and then a call came through and she turned back to the phones. She held some strange hypnotic power over him, perched at her desk answering phones when he walked into the gallery every morning, representing some unattainable idea of detached elegance. Her long neck and dark green eyes reminded him of a woman from a Modigliani painting.

At an opening at the gallery he went to collect some prints from the storage room to show a client, and Holly said she'd help. In the elevator she surprised him by pushing the stop button, then thrust him against the glass in a spontaneous burst of excitement. They kissed. No one had ever thrown herself on him before. After the reception, they continued their buzz and went for drinks at a dive downtown with the others. All throughout the evening her eyes kept finding his and he felt a twinkle in his gut. Charlie slid into the booth next to Holly, and later, when Edward had gone to the bar to get another round, Charlie and Holly slipped out of the booth together to leave. He tugged on Holly's sleeve.

"Why don't you stay for another," he offered. "I'll walk you home."
Holly turned to him. "I'm with Charlie," she said. "Sort of,"
and scooted out. She turned back to look at him when she was
leaving to gauge his reaction. He was a little wasted by then and
proceeded to get smashed.

She had two free tickets to see *Madame Butterfly* at the Met and
asked if he wanted to go. He assumed, because he wanted to, that
Charlie was no longer in the picture. The idea of three hours in a
cramped velvet seat in the middle of the row didn't exactly thrill
him, and he feared he'd forgotten the art of conversation during
his long year of mourning, but didn't want to give up the chance of
spending an evening with her. Once the glittering lights lifted into
the ceiling and the theater darkened and Puccini's music tumbled
into the dark hall he was swept up in the central drama of Butterfly
and her tragic demise. The emotion of the performance gutted
him and he choked up. Holly clutched his arm, which was resting
between them. When the curtain fell she turned and looked at him
with misty eyes.

She invited him back to her apartment on the Upper West Side,
a studio that was conspicuously small given that he'd imagined she
had family funds—someone said her parents lived on Park Avenue
and you could always tell a girl came from money by the understated
but expensive clothes she wore and her pristine and manicured nails.
She sat him down on the bed and slowly took off his tie. A woman
hadn't touched him since Tess. The opera was still in his head, the
bells and gongs, the cries of grief and despair, and as he was pulled
into the canyon of her, smelling the richness of her hair, touching
the soft folds of her body, emotion overcame him. *No, there*, she
said. *Yes, right there.* She had possessed him quickly. Afterward,

alone in his apartment, he told himself he didn't want to open himself to another woman. He couldn't afford to get crushed. But there was her laughter, and the way she tossed back her head, and the shine in her eyes when she spotted him coming into the gallery.

At the gallery, sometimes she came and sat next to him and asked him a question about the work of an artist they were showing. She'd listen patiently while he told her what he loved about a particular painting, transfixed by his zeal. *It's like the way I feel when I watch a horse take off, there is this beauty and intensity that is hard to describe.* One night they went out for drinks with a bunch of others and Carrie Phillips, one of the gallerinas, mentioned that she was dating an investment banker.

Edward turned to Holly. "That's probably what you're looking for."

She looked at him squarely. "That's not what I'm into. My father's sort of a bastard. He buys companies and then hundreds of people lose their jobs."

"So you and your father, you don't get along?"

"It's complicated. I love Daddy. He'd do anything for me. It's just that I don't respect what he does. He's angry because I refuse his money."

"Why do you refuse it?"

"Would you want to be owned?" She rubbed her nose with a forefinger and he felt his stomach drop. "With you, it's different. You love what you do."

The next Sunday he invited her to a Degas exhibit at the Met. They stopped to look at his *Children on a Doorstep*, in which four young children sit in a circle, and Holly said, "I love children. I want at least three." She confided that she'd lost her twin sister when she was nine from a rare blood cancer. "It's strange. Since Lizzie died I feel that there's always someone following me. And at the same time, I have the feeling that someone is missing."

"I'm sorry," he said. They walked past a pastry shop, gazing into blueberry and strawberry tarts, her eyes full of hunger and joy. *What is she so happy about?* he thought when he left the flower shop where he'd gone to get a bouquet for her parents (they were going to visit them for Sunday brunch) and found her sitting on one of the benches on the sidewalk, her head tilted toward the sun, eyes closed, a grin on her face.

At brunch it turned out that Holly's father had known of Harold Darby. They had graduated from the same class at Princeton. "A brilliant man," Frank Moore said, and shook his head. He sized Edward up—Edward had seen the gesture before—as if mental illness in the gene pool might be contagious. Then he cleared his throat.

"Young man, is selling art something you plan to make your livelihood?"

Edward had made a profit for the gallery by bringing in Swartzman and then two younger artists that followed. He nodded.

"Passion is one thing, but don't expect to make a living on it," Frank Moore said, and poured them both a glass of sherry. Edward looked down at his scuffed loafers and then at his white shirt frayed at the cuffs, decade-old blazer, and unwashed jeans and felt himself shrink. Hanging on the living room wall were two side-by-side paintings—in the style of Renoir—of two small girls dressed identically. The faces in the portraits reminded him of the eerie feel of Diane Arbus's figures. The girls were Holly and her twin, Lizzie, dressed in plaid skirts and knee socks. At the table, Mrs. Moore sat rigid and bone-thin in the Louis XVI dining chair as if she were being held up by a coat hanger, straining for conversation. The cracks in her caked-on foundation made her face look like puzzle pieces pasted together. The room was cold and airless. He looked across at Holly, good-natured and pleasant—he didn't know how she did it—and felt a sudden urge to take her away from them.

"Daddy," Holly said impatiently, "money isn't everything."

"Clearly," Frank Moore said, and cast his discerning eye on Edward.

"Let's get out of here," Holly whispered. "Don't mind him. He's impossible."

She took Edward by the hand into her childhood bedroom wall-papered with horses and lured him to her canopy bed.

"I don't want their life."

She said she wanted to live in a little farmhouse in the country with her dogs and horses. Edward looked at her soulfully and kissed her delicious neck. She made him exceedingly happy, even though being happy caused him pain. Everything about her seemed to go against the tenor of his life but being with her, seeing her smile at him, made him feel like he was coming to life again. "Now that you've seen my horror show, tell me about something about you. You never talk about your parents," she said.

He told her how once he had gone to see his father teach his class on Romantic poetry and sat in the back row mesmerized by this person transformed from the slightly scattered and melancholy man he was at home into a dashing intellectual. And then he told her how after his father had gotten sick his eyes lost all their sheen. "They were gray and blank."

Holly looked up at him with her big green eyes. "You're a little mixed-up too, aren't you," she said, lovingly.

He squeezed her close.

"We have a lot in common."

"Do we?" He stared at her with a confused look.

"Loss, dum-dum," she said.

Holly caressed his face and the tension drained from his body. They messed around on her canopy bed, Holly aggressively fondling him (not that he minded) as if to get back at her father, and one thing led to another. Afterward, they went back into the kitchen and made mimosas. Frank Moore wandered in wearing silk slippers and a jacket with the family crest on his breast pocket, a caricature from an eighteenth-century novel come to life. "Mike Fountain says he's waiting for you to graduate from law school. He wants you to join the firm."

"I guess he's going to wait a long time, Daddy." The spark of life shot through her like a cannonball.

After her father left the room she said, "I feel like I'm always disappointing him. They don't give me any space. It's like they think they're going to lose me, too."

Holly scooted him out close to five, saying she had tickets to a jazz concert. The tickets were for her and Charlie. "Charlie?" Edward said. "Are you still seeing him?"

"Yeah. We still do stuff," she said, and peered into his eyes as if she were looking for a response. He wondered if she was purposefully trying to make him jealous. He left feeling soiled by Frank Moore's company and mad at himself for kissing up to him, unable to get the slope of his daughter's perfect nose out of his head.

The next morning Holly sat on her perch in the gallery, a flush on her face, pushing in phone buttons and connecting calls, when he entered the gallery. He walked past Holly at the reception desk and went into his cubicle and turned on his computer. A few minutes later he heard her laugh. He opened the Dunkin Donuts bag and washed down his unhappiness with four powdered donut holes and lukewarm coffee.

That laugh! He could hear it again from his cubicle.

One of the gallery's artists was getting an award at the Academy of Arts and Letters and they were all going that night. He meandered over to the bar in the garden where they held the reception. Charlie and Holly came to join him, Holly a few inches taller than him, her arm locked in Charlie's, watching others do turns around the room. Charlie was a little portly with thick wavy hair and had that sort of Pillsbury Doughboy innocence that some women seemed to like. He possessed a boldness of temperament and confidence that made Edward squirm with envy. Earlier that week one of his artists, a twenty-four-year-old wunderkind straight out of graduate school, had sold a painting to the Whitney and suddenly the four or five young artists who had received Rome fellowships flocked around Charlie. Edward was good at spotting talent—Swartzman and the few others in his stable had created ripples—but he was looking to nail the real deal and take the art world by storm.

Julia Rosenthal was one of the Rome fellows. She sported a low-cut dress and high-heeled boots, a small bag hand-painted with flowers hanging from her delicate wrist. After Edward schmoozed with Julia and tucked his card into her palm, Charlie and Holly waltzed over, Holly in high golden sandals that laced up her ankles like the slippers of a Greek goddess, wearing a frothy thin dress.

"I saw you talking to Julia Rosenthal. You gave her your card, man." Charlie turned to Holly. "Looks like our boy is finally a player."

Holly tugged on his sleeve. "Who's Julia Rosenthal?"

Charlie pointed her out by the doorway. "She's on everyone's wait-and-see list."

Holly onced-over Julia and her face fell into a pout. She pressed Edward's arm and looked at him carefully with liquid eyes.

"Do you think she's pretty?" Holly said. "You probably want to be with an artist, right?"

He stumbled for a minute. "No, Holly, you're who I want."

She grinned, showing her generous, sparkling teeth. "Of course I am."

Charlie eyed Peter Highland, another Rome fellow, in a small cluster next to them. "Excuse me," he said, and maneuvered himself into their conversation. Peter was chatting with Lisel Miller, who covered art for the *Observer*.

Holly hooked her arm in Edward's. She leaned into him and whispered in his ear. "I feel as if I don't really know you," she said, surprising him. "And yet, I do." She squeezed his hand, flirty and a little wasted.

"It's because you're everything to me," he said, because he'd been depleted and like an empty vase she was filling him again. He supposed it was true that he didn't know her either, only what she let him see of her. What mattered was that he was no longer alone.

SIX MONTHS LATER they were engaged. Raised in a modest home on a professor's salary, he was nothing like Holly's father, and while it irked Frank Moore, it thrilled Holly. Mr. Moore insinuated once at a dinner party, after Edward found himself in a mood to explain to one of their guests the meaning behind Duchamp's *Bicycle Wheel* on display at MOMA (it challenged assumptions about the meaning of art), that working at a gallery was for sensitive types. At their engagement dinner, Holly's father took him to the bar and ordered them each a scotch.

"You're against them until you're with them, if you know what I mean," he said, clinking Edward's glass. "Now give my daughter what she deserves and enough fussing over whether a piece of art is good or not. If it sells it's good," he said, and patted Edward's back aggressively. Edward's knee-jerk reaction was to compulsively rattle off the new deals he'd made as if he were still auditioning for the part of Holly's husband, and he supposed he was. Around Mr. Moore he felt like a fraud. "Why don't you just show him your bank statement," Holly said, interrupting their conversation and rolling her eyes.

On the way back from dinner he told himself he would tell Holly about Tess. Occasionally when he'd run into a mutual friend from college and her name was mentioned he felt like he was having an out-of-body experience. Why couldn't he talk about it? It was like there was a pit in his throat.

They walked arm in arm through the park to Holly's apartment. She leaned into him and every few blocks stopped to kiss him. She moved with eagerness, alert and present, quick to brush off disappointments. Her optimism anchored her. He tried to formulate what he would say, but he didn't know how to begin. He didn't know how to explain it right, because he didn't himself quite understand how forcefully Holly had come to mean his very salvation. He couldn't risk losing her—what if she thought less of him or would not want to marry someone who'd been married before? Holly was a purist. And what would Frank Moore think of him, his only daughter marrying a man who'd been scarred first by his father's mental illness and then by this?

He stopped at the Korean market and bought Holly a bouquet of wild daisies that made her blush with happiness, and they resumed their walk together, dodging the sidewalk gratings that he always feared would give way. He'd find another time; they had their whole lives. But as he neared her apartment he felt regret at not telling her. When they got to her doorstep she looked up at him. "What's wrong, honey," she said. "You look like there's something you want to say."

He looked into her open, honest face and felt he didn't deserve her. "Only how much I love you," he said, unaware that the longer he waited, the longer Holly would feel in retrospect that her trust had been violated.

THE WEDDING WAS at her father's club in Connecticut. They honeymooned on St. Barths, an extravagant gift from Holly's father that for once she accepted. When they arrived at the hotel they uncorked the complimentary bottle of champagne waiting in their room and made love on the bed. Holly asked Edward to promise that they would never take money from her father again. "I don't want him controlling our lives," she said, her head propped on her arm, looking at him with her steely, purposeful eyes.

In the mornings they drank mimosas and took long walks to a secluded beach. "Let's tell each other one thing we don't know about each other," Holly said, her coppery skin gleaming in a skimpy bikini. Her revelation: for the year after Lizzie died, she made herself throw up after she ate.

"I told you. I couldn't deal with pleasure."

He wanted to tell her about Tess, he started to, knowing it was wrong to keep it secret. *There was this girl from college, we lived together in New York* . . . but the words stayed in his throat. Instead he said he'd never told his parents that he was kicked off the soccer team his senior year of high school for not going to practice, and when he was supposed to be at practice he hid out in his best friend Bennett's basement getting high.

"Oh, come on," Holly said. "So I married a liar?" She laughed and poked him in the ribs. They made love by the turquoise sea so picturesque and still he thought he was looking at a painting.

At night, after long romantic dinners, he slept beside his new bride in their wide hotel bed with its soft mattress and crisp sheets, feeling her arm hairs brush against his, her breathing melding with the continuous sound of the sea outside their window, aware that his life was not his alone and that whatever he did now would affect her. He watched her slowly coast toward sleep, a foreign being beside him, frightened by her essential unknowability and his own strange unwillingness to reveal himself fully to her. In her sleep Holly slipped her leg between his as if sensing his detachment, and slowly he drifted into a state of calm and then suddenly jerked awake, frightened again. Throughout the nights of their honeymoon the pattern repeated itself, the slow drift toward unconsciousness and then the sudden shock into wakefulness, where a dull seizure of panic took hold of him. In the roll of the ocean, he heard his own fear and pull toward oblivion, moving him forward and then taking him back.

JIMMY OLDMAN WAS in town from Los Angeles. Ran a small gallery there. Pity he had no taste. Jimmy had made a sport out of representing pale, tall women—his newest was called Angel, no last name, with a snakelike tattoo running down the back of her neck, piercings in the nose and tongue.

Jimmy's thick hair crested to his shoulders. It had once been blond but some recent gray had turned it more of a neutral color. He wore a jacket with jeans and cowboy boots, a style that suited him. Edward still wore the same uniform from his prep school days, navy jacket (he'd lost the school emblem on the breast pocket), crisp white shirt, dark jeans, and the occasional Italian suit. Jimmy was endearingly earnest and excitable, always ready for a party, refusing to give in to middle age. He'd come to the work late, a second career that began as a hobby, collecting prints, lithographs, and paintings, turning up at auctions, and only recently had opened the gallery. Eventually he put everything he had into it, though he'd yet to turn a profit. The gallery gave him a second adolescence, jump-starting his professional life and apparently rekindling his sex drive.

He'd been negotiating an affair with high-strung Melody for nearly a year. Strange how none of the women Jimmy slept around with were pretty and his wife, Lucinda, was a knockout. Melody was a young assistant at Betty Cunningham, a gallery in Chelsea. Well, she wasn't exactly young anymore. She was thirty-five, had a gangly son with a spiked haircut and crooked teeth whom she adored (she'd shown Edward his photo on her phone), and had separated from her husband but hadn't officially divorced. She accepted the no-strings-attached concept involved in sleeping with Jimmy—he was married—but she still expected to be texted, that when he came into town he'd get a decent hotel room, and that she'd be invited to stay. There was often a new dustup with her ex over money or custody. When Jimmy was in town, Edward sometimes met him for a drink at the Red Cat. Melody predictably showed up in an intoxicated state after coming from a gallery opening and crashed their drinks date. Inevitably, Jimmy was engaged in a conversation with one of his artists (who also showed up unannounced), lathering on praise in a verbal symphony of adjectives, and Melody privileged Edward with the awkward details of her most recent dramas. She looked just on the verge of a nervous breakdown, spewing without inhibition whatever was bothering her, from the unpleasant side effects of her antidepressant to tales of her delinquent son and play-by-plays of her combative relationship with Jimmy. Edward thought her impulsive and careless need to spill her manic energy into whoever cared to listen oddly comforting.

The first morning back at the gallery after Berlin, Edward wasn't in the mood to find Jimmy, who had been in town all weekend, slumming on the sleek leather couch in his office, answering e-mails on his phone. Familiar, like a brother. Well, it was Jimmy who called them brothers. Edward's office had open windows on one side that looked out into the vast gallery and the flock of assistants facing their computers in small open-cubicle desks. He drew the blinds.

"Don't you have somewhere else to go?" Edward clutched his red-eye, a Grande Sumatra with a shot of espresso in it—he allowed himself one potent coffee every morning, and then something milder in the afternoon—and settled into his desk chair for the morning's long haul. "I have work to do."

"Not everyone has an Agnes Murray on his roster," Jimmy said.

Edward looked up from his steel desk. "A bit early, isn't it?"

"You're cranky."

"Jet lag."

"How was Berlin?"

"Savan was part of the group. Had I known, I would have canceled." Edward raised his head and smiled.

"That ass."

"He can empty a room. You have to give him credit for that."

"Anyone else of interest?"

"Remember Julia Rosenthal? Rome Prize, 1995."

"Really?" Jimmy broke into a grin. "How's she holding up?"

"Pretty well."

Jimmy moved from the leather couch to the chair across from Edward.

"Man, are you holding out on me?"

"Nothing more to say."

Jimmy's phone chimed a rendition of Beethoven's Ninth.

"Hey, babe," Jimmy said into his BlackBerry. "Here with Edward. I think he may have a girlfriend."

"For Christ sakes," Edward said, and shook his head.

"Get a shower and meet me at Gramercy for lunch," Jimmy cooed, still talking into his phone. "I'll see if I can coax Edward to join us." After Jimmy finished the call he turned to Edward. "I'm getting a hard-on talking to her on the phone."

"Jimmy. Could you find another place to entertain yourself? I have work to do."

"Gramercy at one," Jimmy said.

Agnes Murray was on line two. Last night he hadn't slept well. He'd fallen asleep on the sofa in his study after consuming three or four tumblers of whiskey—two was his usual limit—and had awoken with an excruciating headache, as if nails had been lodged in his skull. He was on his second hypercoffee, breaking his rule. He'd had to bribe his assistant to make a coffee run.

He was busy with other artists and clients, but whenever Agnes called he felt he should drop everything and attend to her. Her show had brought in millions and had been a major boon to his career. Some artists wanted to be left alone and others needed reassurance and attention. With Agnes he had to gently stoke the fire to make sure she was happy.

After her show's success, May changed the name of the gallery to Mayweather and Darby, though she was still the controlling partner. His relationship with Agnes was complicated. He knew she was aware that he'd risen on her coattails. He felt he owed her something, and this feeling had placed him in an inferior position, even though he knew that by relinquishing power he was also failing her.

After he secured a show for her at Thaddaeus Ropac, an elite gallery in Paris, she gave him a small abstract painting as a present. It was done in hues of light iridescent green; slowly through a soft play of shadow and light the viewer made out that it was a landscape of sensual green hills. "My father took me to the old country the year I graduated from college. This painting has been in my mind since then. It's for everything you've done for me," she'd said. He mounted the painting in his private space at the gallery and admired it. But it was complicated. Looking at the painting, he felt its subterranean echoes.

The show's success contributed to Nate's and Agnes's spectacular net worth. Months afterward, Agnes and Nate bought a huge loft building on Hudson Street in Tribeca with matching studios on separate floors. They lived in the two floors on top. The building, faced in glass on one side and with a garden in the back, was a modern-looking Frank Lloyd Wright–inspired structure in the heart of the city, meant for viewers to notice—a formidable, glorious representation of money and power.

Months ago, Edward had taken Agnes to Europe to meet a handful of prominent European gallery owners and museum directors. The gallery paid all expenses. On their last day, after a handful of meetings and dinner in Rome, Agnes invited him back to her presidential suite for a nightcap. It was close to midnight. Agnes went into the bathroom to freshen up and came out wearing a pair of navy silk pajamas with her hair twisted in a loose wrap on top of her head. "I hope you don't mind," she said. "I'm exhausted. What a day."

He smiled. "It was a good day."

He looked at the clock on the nightstand. "It's late. I should let you get some sleep."

"Stay. I'm not tired yet. I'm too wound up to sleep." She had tried calling Nate a few times throughout the day and evening, but he'd gone AWOL and Edward sensed not reaching him had made her anxious.

"I'm glad you're here with me. I hate being alone in hotel rooms."

He reclined on a comfortable chair next to the bed. She opened the minibar and took out two little bottles of vodka, poured them into two glasses, and handed one to him.

"To you," Agnes said, and clinked her glass against his. "Do you get lonely when you travel?" She hopped off the bed and trailed to the window to look out at the skyline all lit up.

"I'm used to it."

"I think Nate likes it. The break from the twins."

"Children take up a lot of energy."

"For Nate it's different." She turned toward him again and sat back down. "He already went through being a parent with Liam. He doesn't feel it as intensely as I do."

"That must be lonely."

"Marriage is lonely, isn't it?" Agnes lowered her eyes. She finished her vodka and meandered back to the minibar. "Another?" she said, taking out two more mini bottles of Absolut and handed one to Edward. "This way maybe I can sleep." She propped herself on the bed with the glass in her hand.

"I guess with Nate it's worth it," she continued, as if thinking out loud. "He understands my work. He brings more to the table than anyone else I've been with. I've been thinking. He's the way he is because he's afraid his fame will outdo his talent. He's the youngest of four siblings. His oldest brother runs a hedge fund. The other two are surgeons. His father never approved of Nate. He doesn't understand art. He thinks his son is a fool."

"Is that what drives him?"

"I think so. Only Nate no longer has to prove himself."

"Do you think it ever ends? The desire to prove oneself?"

"Is that what you think of Nate?"

"It's only what you think of him that matters."

"Nate's extraordinary," she said. "I mean, when he isn't being an ass." She looked at him and smiled. "I'm kidding," she said. "An installation he designed has been commissioned for the 9/11 memorial site. Do you suppose we could appeal to the jury to take one of my pieces?"

"You don't think Nate would mind?"

"Mind?"

"If your work outdid his?"

A small smile crept into her face and then, catching herself, she bit her bottom lip. "Nate isn't competitive with me. He's my biggest fan. Let's try calling him again." She sprung out of bed and balanced herself against the nightstand, tipsy from the vodka. "I want to tell him about all the meetings we had." She reached for her cell phone, got his voice mail again, and with a frown hung up. "He's probably out with Frederick."

"I should go," Edward said, stretching.

"Stay a little longer. If I'm alone I'll start thinking too much. And worrying."

"About what?"

"You mean, what don't I worry about? That the work won't hold up. That Nate will tire of us—the girls and me. Sometimes I wonder if I even like him."

"Nate?"

She nodded. "I don't always know if Nate's a good guy. He's got too much on his plate," she said, and yawned. "I don't know why I said what I just said. I'm crazy about him. I'm tired." She crawled underneath the covers. "Do you mind staying a little longer? Until I fall asleep?"

"Of course." He dimmed the lights and in the upholstered chair by the bed he studied how the shadows from the lights outside fell in the room. He thought about Agnes and Nate. They were intensely intertwined. They flirted, bantered, fought, and made up. Their charged connection fed their artistic fires. But lately he'd noticed something new: Agnes liked to subjugate herself to Nate's dominance. It turned her on. He glanced at her curled into her pillow like a little girl. He quietly slipped out and went back to his hotel room, glad the European trip had been successful but eager to return home.

WITH AGNES'S NEW show on the horizon, he had to tread carefully. He told his assistant to tell Agnes he'd return her phone call that afternoon. He'd tackle it after lunch. He suspected she was ready to talk about the new work. Agnes's expectations were high and so were the stakes. It was sometimes difficult for an artist to produce after a successful show. Though she had invited him to the twins' christening, the only person outside her family in attendance, she'd gone uncomfortably quiet on him over the last few years, emerging to write or answer the occasional e-mail for business purposes when they needed to be in touch, or to check in on her assets, every few months meeting him for lunch or a drink. The last time he saw her she went on about Nate. She mentioned that Nate's gallery in Paris had done a redesign of their website and that Nate was on their home page. She wanted to know whether the gallery ought to redesign her page.

"I'll take a look," he'd said. Even though she didn't want her work compared to Nate's, she made sure that what he got, she would get too. Though Agnes worried she'd be perceived as having married Nate to better her reputation, she secretly enjoyed the association. It allowed her to be a figurehead of her generation. Without gossip from the press, she'd be shelved in obscurity like most artists.

He'd learned to tolerate the fast-and-loose way Agnes had of obtaining what she wanted, sometimes stretching the truth so that it suited her desires. She was successful but didn't have quite the same degree of star power as Nate, for one reason: she was a loner and people made her uncomfortable. Part of being successful was allowing the public to have a piece of you. Edward felt for Agnes. He was a loner too.

He decided to skip lunch with Jimmy and ordered in a sandwich. He could abide Jimmy and Melody, but not when he was sober. He told Jimmy he'd meet them after work for a drink before he took the train home, and then attacked his waiting e-mails.

May walked in dressed in a light pink Chanel suit, with a strand of oversized pearls around her neck. "How was Berlin?" She was just a little over five feet, with nut-brown eyes and a nervous habit of pushing back the thinning silver hair cut in a pixie from her forehead.

He'd met May almost eighteen years ago when Gertrude Silverman asked him to attend a fundraiser at the Met on her behalf. During his apprentice years he'd spent many evenings doing things Gertrude's demanding schedule no longer permitted her. It had given him an opportunity to advance himself even though at those opulent functions he'd always felt like a kid in a tuxedo.

He had been seated at May's table. The place next to her had been reserved for a Guggenheim heir who never showed up. Edward scooted over to May and introduced himself. People genuinely liked him, and she had brightened immediately. He was the kind of man who grew more attractive when he smiled. His mother told him that because he was delicate his handsome face would take him far, and especially then, when he was starting out, he'd hoped she was right.

"That's an elegant name," May said, from the first moment a charmer. The diamond choker she wore must have cost three times his yearly salary. "It reminds me of a name from a Henry James novel. Are you Jamesian?"

"How would you describe Jamesian?"

"Work that's interested in consciousness and perception."

"I guess that's the kind of art I love."

"If you love art then you'd better get out of the business." May threw back her head and let loose a deep, throaty laugh that crackled as a result of years of smoking, and he laughed too. A few days later May invited him to lunch at the Colony Club, and shortly after asked him to come run the day-to-day operations of the gallery. She felt they had connected. So had he. She mentioned to him that Charles had hoped to leave the gallery to their daughter Abigail, if she ever got sober.

Unsure there'd be room to move up in Gertrude's shop, and newly married and eager to advance, he had accepted the opportunity. Edward and May trusted each other. He was careful about the artists he took on, and if they lost money on someone he took it to heart, as if he were personally taking cash out of her pocket. They became close.

"Berlin was good. I closed the deal with Henning. And we're narrowing in on a huge deal for Murray."

"Good," May said.

"Everything okay here?"

She nodded.

"What's wrong, then, May? You don't look well."

"It's Abigail again. She left rehab. I thought this time would be different. I don't know where she's gone."

"I'm sorry."

"Charles and I gave her everything." She lowered her head. "What good did any of it do for Abigail? She's been an addict since she was fourteen. I've been trying to reflect upon the way in which Charles and I let her down."

"I wish my mother had your sense of reflection."

May looked at him warmly and he felt himself being pulled into the vaulted and privileged sanctuary of her trust. For some reason he could confide in May, whereas with his own mother he'd always kept a distance. "I miss Charles every day." She reached out her bony hand to touch Edward's sleeve. "You're my family now, Edward." And then quickly, as if aware she'd let down her professional guard: "What's on the agenda this afternoon?"

"We have a budget meeting at two. And Agnes. She called this morning. She's on the agenda."

"Better get to it. She's paying our salaries," May said.

BY FOUR, LESS anxious and settled into his routine, he secured his mental resources and called her.

Agnes was around the corner and asked if she could pop in.

He got off the phone, went to the men's room, sprinkled water on his face, and redid his tie.

He greeted her in their lobby. She looked thin and pale. Dark circles lined her eyes. He invited her into his office and offered her a seat on his couch.

"It's good to see you, Agnes. In Berlin your work is creating quite a stir."

"I'm glad." She smiled with tight lips.

"It's a good sign." He stood up from his desk and took the seat next to her.

"I hope so. I've pushed hard."

"What's it like? You've been secretive."

"I've tried to keep myself in the dark as much as possible. The short answer is that the work is about artists and historic oppression. I suppose the real question is whether art can be owned. I hope the conceptual elements I've chosen, the textures and materials, convey that anxiety."

He listened carefully. Most artists weren't as articulate about their work as Agnes. She had a habit of lecturing, but he didn't really mind. Not all of the time.

"I want to call the show *Things Fall Apart*. It's from Yeats's 'The Second Coming.' The new work is nothing like *Immortality*. It's painted with a darker and more conceptual edge. And I'm using other materials beside paint."

He had hoped for something with perhaps more levity and playfulness. They'd budgeted for the revenues it would throw off and had been counting on them for the following fiscal year. It bothered him that he had to think about the marketplace. Before Agnes's success he hadn't thought about it much, but now that the gallery had profited and been taken up a notch, he had to make sure it stayed that way. It was a struggle, knowing how to make sure an artist wasn't compromising her talent for the marketplace, but also ensuring that the work would sell.

"My paintings are about the way in which art can express a moment in time. If it exists on the canvas, then it exists in history. The understory is about the oppressed and their unwillingness to forgive. 'One wants from a painting a sense of life. The final suggestion, the final gesture, the final statement, has to be not a deliberate statement but a helpless statement. It has to be what you can't avoid saying.' Jasper Johns said this. I've had the statement pinned on the wall in my studio."

She suddenly rose, wandered to his window. Though she was dressed in grunge wear—an expensive-looking army jacket, jeans, and low-cut work boots, and her hair tied back with a swath of a pink rag—he noticed the understated emerald pendant she wore on a black string around her neck. It must have cost a pretty penny. She turned around and her eye lit on the painting she'd given him when they first signed and her lips widened into a smile of satisfaction. *A bitch,* one of her European dealers had called her, and he supposed the dealer was right—but beneath it all there was a stream of sweetness.

"I'm at your disposal. What can I do to help?"

She sat back down and crossed her legs. "I think you'll understand what I mean when I say this. You have a daughter. I'm interested in the idea of that primal fear in the work. The fear of losing them, the twins. Nate thinks I'm paranoid but he's wrong. And of course it ties back into 9/11. How vulnerable we are."

"Of course."

"It's complicated, because that's what's making it difficult for me to contemplate letting go and showing the work. Even to you. It freaks me out. It's that same vulnerability that is my subject."

"You have nothing to worry about."

"You heard about Nate's latest show, right?"

"It was called *Necrophilia*, wasn't it? It was in the air." Of course he'd heard about it. Who hadn't? It outdid his previous show in provocation and profits. An artist could be dismissed by the press, and by his contemporaries, and still wind up the most prized artist at the Metropolitan Museum of Art. Or not.

"The press can't come after me. Can they? I mean, my work is nothing like his."

"The work is all that matters," he said, deciding to take the high road.

"The critics called Nate's last show offensive, demeaning, and vulgar. But it was his most successful yet. He's review-proof. The public adores him. Men can be provocative and unsettling, but when a woman painter goes after the same effect it's considered derivative."

"Your work isn't provocative in the same way, anyhow. It's more complex."

"Abramović said a woman had to be like a man if she wanted to be an artist. Do you believe that? I wonder if being a mother has hurt my work."

"Or deepened it."

She looked at him and smiled.

"It doesn't have to be all or nothing, you know," he said.

"The truth is, I'm terrified. I've worked on the paintings in utter isolation. I need to be alone with my materials. Beauty and seriousness are all I have to work with. Nate is different. He's out nearly every night going to openings, back and forth to Europe to see private clients all the time. He doesn't need it the way I do."

"You have nothing to be afraid of."

"You think so?" She tucked a loose strand of hair behind her ear. "Thanks. I'd be nowhere without you."

He undid his tie and opened his top button. How did Nate put up with Agnes's neuroses? From time to time Edward wondered what kept Nate enthralled. He supposed it was her beauty and her money—her parents had underwritten a concert hall in Lincoln Center dedicated in their name—or the fact that her extraordinary talent kept him on his toes. Perhaps he was drawn to her neuroses, too. Maybe Nate got something out of feeling needed in this way.

"Have you run into Nate lately?" Agnes said, as if reading his mind.

"I haven't. Why? Is something wrong?"

"He's been distant. Something's going on he won't tell me about."

"It's like that after a recent show. I've watched it happen. No matter how successful, there's an emptiness that comes after it. It's like postpartum depression, isn't it?"

Agnes's face broke open and she burst into tears.

"What's wrong?" Edward moved next to her and she crumbled into his arms. Her shoulders were bony and fragile. He felt as if he were holding a skeleton.

"Of course you're right. I always feel empty after a show." She hugged him again and then let go and wiped her eyes with a Kleenex from her handbag. "It's all the isolation that's getting to me."

"Are things good with Nate?"

"They have to be. With him I'm like his child, his mother, and his lover. Sometimes I don't know what role he wants me to play."

"Then why . . . ?"

"Nate knows everything about me. It's intensely erotic to be known in that way. It's the closest rush to painting. He's good for me. Who would I be without him? How would I manage all this?"

"We won't let you down, Agnes. You can consider the gallery your second home. We see you like family. Everyone here does."

"I feel that way too." She stood up to leave, still sniffling.

"There's one more thing," Agnes said as he walked her out to the lobby. "Alex Savan called from Berlin. He saw a painting of mine and gushed about it. He said he'd been talking my work up to every impressive gallery in Germany."

"I have two deals pending in Berlin. I was waiting until we'd gotten final terms to put you and Reynolds in the loop. Galleries want exclusivity. And trust. I don't need Savan mucking it up. I'll take care of it." Goddamn Savan, he thought, trying too hard again and screwing things up.

He said good-bye, kissing her first on one cheek and then the other. When the elevator door closed, he was glad she'd gone. Back at his desk, he picked up the phone and called Leonard. They had bonded over the careful handholding Agnes required, and even though Leonard was no longer her manager, Edward often consulted him. Six weeks before her first show at the gallery, Leonard's wife had left him. His young son suffered from anxiety and wasn't doing well. Leonard had taken him away skiing. Agnes was nervous about the opening and kept calling his hotel and leaving urgent messages. When she finally reached him, she lit into him, saying she needed him in New York. He said if she wasn't happy she should find another manager. It was one of the occupational hazards of dealing with an art star. They forgot you had a personal life. Agnes hadn't taken it well. Shaken, she'd fallen into a depression, and for a few days, having momentarily lost her confidence, threatened to postpone the show. She called the gallery four or five times a day, asking Edward to walk her through every painstaking detail, and then broke down. She said that Leonard knew everything about her. Every collector. Every interested museum director. She was angry that he'd cut her off and was seemingly unaware of her neediness and solipsism. She spent weeks interviewing managers, until she decided on Reynolds, calmed down, and allowed the show to open as planned.

The result of being left by his wife, and then cleaning house of his most valuable client, was that Leonard saw others with a kind of knife-sharp perception Edward found nearly profound, as if by being betrayed Leonard was alerted to character nuances he had hitherto never been privileged to see. There were those who preferred not to see and those whose need to see at times made life unbearable. Edward did not know which camp he belonged in.

"I just spoke to Agnes. She's getting ready to show me her work. She's incredibly uptight. I've never seen her like this. The last time was after you let her go. The work didn't come easy. It's been four years. What if, you know . . . It will be brilliant, won't it?"

"Has she given you reason to doubt it?"

"Not exactly. She's been quiet about it until now."

"Regardless, tell her you're blown away. Don't let her walk you into a corner."

"I have to be honest with her. She trusts me."

"She trusts no one."

"That's reassuring after all these years."

"Your problem. Not mine," Leonard said, almost gleefully.

Edward packed up his briefcase, eager for a drink.

MELODY WAS WEARING a tight T-shirt without a bra—Edward had thought that braless had gone out with the ushering in of the eighties—and it was impossible not to notice her nipples were at attention. She was drinking an extravagant cocktail, something cranberry-colored with a twist of lime, and her fargone eyes had the glassy sheen of marbles; they'd been drinking since lunch. Jimmy, earnestly enthralled, made Edward squirm. He touched her arm, her hand, then leaned over to kiss her neck. You'd think he'd nabbed Natalie Portman instead of Mel, with her boyish haircut and piggish nose. She was British. Perhaps that was part of the appeal.

Melody greeted him and planted a kiss on each cheek. That she seemed especially glad to see him lifted his mood. "Darling," she said, once he sat down. "Jimmy says you're in love."

His face broke into a grin, thinking of Julia and then, realizing it, he recovered quickly. "I'm married, Mel," he said, soberly.

Jimmy glanced at Melody. Her face dropped and she straightened herself and took a sip of her cocktail. "The pieces are coming together." She moved her shoulder away from Jimmy's. "Jimmy likes being married. That's why he won't leave his wife. It makes things more intense when we're together, doesn't it, darling?" She bounced her leg, unable to keep still. Edward looked at the hipsters in leather jackets and trendy haircuts at the bar and felt old and out of place.

"Mel," Jimmy said, "I'm crazy about you."

"Let's talk about Edward. You never change. Edward, on the other hand, has been transformed." She touched Edward's arm. "I could tell when you walked in the door that something was different. How terrible is it, darling?"

"Tell what?" Edward said. *Was it really that obvious?*

"I could make a building out of my knowledge." She raised one eyebrow. "Jimmy said you met someone."

"Jimmy," Edward said, and shook his head. "Get us another round, would you?"

Jimmy got up and headed toward the bar.

Once he was out of range, Melody put her head in her hands. Edward rose and moved into the booth next to her and touched her shoulder. "Mel," he said, genuinely moved. "What's wrong? You and Jimmy are perfect."

"Are we? If you commit one sin, then you commit them all."

In Los Angeles Jimmy had a wife and two daughters he worshipped. Edward had been to their home with a swimming pool that overlooked a canyon and a magnificent house with one side made of windows. He'd suspected something was up with Jimmy after he showed up in New York for the Armory Show, then a month later an auction, two weeks later to go to an exhibition. Jimmy said he'd fallen in love. Edward wondered whether he had meant with Melody or with the intoxication of the New York art scene and the people who were part of it, or if they were both the same for him, an adrenaline-inducing fictional world (for art could only masquerade as reality) where he could reinvent himself. Before

Melody there was a girl, an artist, with hair cut shorter on one side than the other, which had made Edward just a little dizzy when he looked at her, and then there was Julie Johnston, an art critic for the *Times*, and briefly a slim Italian art dealer. Melody was the latest. She was overstimulated and—Edward could tell—highly sexual. It was what Jimmy saw in her.

"But you're the one he's with now," Edward offered.

"What's she like?"

"His wife?"

She nodded, and bit her bottom lip.

"You don't want to know. Best to not know anything. This is what's absolute. You and Jimmy are good together." He didn't know if he really believed this or not, but he wanted to—just as much as he wished he were more free and easy, like Jimmy, who didn't stop to think about the consequences of his actions, or if he did, was willing to risk it. And poor Melody—she looked so strung out, he had to say something.

"So you approve?"

"How many absolutes do we have proof of? We don't even know what color the sky will be on any given day."

"You're masterful," Melody said, and sniffed back her tears.

He didn't think so, or believe really in what he'd said, but her mood lifted and it made him feel better. Jimmy returned with drinks and Edward rose from the booth so that Jimmy could sit beside her. Jimmy slid in close and kissed her. Then her hand reached under the table. Edward excused himself to catch his train.

Outside it was dark and the wind blew in swirls. A loose piece of paper skimmed his cheek. The buildings loomed overhead. He walked over a sewer grate and felt it tremble under his feet. A homeless man dressed in rags picked at a half-eaten sandwich in the garbage can. Traffic went by in an unremitting flow down Fifth Avenue. He walked swiftly to the station, pulled by its powerful force. He thought about Julia and wondered if Melody was right. Had meeting her changed him somehow?

He found an empty car at the back of the train. The severe light exposed sections of newspaper, soda and beer cans, and sandwich wrappers strewn on the floor. The cheap upholstery was ripped. The train pulled off, rattling the cans, and the lights dimmed. Rain appeared on the window, and as he listened to the stop-start patter on the glass, pressed against the side of the darkened car, he retreated into its sound.

Like Jimmy, he had had opportunities. He supposed there always were if one wanted only sex. Once an ambitious assistant shocked him by coming up to him at a reception and asking him point-blank if she could give him a blowjob. He had refused her, awkwardly heading toward the door of the gallery claiming he had a train to catch. Had he given off the vibe that he had been attracted to her? He wasn't sure he had been, though he'd noticed the way her body moved when she walked in and out of his office. When he was outside, he had broken out in a rash of perspiration, wondering if he had led her on. In the coolness of the night, away from the warm bodies standing arm to arm in small clusters, he had wanted to go back in and find her. On the train home he fantasized about inviting her into his office the following morning. But when he got there, bright and early, he avoided her and was glad when a few weeks later she left to take a sales position at Sotheby's.

He watched the lit houses near the tracks rush past. Then a long ravine. A cemetery. The rain made him relax and for a few moments he retreated into a rich forest of fantasy. He thought of Julia next to him in the dark car and his hand went to the empty seat at his side. In the forty-eight hours since he'd been back from Berlin he couldn't shake her. He closed his eyes and breathed.

The train came to his stop and he robotically rose, reached for his briefcase, and departed. He felt inside his pants pocket for his keys, opened the car door, slid inside, and sat for a few minutes before he turned the key and the car accelerated. The streets were dark and wet. He pulled up his driveway. It was unbearably quiet, with no sense of the trees as companions, no sense of any living thing, not the deer that had begun to deplete his garden or the occasional fox that ran through his yard. The rain stopped. The house seemed to belong to ghosts.

12 CONNECTICUT

A T THE ACKERMANS' cocktail party he watched Holly in a short black dress, snug at her hips, and high pumps. She looked amused conversing with Tom Drury. She and Tom had been close friends as kids, and now he owned the barn where she and Annabel rode. Holly was flirting with Tom, Edward observed, almost abstractly. They were such old friends it didn't worry him. Hand on her hip, high cheekbones, square chin, and hair cut in a long bob, she caught Edward's eye and he returned the glance. They both smiled, and he brightened. It was a rare moment at a crowded party to get a moment of her attention. It excited him, seeing her across a crowded room like that, even after all these years.

In the car on the way home, Holly was tipsy. "Did you see how much weight Irene lost? I bet she's having an affair. She has that rabid look on her face. If Mark finds out, he'll throw her out."

"Aren't you being a little harsh?"

"You'd throw me out, wouldn't you? If I were cheating on you."

"You'd probably throw me out," Edward said.

"Did you hear that Sally left Tom?"

"No, since when? Why didn't you tell me?"

"I didn't want to betray Tom's confidence but now it's out in the open."

"Why do you suppose Sally left him?" He took his eye off the road and looked at her.

"Because Tom lost interest. Isn't that how it usually works? Sally—do you find her attractive?"

"Sally's not bad."

"Tom said that he doesn't know if Sally ever really loved him." She scooted closer and rested her face against his arm. "I never liked Sally." He smelled the evening's wine on her breath; her words were slow and languid. "She was always critical of Tom." She curled next to him. "I think we need to spend more time together."

They pulled into the drive. Sometimes returning from a party he wandered the downstairs of the house or took the dogs for a long walk through their quiet streets to settle his thoughts. But before he could get the leash on the dogs, Holly led him up the stairs by his hand. He couldn't remember the last time she'd wanted him. The years after Annabel, when they were trying to have another baby, he had to perform on demand when Holly was ovulating. Since then sex had become freighted. All these years later and they hadn't quite figured out how to get their rhythm and spontaneity back. Maybe she sensed something.

She went into the bathroom. He undressed and lay on their bed reviewing the night in his mind. Throughout the evening he had observed his neighbors' lives, comparing them to his own rather than enjoying himself. Phil, two houses down, was in mergers and acquisitions. There was always some new possession he made you aware of, a Mercedes or an antique rug. His recent purchase, an estate in East Hampton. Chip Lawson boasted about his twin boys who were both on the hockey team at Harvard, and though he liked the boys he wasn't interested in hearing a play-by-play of a hockey game. And Tom Drury was getting divorced? Tom ran three different horse farms in Connecticut. He and Holly were close. He'd known Lizzie too, and for that reason Tom knew Holly in a way he never would and every now and then Edward found himself jealous of their closeness. He had always thought Tom and Sally looked happy. Thinking about his neighbors, he realized that though he wanted to connect with them, he felt separate and distant. They had little in common. He was more like his father, who rarely socialized outside his field and groused when his mother had wanted him to go out with her friends.

Holly came out of the bathroom, her hair pulled back in a ponytail, in a black satin nightshirt that brushed her thighs. She folded into her side of the bed and turned to him. Her hand reached between his legs and she touched him and he thickened against her. "You're sure you're not too tired," he asked, guarded from the nights he'd gotten aroused and she'd rolled into her pillow longing for sleep. The moonlight through the fold in the curtains shadowed her face, her skin warm and slightly damp. "No," she whispered in his ear. He moved closer to her and slid her nightshirt up to reach her skin and slipped down her panties. He felt her come loose in his arms as she moved upward to meet him. He was aroused by her overnight smell, her slightly sour breath mixed with the faint odor of the evening's perfume. She fondled the back of his neck with her fingers, like she always did, and moved her mouth to kiss him and soon her skin began to perspire, her body warm like fever. After, they lay on their backs next to each other for a long time in silence. He sensed Holly was thinking the same thing he was—their love-making, though pleasurable, had become routine and familiar, and though it should have brought them closer, he felt far away from her. It seemed it ought to be simple to get back what they once had, and yet, it wasn't.

He kissed her forehead and tried to coast into sleep, telling himself that it was what happened in most marriages. Holly turned into her pillow and before long he heard the recognizable sound of her slow sleep breathing. His thoughts drifted to Julia. Since Berlin his thoughts kept turning to her. He climbed out of bed to take the dogs out.

JULIA'S STUDIO WAS in Soho, one of the last of the rent-controlled holdouts, and his gallery was in Chelsea. She only had an hour or so for lunch, and had an afternoon meeting near Grand Central, so he'd come up with the idea of meeting at the oyster bar in the terminal, which was centrally located (he mentioned he might afterward pop into Christie's, where there was a print auction going on) and quick and, Edward surmised, not the sort of place where one made love to a woman. Men and women mostly dressed in business attire sat on stools eating oysters or clam chowder. The waitresses clashed dirty plates down in bins one after the other in an orchestra of angry sound. It smelled slightly rancid, like urine covered over with a strong cleaning product. The smell of the shellfish reminded him of the summer they'd rented a house on the Cape for a week and grilled lobster on the deck and even the next morning the smell was still on his fingers.

He looked out for her toss of hair streaked with locks of blond. She arrived in the midst of some mild state of confusion, looking as she did at Hamburg airport that day when she thought she had lost her passport. "I got on the wrong train. I thought I was late."

He smiled. "You're not late."

They greeted each other briskly and then he stopped a moment to admire her.

"You're looking well," he said. It had been months since he'd last seen her in Berlin, and face to face he was struck again by her radiance. She had just gotten back from Japan with her husband, who had business there. He asked her about it.

"I love Tokyo. The Japanese have a minimalist, poetic culture. What are you having?" she asked when the waitress arrived, holding out her pad and impatiently tapping her pencil on the counter, to take their order. The menu was as dense as the phone book. "I'll have the shrimp salad. No, I'll have the crab cakes. Should I have the salad or the crab cakes?"

He smiled.

"I'll take the crab cakes," she said. When the waitress left she turned to him. "I feel like we're back in Berlin. Our waitress looked German, didn't she?"

They laughed.

"Did you see Flammarion's show at Gagosian? Some people find his work derivative and overhyped. Derivative or not, that last painting made me cry." Her cheeks reddened. She was more comfortable talking about other artists' work than her own, which made Edward like her more. She was so unlike Agnes. She looked up at him, suddenly embarrassed by her burst of passion. "Why don't you stop me?"

"I like hearing you talk."

"Are you going to the London Art Fair?" She sipped her glass of seltzer, lime, no ice, from a straw.

He was so absorbed by how pretty she was and by the hint of cleavage from her V-neck sweater when she leaned over that he couldn't concentrate on her words and didn't immediately realize she had stopped talking and was waiting for a response.

"London? Are you going? Watkins is taking my *Dancers*." They were Giacometti-like figures in unusual, uncomfortable poses. Her sculptures were shown by Watkins and Rogers, one of the hipper but lesser-known galleries in Chelsea. "Seriously, is your gallery showing anyone in London this year?"

"Yes, I'm taking Tony Henderson's paintings."

"So you're going, then?" She glanced up at him and stroked the side of her jaw.

"Of course. Unless May shuts us down before then."

"Are you worried?"

"The last two quarters we've been down."

"Hasn't everyone?"

"Everyone except for Savan. He said his revenues were up sixty percent."

"He is the art world macher, isn't he? Or at least he thinks he is."

"I suppose he is."

"But you're more talented," Julia said.

"Why do you say that?"

"Because you don't boast. People boast only when they need to prove something."

"The irony is that it works for him."

"Do you think so? I'm not so sure."

"Well, no one could say that about you. You're extremely modest." His arm brushed hers when he reached to take a sip of water.

"I'm my own worst critic," she declared and shook her head.

"You shouldn't be."

She stopped picking at her lunch and touched his sleeve. "You're sweet to say that. When we were in Tokyo I went to Zojoji, a temple where the Japanese worship babies that are a result of miscarriage or don't survive childbirth. Remember, in Berlin? When you wondered what was wrong? Roy and I lost a baby a few years ago. She was born still," Julia said. "She wasn't, though. She was alive inside me. She was my baby." She took a sip of water. "It was her birthday. Roy and I always make a point of acknowledging it." She looked at him and then looked down.

"I'm sorry. How are you doing now?"

"My work helps. I've started something new. It's still in the drawing stage. But the idea compels me. It's not the work," she said, glancing up at him. "It's the future that scares me. Since we lost the baby, it's hard to talk to Roy. It's like we're on eggshells with each other."

He looked at her silently.

"Have I said too much?" she asked, breaking his thought.

"I was just thinking how brave you are." Holly's modus operandi was to delve into a project like painting the shed or taking on more hours at the refuge when she was upset or on edge. His mother never talked about herself. His father had been secretive and cryptic. After his breakdown he spent afternoons sitting in his study lighting one cigarette from the dying embers of another. The medications he took made his hands shake. His mother sometimes turned out the light, so that he had often found his father sitting by himself in darkness. After he got sick, his mother reverted to talking to her professor husband as if he were a little boy. *Finish your milk, Harry. Oh, that old sweater of yours needs to be thrown in the trash.* He retreated to his bedroom or over to Bennett's house to get high in their basement. At thirteen he began counting steps. And then the tiles on the bathroom wall when he was taking a shower. The methodical organization of a painting soothed him. He wasn't used to talking openly about things most people never talked about.

"Enough about me. You look tense," Julia said.

"Do I?" He took a bite of his lobster roll. "It's been months since I've found anyone, well, worth signing. Or anyone we can afford. The larger galleries are able to offer better terms. And Agnes Murray has me on edge."

He rarely talked to Holly about his work. After Holly quit the gallery, they'd lost that as a mutual interest. Holly had become more involved in their life in Connecticut and he found that when he came home from the gallery, his artists and his work were the last thing he wanted to talk about. Being with Julia, he saw how separate he and Holly had become. He rotated his stool just slightly so that his knees brushed hers.

"It will pick up," she said. "And besides, like you said, you represent Agnes Murray."

"Do you know her?"

"I know her work. She's incredible. And brave."

"Why do you say that?"

"To have married Nate Fisher. I knew him before he was famous. Now he's part of the establishment, the old guard. And Agnes represents the new guard. Soon she'll supplant him. It will be interesting to see how he weathers it."

"So you know Nate?" Edward asked.

"Well, I can't say I really know him. I once dated one of his students. Frederick Jackson."

"You're kidding."

"You know him?"

"Only his work," Edward said.

"It was ages ago," Julia said, and reddened, as if having dated him embarrassed her.

The mention of Frederick piqued his interest. Frederick was naturally good-looking, the kind of man whose easy banter made other men jealous.

"Will you have dinner with me in London?" he surprised himself by asking.

"Friday night is the gala. Saturday, then?"

"Saturday," he said.

"So have you been reading the odes?" she asked suddenly. "I've been wondering about those lovers. You know, in 'Ode on a Grecian Urn.' I mean, if eternity is all it's cracked up to be." She wiped her lips with her napkin.

"I think Keats is saying that the promise of eternity offers comfort. The lovers have been immortalized through art."

"Is that 'sweet comfort'?" She dropped her napkin and in picking it up brushed against him. He smelled the perfume off her sweater and remembered Berlin again. Her scent was dark and heady, some combination of lavender and musk.

"The lovers are frozen in time. They'll never experience suffering," he added.

"But it is only through suffering that we grow. I have to think that way." Her eyes filled and she gave him a tired smile.

"I'm sorry," he said. She moved him, not because she lacked pity for herself but because she had confided in him.

The waitress, in a blue uniform that looked like it was made for a cafeteria worker, approached and interrupted the flow of their conversation. She poured coffee into their empty cups, spilling it over into the saucer. He drank his black and Julia asked for skim milk, not cream. He liked knowing this small detail.

After the waitress cleared their plates, she took a small tube of lotion from her purse and rubbed it on her hands. It was green and smelled like avocado. "Do you want some? My hands are dry from washing them all the time in the studio," she said, holding out the tube.

"No. I don't want any," he said, wanting suddenly everything.

Julia turned her stool slightly to look at him. "I knew the minute I saw you that we'd be able to find the thread with each other again." She was referring to their last conversation, when they'd said good-bye at the hotel in Berlin.

"How did you know?"

"Because you said so. You said you were offering me friendship. At the hotel. You said you wanted to be friends."

"And?" He was interested in what she meant.

"No one declares friendship as if it were love."

He was silent for a moment. "I don't understand exactly what you mean. What you said about friendship."

"Yes you do." She took a sip from her water glass and then looked at her watch. "I have to go." She put her credit card down over the check. And then she stopped and looked at him with new emotion.

He wondered whether she was flirting with him.

"No, let me." His credit card was already in his hand but, distracted by her, he had neglected to assert it. He put it on the check and gave back her card. He had forgotten that stimulating conversation could be a pastime.

"Only if you let me pay next time."

After the waitress returned with his credit card and he signed the receipt, they stood up and grabbed their coats. She struggled to put on hers and dropped her scarf. While her back was turned he picked it up and momentarily held on to it before reluctantly handing it back to her.

Silently they walked out of the oyster bar back into the subterranean terminal, she to go one way, to the subway train downtown, and he up the ramp and out into the shock of daylight. Before they turned to go their separate ways she tugged on his coat sleeve and kissed his cheek. "It's good to see you," she said. Something had changed in her. He noticed it. She'd dropped her guard and her former reluctance had opened into trust.

HE WALKED SLOWLY, filled with her. After the first unsettling weeks since they parted in Berlin sometimes words or sentences she'd said came to his mind. He had been content to think that he'd made a new friend and that they'd see each other when she returned from Tokyo. But seeing her again, the excitement he'd felt in her company in Berlin came back to him. He thought about the proposal he had made, to have dinner together in London. There was some unspoken idea that once you were married you no longer derived pleasure or excitement from the look of an attractive or interesting woman. He supposed he had shut himself off to other women during the early years of his marriage. Occasionally he formed a harmless crush on a colleague or an artist but he knew better than to have an affair with a colleague. He saw what it had done to others. With Julia it felt different, less harmful.

His BlackBerry rang. He took it out of his breast pocket.

"Dude," Jimmy said. "Going to London?"

"Yeah. I'll be there."

"You okay? You sound strange."

"I had lunch with Julia."

"Rosenthal? Good for you."

"She'll be in London. I asked her to dinner. And now I wonder whether I should have."

"If it's real then you can't walk away. How often does it come around?"

"It's not like we're kids, Jimmy."

"Like I said. How often does it come around?"

"You should know."

"Hey, man, Lucinda is the only woman I've ever loved."

"Then why . . ."

"Because I love my wife."

"That doesn't make any fucking sense."

"Yeah, well, whoever said I ever made sense," Jimmy said before he hung up.

He thought about what Jimmy had said and shook his head. He was nothing like Jimmy. Instead of going straight back to the gallery, he decided to take a walk up Fifth Avenue, enjoy the shops, and maybe stop at Christie's for the afternoon session. He lingered by the show windows at Saks. The handsome mannequins dressed in sleek Armani and Louis Vuitton seduced him inside the store. He walked through the narrow and overly lit aisles admiring the artistry with which a perfect object was designed and the fabric chosen to accentuate it. The exacting design of a watch thrilled him. The feel of a soft cashmere scarf put him in a mood of extraordinary calm. Some men liked to work out, or watch sports, or build stuff. He liked to look at beautiful objects.

To get to the escalator he ventured through the cosmetics aisles and into the cloud of perfume the sales clerk was spraying onto strips for passersby. It was Bulgari Notte, meant to be worn after dark, the sales clerk with overly made-up eyes suggestively told him. He read the packaging. *Bulgari Notte's blend of galanga, iris and dark chocolate embodies refined seduction, along with the mystery of the night.* On a whim he bought the perfume. He wandered to the men's section and began trying on gloves. Happiness filled him. He thought of Julia again and felt as if he were walking outside his body, floating on air. He decided on a pair made from the finest leather and cashmere. He told himself he wouldn't buy them and put them back. They cost a thousand dollars. He walked away from the counter and in a few moments wandered back and purchased them. He strolled to the scarves and bought an Italian gray cashmere for nearly twice the cost of the gloves. The purchases made him feel new again.

He decided to skip the auction and took a cab back to the gallery. The leaves on the trees lining the streets had turned late this year, flaming orange and red—how come he'd never noticed their depth of color? He perceived everything more intensely. Back at his desk, he looked at his picture of Holly and Annabel dressed in matching riding gear at the stables, on the steel-gray blotter Holly had bought for him one Christmas. Holly. He hadn't thought of her or Annabel all day. He looked at the bag from Saks propped on his desk and regretted his purchases. It was a compulsion, buying things like this; he didn't know why he did it. He opened the black box with the gloves in tissue paper. *The natural softness and elasticity of the Italian deerskin makes these gloves a perfect fit for your hand. They come in black or chocolate brown,* the sales clerk had said. *Feel them. Put your hands inside. They're lined in cash-mere. Every pair is hand-sewn.* He tucked the box of gloves and the scarf in his closet, next to the five-hundred-dollar Paul Smith tie, the turquoise box with the silver clock from Tiffany's, and the jewelry box that housed the exquisite Locman automatic watch called the Latin Lover: *a statement of precision and elegance with reptile band and curved, scratch-resistant rectangular face outlined in stainless steel. Made with only the best materials from around the world and designed and then assembled on the Tuscan island of Elba. Gift box included. Made in Italy.* He'd bought the watch online on Forzieri. He'd read over the selling copy as if it were lines of poetry. The cadence of the words relaxed him, as did the idea of comfort and elegance, of a world clean of decay, mediocrity, and shabbiness. He took out the bottle of perfume from the Saks bag, and though he wanted to remove its seal and open it, he forbade himself to do it. He put the bottle in the cabinet of luxuries and locked it for safekeeping.

CLARA FEINMAN, HIS therapist, was Jewish. On her bookshelves were volumes of Freud, along with works by Carl Jung, D. W. Winnicott, William James, Virginia Woolf, and Kierkegaard. He had spent silent moments looking at the spines. He hadn't been feeling right since Berlin. He didn't understand the loneliness that seized him sometimes traveling to and from the gallery on the train, the waves of anxiety that flooded him in moments in the office, and the inexplicable sensation now and again that his life was a fraud. After Julia mentioned that he should consider therapy, the idea had stayed with him. He had his yearly checkup a week later with their family doctor. Rothman wrote Dr. Clara Feinman's phone number on a sheet from his prescription pad. After days of considering it, he unfolded the prescription from his wallet and made his first appointment. The first two or three sessions were difficult. He wasn't used to talking about himself, or thinking about himself so closely. But Clara seemed so genuinely interested in him, and in the work they were doing together, that he slowly began to take the work—probing the minefield of his interior life—seriously too.

He liked her office. He thought of it as a place where he could go to hibernate for one hour twice a week. She had photographs of Rome—his favorite city—on one wall of the office and matching Shaker furniture: a smart cherrywood coffee table and two end tables, a desk and a mirror. Something about the unpretentious, clean lines of the wood and the furniture's slender, deerlike legs and the perfect shape of the vase on the table and her library of books relaxed him.

Once he'd gotten comfortable in the leather chair and began to talk—those first words were always the hardest—he said he didn't want to go home that night.

"Really? How long have you been unhappy at home?" Clara asked. Marriage had been the grand theme of their last few sessions, after they had begun to probe his childhood and the lack of meaningfulness he sometimes experienced as of late at work.

"I'm not sure." He hadn't realized till this moment that he was truly unhappy. For so long he'd justified his marriage.

"But you and Holly have been happy before?"

He studied the bracelets she wore and the thin watchband on her left wrist. Her hair was silvery white and wavy around her face. Wrinkles had formed over her lips and around her eyes. He was amazed how long he could look at the different parts of Clara and not feel he had to turn away. What else could you do, trapped for fifty minutes inside the small confines of the soundproof room, besides occasionally study the pattern on the kilim rug or her long neck and the pinches of rolled flesh when she dropped her chin, the motor of her mind turning in her intelligent eyes.

"Yes. We were happy." He thought about the times when they used to spend a Sunday holding hands walking through antique shops to furnish their home. Or stopping at their favorite diner for burgers and splitting a plate of fries. How they couldn't keep their hands off each other. "But, now—I can't explain it. I don't feel close to Holly." He looked down at his hands. "I wish I had more space. I mean, that we could take a break and I could figure it out and it would be all right."

"Is there someone else?"

"No. Not really." He looked above him at a photograph of the crumbling walls of the Colosseum. He couldn't bring himself to tell Clara about Julia. That would make it too real.

"You don't think it would be all right if you had a break from Holly?"

"And risk losing her?"

"So you don't want to lose her?" Clara said, in that way she had of making a statement into a question.

"She's my wife." He looked at Clara and then back at the photograph of the Colosseum, and then back at her again. "I love her. I don't want to hurt her or leave her."

"And?"

"And there's Annabel."

He paused, started to say something, and then stopped. He could not formulate his thoughts into words.

"What's wrong? Did something happen you're not telling me about?"

He shifted uncomfortably. "I had a lunch that unsettled me. I went to Saks and bought a pair of expensive gloves and a scarf I don't need. I do that sometimes. When I'm anxious."

"What else have you bought that you feel guilty about?"

"There's an Italian watch I bought online. Sometimes when I travel . . . I keep them in a closet at the gallery."

"Why? You mean you buy things you don't use?" Clara probed.

"There's a Matisse drawing I bought after we closed a big deal in Paris for Agnes. And a Homer watercolor of the sea. Holly would kill me if she knew how much I paid. She doesn't understand that art . . . well, that for some of us it's more than a beautiful image. I don't mean to be patronizing."

"Why do you think you do it? Hide things. Is it because you feel deprived?"

"Because they make me feel better."

"But why keep them in a closet? Why not enjoy them?"

"Then they'd be ordinary, like everything else." He looked into her face for reassurance. "I could be buying crack or heroin," he said with a smile. He shifted in his chair. He was too uptight to master the couch. "We go to the Cape every summer. We rent the same house. Every year Holly makes the same Thanksgiving dinner. She's bought the identical white sheets for our bed since we were married twenty years ago." He pondered further. "Everything seemed good between us. Until . . ."

"Yes?"

"A few years after Annabel was born. We were trying to have another baby. Everything changed."

"Do you want to talk about it?"

He didn't think he could go there. He couldn't explain how having sex when they were trying to get pregnant suddenly seemed mechanical. He'd wanted to take her ovulation thermometer and break it in two. He'd watched as she drifted off in sadness when she got her period, and then a week or ten days later she'd begin to feel hopeful again, until her period came. And once they stopped trying, sex no longer seemed to interest her in the same way. Nor him, if he was honest with himself.

Initially, therapy had seemed an indulgence, but within weeks he found himself looking forward to his sessions. He discovered terrain inside himself he had not known existed.

"I can't."

"Is there a reason?"

"I feel if I talk about it—I don't know, that I won't be able to contain it. That I'll snap or something."

"Like your father?" Clara searched.

"They weren't happy. My parents. Everything changed once he got sick."

"The items you've purchased. Do you think you keep them a secret because you're frightened?"

"Of what?"

"Of being fully known."

Edward looked at her thoughtfully.

"There were a lot of secrets at home, weren't there?" Clara asked.

"My father's illness?"

She nodded. "Did your father's illness frighten your mother?"

"I suppose so. My mother's father committed suicide when she was a child. I never thought about her being frightened."

"Did you marry Holly to please your mother?"

Edward pictured his mother, whose face over the years had hardened into an iron mask of disappointment. He felt a tiny crack in his chest. It was true that his mother had approved of Holly. It was true, too, that when his mother was happy, he felt free of her sadness. His mother made him feel, because she was distant, that he was too emotional. She, by contrast, was impenetrable. He didn't like this. When Clara brought his mother up he felt ice jams beginning to break loose inside him. He married Holly because he was in love with her.

"Do you blame your mother for your father's illness?" Clara said.

He flinched. "I'm not sure."

He looked at the clock on the wall and watched the second hand go steadily around the numbers, one after the other.

"But why do you hide them? You buy things you love and you don't enjoy them. Are you afraid to come out of hiding?"

"I'm not hiding." He cleared his throat. He felt as if he couldn't breathe.

"Are there other things you're keeping from Holly?"

He thought about Tess and how he'd never told Holly about her. He hadn't thought about it in a long time, as if he had been willing it to all disappear, until he first saw Agnes's work four years ago and the figure in the painting that reminded him of Tess, then his abrupt confession to Julia. Suddenly the terror of how Holly might react seemed bigger than he'd thought. A prickle of fear went through him.

"Tell me more about what it's like at home. So we can figure out what it is that's frightening you."

"It's a nice house. Everything we saved for has gone into it. It's hard to describe. It's not extraordinary. We have three bedrooms. A third floor. A garden."

"Tell me what it's like when you're at home. Let me picture it," Clara asked as she looked at the clock and noted the session was ending.

"Picture what?"

"Your home. I know you don't want to go home tonight. But perhaps we can conjure one image that makes you feel safe enough to return. At least for tonight."

He felt a lump form in his throat. "I can't picture it."

"Try."

Instead he remembered Berlin. He closed his eyes and sank into the memory. He and Julia exchanged glances in the open white room of a gallery. She was talking to a small party of others, and he had felt excluded and agitated watching her and not being part of her conversation. The light in the gallery made her skin pale and almost translucent, and he had wanted to walk into the circle of friends around her and embrace her but he couldn't move.

"Where did you go, Edward?" Clara had been patiently waiting for him.

"Sorry."

"Just then. Where were you?"

"Home," he said, his eyes stinging. "You wanted to know about home."

15 CONNECTICUT

TREES, RAMSHACKLE HOUSES, empty streets rushed by the train window. Slowly the stress of the day fell away and he eased into solitude. He needed to slow down. Recalibrate. Agnes had promised to let him come to her studio to see the new work soon. Before Christmas. He had to gear up. Begin conversations with collectors. He couldn't afford to be distracted. One of the things he loved about being a dealer was to see an artist grow over a period of years, to take the work to a new level and challenge her own history.

He thought about the lead-up to the last show he'd mounted for her. She'd called it *Immortality*, which struck him as slightly grand, but he felt Agnes could get away with it. When the show opened, the first review in the *Times* compared the work with Fisher's. Agnes had made sure in all their marketing materials that they distanced themselves from Nate's work. If anything was worded in a similar way to how his work had been described, she demanded they change it. The show was timed, as Agnes had requested, so that it would not overlap with Nate's.

Agnes Murray's second show, 'Immortality,' bears an uncanny resemblance to 'Falling Man,' by her better-known husband and former professor, Nate Fisher. It is unclear

*whether Murray is paying tribute to Fisher or attempting
to outshine him. One wonders whether it is self-indulgence
rather than historic guilt that fuels the work—the guilt, of
course, of those who escaped unscathed—and whether it is
appropriated guilt or appropriated subject matter.*

Edward thought they'd be hung out to dry. A scathing *New
York Times* review could ruin an artist.

Agnes had dated the reviewer years before and had left him for
Nate. She blamed the gallery. She thought the review was a breach
of ethics and that they should do something. Edward recognized
that Agnes sometimes functioned better when she was angry and
he allowed her to vent—not that he could have stopped her. He
explained that the gallery couldn't control whom editors assigned
to cover the work.

"Why can't you?" she responded, never missing an opportunity
to let him know she was disappointed.

They recovered once a three-page rave in the *New Yorker* hit
the stands, a few more positive reviews trickled in from influential
papers and journals, and the paintings sold quickly—though one
cynical rival had said in print that the reason Murray's show sold
out was that the consumer wanted to be in the same company as
Fisher and thereby be touched by his genius.

It took a month or two after the money had started flowing in
before Agnes calmed down and realized that the response to the
show had changed her stature. One critic said she was "an artist
who transformed her canvas into a modern-day theatre wherein
a conflict between man and history might be rehearsed." While
another painter might have received the statement with humility,

for Agnes it set the bar and as a result she grew more controlling and irrational. Mounting the new show was going to be rough sailing. If Agnes had demanded a lot then, now that she had more at stake it would be more difficult to please her. He took out his notepad from his breast pocket, suddenly remembering a few phone calls he had to make, before he forgot them again. He reached for his Mont Blanc fountain pen. Agnes had given it to him after a review in *Art News* praised the exhibition as the most outstanding solo show of the year. He read the inscription: "Together we have realized the essential rhythms of art."

He looked up and noticed that the train was heading into his station. Passengers shoved past him to get off. He put the pad of paper and pen away and grabbed his briefcase and newspaper and exited the car. He stepped onto the platform, slipping into the anonymous flow of strangers.

N ATE AND AGNES, embroiled in a heated discussion, surprised him, sitting on the couch in his office when he strolled
in a week or two later. Nate's hair was unwashed. He hadn't
shaved. His wrinkled clothes looked slept-in. He passed the hours
of the afternoon and night in his studio or out and about and was
not the kind of man usually seen in broad daylight before noon.
Something was up. He was manically chewing gum, one arm strung
over the end of the couch. Agnes looked uncomfortable.

"Did I miss something on the calendar?" Edward shook Nate's
hand and kissed Agnes's cheek as they rose to greet him. "Have you
been waiting long?"

"I wanted to call first and Nate thought we should just drop in.
I hope that's okay. We've been up half the night talking."

Georgia brought in coffee and placed the mugs on the table in
front of the couch. Agnes held hers between two hands. She rose
and stood in front of the window and looked out at the cityscape,
pensive, her sprawling hair in a cascade down her back.

Nate started. "Look, Edward. Might as well get down to business. We're here about the *Vanity Fair* profile." Cynthia, the gallery's publicist, had arranged a profile for Agnes to keep her in the
limelight before gearing up for her new show and she was thrilled

about it. "Now isn't a good time for a journalist to go poking around. I don't think Agnes should agree to the interview."

Edward had heard from Leonard that Nate had been struggling with his own work as of late. The extraordinary auction prices, over-the-top attention from the critics, and international success had him in a holding pattern. He was an academic painter who'd taken a risk by taking iconic images of the Twin Towers—the buildings slanted to the sky against the pure blue light of day, the explosion of flames, American flag, falling man—and painted them in a style so polished and pristine that they looked synthetic. Their bold emptiness was part of the statement. A high-powered gallerist happened to be at Columbia and had seen something in the work he could manipulate. The rest was history. Whether Nate believed in what he was doing or what he had achieved wasn't clear, but nevertheless the work was understood to be part of the history of our times. Nate didn't want to repeat the work he had already done and was at a crossroads. When he wasn't working well, he partied too hard and went on all-night benders. No wonder he looked like crap.

Agnes returned to sit next to her husband. "But I want it," she said, with childlike steeliness. "Edward said it was important." She took Nate's hand again. "To create interest for my new show. Is there a way we can control the content?"

"The short answer is no. Not if the journalist talks to other people for the profile. Is there something I ought to know? Something you're afraid might be exposed?" Edward adjusted his pant leg, which had crept up when he sat down.

"Edward should know everything, Nate," Agnes implored. She touched his thigh. "Otherwise he can't do his job."

Nate leaned over and kissed her. "I'm the only one who needs to know everything about you, baby. Go ahead, tell him then."

Agnes blinked her eyes. "It's about Liam, Nate's son. He stole a drawing of Nate's and sold it on the black market and took off for Europe. He's been in trouble lately. Nate doesn't want the press to pick up the story."

"My concerns are real. He's my son," Nate added, soberly.

"We can wait until it blows over. I'll tell Cynthia to reschedule the interview closer to the opening. It shouldn't be a problem. Look, I haven't seen the new work yet. We've got time." Edward looked at Nate. "I'm sorry about your son, man."

Nate nodded. "Thanks. He'll be all right. He's still a kid."

"He's my age, baby," Agnes reminded him. She reached up and smoothed his ripped-at-the-neck T-shirt.

Once they left, Edward retired to his desk. He swiveled his chair to look out the glass window at the gallery. He watched the junior associates on the phone to clients and assistants typing at their computers and sat back and thought about how he had built up the gallery's staff and stable of artists and how incredibly personal it all was. He'd fostered relationships, some more profound than others, with colleagues and artists and collectors in hopes they would extend over time and they had. Unlike Savan and others in the business, he never aspired to hang out all night with his artists and flit off to the South of France and get trashed on a weekend bender. He never needed that. He was looking for artists who were extraordinary and singular. He believed that art offered a refuge from the trouble in the world, or at least allowed the culture a way to think about it. Sure, he'd made some mistakes—passing up artists whose work he didn't get and watching their star rise under another gallerist. He was looking for work that could only have been made by that particular artist. And he hoped and wanted them to be forward-thinkers. There was a train of art history and hopefully some of the people he worked with were moving the train forward. He thought Agnes was, and maybe a handful of others, and for the first time in a long while he actually felt himself getting excited about her new work. He liked shaping and mounting a show and all the hoopla surrounding it. This was going to be big. Sure she was nervous about it. And so was Nate. No one wanted bad publicity before a new show. It was his job to do damage control and not let all the noise infiltrate her studio. He had to calm down and focus.

17 CONNECTICUT

H E AWOKE TO the ringtone of his BlackBerry on his night-stand and glanced at the clock. It was three thirty in the morning. He looked at the caller ID. She rarely called him on his mobile. He put the phone to his ear.

"Agnes? What's wrong? Wait a minute." He struggled out of bed and walked into the hallway to not wake Holly.

"I'm sorry to call so late. I needed someone to talk to. I'm shaking."

"What is it?"

"Nate's out of control. He was out drinking and doing God knows what else. He came into my studio and trashed it. The paintings. Thank God." She took a long breath. "They were untouched."

"He trashed your studio? Why? That's crazy."

"He's freaked about Liam. And he's not working well. Then he goes out and gets wrecked. He said our art is ruining us. Sometimes he gets like this, but he's never trashed the studio."

"Do you want me to come over? I'll drive in."

"You'd do that for me, wouldn't you."

"You know I would."

"That's why Nate doesn't trust you."

"He doesn't trust me?"

"He doesn't trust anyone. Really. And he knows you'd come if I needed you. He still thinks I'm his student. He doesn't want anyone to usurp his place."

"I'm your dealer, Agnes. It's different."

"I know. Of course it is. But not to Nate."

"Do you want me to come? I can get there in less than an hour."

"It's not necessary. I feel better, just hearing your voice."

They hung up and he wandered back to bed. He'd always thought Nate was obsessed with himself, but violent? That was something new. The two of them were going to destroy each other. Before, he'd been envious of their intense and charged relationship. Seeing the fallout, now, he wasn't so sure. He'd found himself wondering since Berlin what it would be like to be in a marriage like theirs—what it would be like if he were married to someone more like him, like Julia. Seeing her again in New York for lunch—open and vulnerable—he couldn't stop thinking about her. He closed his eyes and willed his mind to go blank.

IN THE MORNING after breakfast, ensconced in his study, he called Agnes to check in. It was late November and they were expecting snow. He felt it in the air.

"Nate brought me two dozen yellow roses this morning. They're my favorite. It's like it never happened. He likes those drag-down fights. It fuels his work. He's been painting like a maniac all morning. He called two of his assistants to come by and stretch canvases and mix colors," she said—a little too gleefully, he thought, and shook his head. What would it be like for Nate, Edward wondered, if her work outshone his? He agreed with Agnes that being a woman artist made things more complicated.

Not in terms of the work itself, but in the way in which the work would be perceived and noticed by the critics. Men were used to pushing their work forward. Women artists tended to be more uncomfortable in the spotlight. It was part of the ambivalence he'd noticed in Agnes and, he assumed, why she was nervous about letting go of the new work.

He powered off his computer and went back downstairs to find Annabel in the breakfast nook doing homework. He sat next to her and restlessly attempted to read the paper. Annabel explained to him the Pythagorean theorem. A squared plus B squared equals C squared—it brought back his own days in geometry class. He looked out the window distracted.

"Dad?" Annabel said.

"What is it, Annabel?"

"Can I go to Danny Wasserman's house Friday night?"

"Sure." he said. "If your mother says so."

"Dad?"

"What, darling?"

"You need to talk to Mom more. I think she's lonely."

"Why do you say that?"

"She always wants to be with me," she groaned.

The phone rang. Annabel leaped at it as if she'd been waiting. She held out the receiver and asked him to hang up once she had gotten to her room. He put the phone to his ear, waiting, and recognized the slow breathing of a boy at the other end and felt a catch in his throat.

"Is it you?" Annabel said when she picked up.

"Yeah," the boy said, in that languid tone Edward recalled from when he was that age. "What's up?"

Years ago Annabel used to crawl into his lap and put her tiny arms around his neck. Her face, rosy and unblemished, had taken on contours. She'd grown long and thin and had breasts. He did not know whether he was supposed to observe her changing body, but he had and it unnerved him. He thought about her sudden infatuation with boys. Everything was shifting just a little bit away from him.

He went up the stairs again to check e-mail. He was expecting a deal to come through from London. He opened his laptop and logged in. He looked out the window at the cloud formations building in the sky and sensed the coming snow. His assistant had sent him a message that Agnes wanted him to secure a deal with a gallery in Madrid. Nate had two galleries there interested in his work and his prices had skyrocketed. What was it like for them working in private studios in the same house, always comparing? Talking about every deal? He thought again about Nate trashing Agnes's studio. Nate was losing his way. He'd seen it happen to other successful artists terrified that there was nowhere to go but down. Years ago he had mounted a first show by a young painter, Miles Mahoney, and it had gotten favorable write-ups, and though the work hadn't generated nearly the amount of excitement he'd gotten for Agnes Murray it had been respectable. Two years later and the new work was shit. It was all a crap shoot.

He looked at his father's paintings on his wall—all that unrealized brilliance. What happened to him? At dinner with John Kincaid, gnarled in an argument about the interpretation of a poem, they could go at it for hours. His study crammed with three decades' accrual of books, couch and desk stacked with works in progress and students' papers. His father was obsessed with his work. "It can't be just about this," he once said, when they were lingering at the dinner table and his mother was cleaning up.

"What's wrong with this?" his mother said.

"There has to be more," he'd said, looking into his coffee cup.

"The more you search, the unhappier you are," she muttered.

His father's last years teaching, he grew paranoid. Awarded a prize for a book, he felt that the other books that did not get prizes were better and didn't trust the praise. Preoccupied at home, he snapped at Edward or his mother if he couldn't find a misplaced book or paper. If one of his students failed an exam his father took it personally. Edward's mother passed her evenings knitting. She looped the yarn over one needle, stretched it over the forefinger, and stabbed the other needle into the wool.

Edward closed his laptop and went downstairs, restless. In the kitchen Annabel vigorously erased marks from a problem on her math sheet. Holly was unpacking groceries.

"I'll be back soon. I'm going to visit my mother before dinner," he said. A sudden desire to see her overcame him. He'd been thinking about her a lot since he started seeing Clara.

"That's brave of you," Holly remarked.

His mother had recently moved into the assisted-living section of the retirement community where she lived, forty-five minutes away. She'd started forgetting things, and once had left the stove on and nearly burned down her kitchen. He'd dragged Annabel and Holly with him a few times and they'd had lunch with his mother in the overheated dining hall, but they complained about going and now he usually went alone. He hadn't been in weeks. He avoided spending much time there, stopping in to bring over papers that needed to be signed, or her medications and toiletries from

the pharmacy, sitting a few minutes before abruptly rising with an
excuse that he had to run to the city for a meeting. Afterward it
took him days to shake free of her.

H E FOUND HER in the game room, smaller than in his memory, playing cards with a group of other residents before dinner.

"Edward," she said, happy to see him. "You didn't tell me you were coming." She turned her cheek for his kiss and introduced him to the others at the table. "The snow's supposed to get worse. Was it snowing when you drove in, darling?"

"Not too bad yet." It was the first snowfall of the season.

Rising unsteadily, and more slowly, she reached for her cane. He hadn't noticed it before. He held her arm and led her to the sitting room, which smelled of decaying fruit. On the sofa an elderly man slept sitting up with his mouth open. A woman in a wheelchair stared into the fireplace. This is what the end looks like, he thought. They found two empty overstuffed chairs in a corner of the room. The afternoon light slowly faded from the window.

"Get us some tea, darling." She pointed to a narrow table near the entrance to the room where tea was set out for the residents.

She was small and neatly groomed, dressed in a plaid wool skirt, blouse, and cashmere sweater, a Kleenex tucked into her sleeve. He leaned over to hand her a cup of tea. A musty smell rose off her sweater. Sipping her tea, she ran her eyes along him as she had when he was a boy, remarking if his hair was too long, or a pimple was on his chin. She never missed a beat. When he was a boy she was happiest, his father was happy too—Sundays in the park, walking to school, his father on one side of him, his mother on the other, each holding one of his hands, their long car rides to the city to see a concert or go to a museum.

"How are you?" He unbuttoned his jacket, reluctant to take it off.

"I'm fine, darling. And you? You look tired." She brushed her hand across his temple. "You're not giving Holly any trouble?"

He raised his eyebrows playfully. "Maybe a little."

"And my granddaughter?"

"Growing up. Almost sixteen."

She smiled and smoothed her skirt over her lap. "I'm knitting her a sweater for Christmas." He glanced at his mother's hands. Blue cordlike veins, blotches of age spots. The flesh had fallen off her bones. They'd have to eventually cut off her wedding band, he thought morbidly; it was trapped beneath an arthritic knuckle the size of a garlic bulb.

"Your father didn't get to see you become a man, and look at you now. You look so handsome, darling. And your work is going so well." She spoke to him as if he were still her little boy. Her eyes shifted to the wall above him and then filled with tears.

"Always in that dusty study like some nocturnal creature." She shook her head. "I used to wonder what he'd be like if he spent more time with us."

Edward remembered coming home to his mother in the kitchen preparing supper or doing laundry, one day indistinguishable from the next.

"Dad was an intellectual. He needed solitude to write his books."

"Of course he did. But success, brilliance, they're a completely abstract thing. You don't have to make excuses for him. You always defended him. I suppose a boy does with his father. He was looking for things that didn't exist. He was happier when I could get him to forget it all."

"Was he?"

"He wasn't teaching the Romantic period—he lived it. Or wanted to. I don't know which was worse."

Outside the window more clouds had muscled through. A rash of heat swept over him. He didn't know why the tight black box where he'd stored his parents' marriage was opening and why it suddenly seemed important to have this conversation with his mother. But it did. How and why they met and married made no sense to him. No one could predict how a marriage would wear into an unknown future. That was what made it interesting, he supposed.

"I wish you were happier. You made each other miserable."

She picked a piece of lint off his jacket. "Who are you to judge us, darling? Your father was sensitive. He felt everything too much and couldn't filter it out fast enough. It's what made him a brilliant man, I suppose."

"He didn't make you happy."

"I didn't make him happy? Is that what you mean?"

He flinched. "That isn't what I meant."

"They don't give out prizes for the woman who organizes the home, makes the bed, cleans out the closets." He remembered how his mother laid out his father's clothes in the morning, packed his lunch. Edward shrank from her eyes and looked out the window. More clouds.

"No, they don't, Mom." He looked at her tenderly.

"When you live here, there's plenty of time to think." She touched her pearl earring and twisted it. "He was lost in himself. It was hard to get used to. But you can get used to anything." She took a sip of tea. The china teacup trembled in her hands. "He was his own worst enemy. I suppose all of us are."

The smell of evening dinner rose from the kitchen. He looked at his watch. Quarter to six. He'd have to leave soon. Other residents shuffled toward the dining room.

"Walk me to dinner, darling. When you live here it's like a prison. The staff needs to get home early. And stop being judgmental. It won't get you anywhere. The snow's supposed to get worse. The roads will be slick. You'll drive slowly, won't you?"

He nodded and buttoned his coat.

"You'll come again soon?" She grasped his arm. Her eyes were suddenly black with fear.

"Soon." He kissed her cheek. "I'm sorry—in there." He nodded toward the drawing room. "He'd have been nowhere without you."

"The love of my life," she said, touching his cheek.

OUTSIDE, FREE OF the emotions binding him, his movements came more easily. He took in the cold air and let out a long breath. Everything was quiet and still. He turned back and saw his own shallow footsteps. The snow blanketed the shrubs. He turned back to look again. The roof and branches of the trees surrounding the retirement house were almost completely covered in snow. It clung to the railings, forming a lace of ice, and settled into the empty windowboxes clinging, holding on. Wind shattered the icicles along the gutters and they fell silently to the snowy ground.

In the car, snow came at the windshield. He drove slowly, barely able to see, the snowflakes coming at his eyes in a whiteout. The roads were slick and wet, with few drivers. His wheels spun on an ice patch and the car careened toward the curb. He turned the wheel into the slide and slowly came to a stop. He put the car in park and for a moment laid his head on the steering wheel, shut inside the silent temple of his car. He had a beautiful family. His mother was safe and well cared for. Why did he feel like all of it was going to unravel? He lifted his head. The ice on the windshield formed a long vein and then slowly began to blister and crack. He put his hands on the wheel, put the car in drive, and slowly accelerated again. He coasted past the pond near the roundabout to his house. The pond was frozen over except for a patch where a swan stretched its neck and shivered. He stopped the car and looked at the swan, trembling, unable to shake the fear of death he saw in his mother's eyes.

EXCEPT FOR LAST-MINUTE shoppers the city was beginning to empty out. It was the week before Christmas. The morning air was colder than it had been in months. Above the buildings, the sky was gray and all the sounds of the stirring city seemed to rise toward it. Edward took a cab from the gallery to Tribeca, to the loft building where Agnes and Nate lived and worked. Once out of the cab, he looked at the intimidating building, at its huge windows and steel frame, and was reminded, as he always was when he came to see her, of their staggering wealth. He walked briskly to the sidewalk gate and took a breath before climbing the steps to the front door, which was decorated with a pine and berry wreath.

He had spoken to Ryan Reynolds earlier that morning and Reynolds had put him on edge. He said Edward should be clear about expressing exactly how he felt about the work. "We have to be tough on her. This show is too important."

They'd never worked together before. Reynolds's artists typically showed at the powerhouse galleries. Over the years he had forged a coterie of close-knit relationships among dealers and artists to leverage his power. The first time they met, Reynolds had greeted him from a booth at the Regency wearing an Italian suit and a crisp white shirt, his dark hair slicked back with gel, and though Edward was dressed in one of his favorite suits, he'd immediately felt inferior.

Reynolds spoke in a soft whisper so that Edward had to lean in to hear and often wasn't sure exactly what was being said. Reynolds said barely anything at all, so that it was Edward's job to keep the conversation going. It was a passive-aggressive move by Reynolds to make sure he was the one in control. Edward had been careful not to give too much of himself away. He, too, knew something about leveraging power, but even so he was glad when the lunch was over.

HE ADJUSTED HIS tie before buzzing Agnes's bell. She welcomed him, planting a quick peck on each cheek, and they exchanged pleasantries. She was dressed in a long white blouse she wore with black leggings. Her hair was in loose braids pinned on top of her head Heidi-style that, on her, looked avant-garde. Nate came in to say hello carrying a coffee mug. It looked like he'd just woken up—jeans, untucked shirt, and bare feet.

"Are you ready for your mind to be blown?" He winked and shook Edward's hand. "Everything good at the gallery?"

Edward nodded. "All good."

Agnes excused herself to give the nanny instructions upstairs.

"I'm glad you're finally doing this. These last few weeks have been killer." Nate shook his head. "My wife. With her there's no boundary between church and state. She'd throw me out the window for it, but she'd throw herself out first. Go easy on her, will you? I'm out the door in a few minutes. I've got a meeting uptown."

"Good to see you, Nate."

He entered the studio cautiously. The space was white-walled and soundproofed except for the whir of ventilation. A modern daybed was pushed against one wall and against another was a long white picnic table with a matching white Macbook adorning it. On the windowsill there was a row of carefully arranged red poinsettias in flowerpots to mark the holiday. He sat on the painted white bench. The meticulously choreographed room reminded him of Agnes and Nate's wedding. Everything was perfect, from the white roses on the tables to the lanterns in the garden. Nearly every important person in the art world had attended. At the wedding reception guests were passing out business cards. Agnes was barely visible. She emerged from the main house holding Nate's hand to do a quick obligatory tour around the tables. She was tense and very thin, her skin stretched taut over her frail arms. She held Nate's hand a little too tightly and breezed through the tables as if she were annoyed she had to share him with her guests.

Agnes appeared out of breath. "You're finally here," she said. "Do you have plans for the holidays?"

He explained that they were staying at home but she didn't seem to have heard him. He didn't bother to ask about her plans. She had once told him that she didn't believe in vacations, that she didn't like to be away from her work, and he imagined she felt the same about holidays.

"Shall we?" she said, inviting him further into the studio.

"How are the twins? And Nate?"

"The girls are good. Nate, I don't know. He's putting a lot of pressure on me. He's over his head financially. He always overextends. I think it's the thing that presses against him. I suppose one can't make great art without it."

"Well, you would know."

"You'll have to tell me if I have."

"Have what?"

"Made great work."

THE PAINTINGS EVOKED an ominous mood. They were less realistic than her previous work, more abstract and brushier.

She quietly followed behind him as he toured the space. Her studio was immaculately clean, as if she had purposefully hidden away the debris of the painstaking hours of creativity: encrusted paint; abandoned canvases; ghostly dustcovers; stretcher bars and turp-covered rags. He remembered her modest studio in Bushwick where he'd first met her years ago, before she married Nate, and noted the contrast.

One painting was called *Aftermath*. The large canvas taking up almost half a wall was washed in hues of gray and white and found materials were layered into it. Underneath layers of paint was a faint shadow of the towers.

"I'm after a sort of internal tug-of-war of elements. I want the work to lead the viewer through a place of non-thinking. Looking only at the thing before you."

In another, she'd taken earth, ash, cement, pieces of glass, newspaper, fabric, and painted over them, so that it looked as if debris from the fallen buildings had been painted into the canvas. She carried the image through a sequence of permutations using a variety of techniques to "reveal the many starts and stops and dead ends," she explained.

"Your technique is different," he said. "The paint is applied thicker. Less precise." He nodded his head.

The Rescuers consisted of panoramas painted in hues of red, orange, and brown creating an image of fire and destruction. Pieces of burnt paper, ash, brick, and debris were thickly painted over on the canvas and in the swirls of color there were ripped and charred pieces of cloth. Again, the ghostly image of the towers was in the background. This one made him a little nervous. He wondered whether Agnes had pushed the conceit too far.

"I'm interested in the way problems and solutions develop from one canvas to another and the interplay of materials. If the towers still exist in the viewer's mind, even as ghostly shadows, then what's really been destroyed?"

"I like the statement. Art doesn't forget. It invites the viewer to question the role of the artist in the preservation of history."

For a moment her face broke free of seriousness. "That's it," she said. "I wouldn't have put it that way, but I like it."

"I do too. But is it perhaps too grim for the viewer? Let's think about it."

"Really? I find this one exciting. To take that risk." She challenged him with her eyes. "Joan Miró created his series of 'Burnt Canvases' as a response to the Spanish Civil War. It's an artist's responsibility to respond to desperate circumstances."

"You certainly have," he agreed.

He took another turn around the studio. Agnes followed, her breath at his neck. "I want the entire gallery space painted white. We have to get the paint from Italy. Have you seen the white walls in galleries in Rome? It's different."

An hour passed. Occasionally he attempted to put into words his thoughts, but he was cautious, knowing she held on to each one. Another large canvas was painted in hues of white and gray. In the swirls, underneath many layers, were the shapes of hundreds of faces. Again she had used materials such as plaster, wire, and insulation in an attempt to give the canvas texture and depth.

"In these ghostly images you bring grace into the canvas. The viewer's eye can't escape the look on those faces. It's haunting." He said it more to placate her. As he looked more closely, he did not feel that zing that shot through him when he was in the presence of transcendent work. He felt himself begin to perspire.

Agnes arched her brows. "I didn't see that, but I can see it now. Part of my process has been about learning to trust what the painting will reveal to me."

"Brilliantly done." Edward looked around again and considered the impression. The paintings were beautifully made but nevertheless unease filled him. They strained toward recognition.

His instincts told him that there was some revelation that as yet eluded Agnes, and that she should be braver, take more risks to get there. He wondered too whether the images were reaching toward cliché. She was struggling too hard to make a statement that her work was art with a capital A. He would have to figure out a way to downplay its self-importance. Yes, something about the work seemed derivative and simply left him cold. It was as if she was afraid that if she went back to what she did best—paintings that were classical yet completely contemporary—she wouldn't be taken seriously. He had to figure out a way to express both his admiration and his hesitations. If he let it go, it would only come back to bite him in the ass. It had happened before, when he first started out and was too timid to express his doubts.

"THERE'S TEA AND scones for us upstairs," Agnes said carefully. "I want to hear your ideas. Do we have a time frame yet?" They rode the elevator to the living quarters. The tonal sound of the music of John Cage streamed into the room. "We're thinking late March or April, right? I believe that's what Ryan said."

Agnes poured them green tea from a Japanese set. She described her process. How she'd collected fabrics and paper and other debris and materials from building sites and painted them onto the canvas to give depth and texture and to call to mind the ash and wreckage of 9/11.

"What's your impression?"

"I need to think about it more. I'm still taking it in." He smiled, looking at the walls of the room painted in shades of gray.

"Nate said that a dealer's job is to put art in production. That's a crass way of putting it. But Nate's gift is that he knows how to make his art sell."

"They'll sell, but the viewer may need a bit of help."

"Really? Nate said he liked that I didn't completely connect the dots. He said the work was about the nihilism of culture. He thought the paintings were self-explanatory."

"Well, they are," Edward fumbled. "Of course they are. But the viewer isn't always as attuned to nuance as Nate."

"But I'm not painting for the average viewer. That's not my intent." She took the pins from the top of her head, let loose the braids, and shook out her hysteria of hair.

"Look," Edward said, leaning forward, "the critics bring out their knives, especially after a successful last show. We need to consider everything. I'm your first pair of eyes." It was as if she had chosen to sacrifice irony and provocation for seriousness in order to distance her work further from Nate's. "We need to come clean in our copy that the work, the use of recycled materials, is a nod to Rauschenberg and Johns. To not deny the influence."

"Rauschenberg? Really? I didn't think of him. Johns? You mean his use of found materials. But if the compositions are brilliant, why would anyone object?" She pulled at the skin on her neck. "We're constantly ripping each other off. Every conversation or representation is a rip-off. Language is not authentic. Nor is painting." She aggressively stirred the tea in her cup.

"I'm just wondering. What if you pushed the work a little more toward your intentions? Softened it a little, worked more from an emotional place? If I don't tell you this, no one will. It's what I'm here for. Paint what you can't forget, right?"

She acknowledged the source of the comment and paused and lowered her gaze. Silence filled the room.

"I suppose so," she said, reluctantly. "I'm so very tired, Edward."

"As you should be. It will be magnificent. It's almost there."

It wasn't exactly what she wanted to hear, he knew it, but he also knew in his gut that it was what the work needed in order to hum, and he believed that she would come around. She trusted him. "I'm just saying we should look at it from all sides. That's what I'm here for. In the end it's your work, but my job is to tell you what I see."

"Excuse me a moment," she said, and turned abruptly away so that he could not see her face. "I have to check on the girls."

He heard her in the next room on the phone. She sounded agitated. Minutes later she returned and paused for a moment before entering the vast, sparsely furnished room. She looked betrayed, hurt, and defensive all at once. He wondered whether she had called Nate.

"I have to take the twins to the pediatrician. I'll have Ryan call you and we can discuss the details."

"The work is brilliant. It's going to be huge. It's been worth the wait."

She walked him toward the steel door and a large mirror where they both stopped to see themselves in the glass, clear and without pretense. "Do you think it's been too long between shows? Is that what you mean?" she asked boldly to conceal her fear. "I have to know."

"There are ways to get around that and make it an advantage. The work is powerful. Really, Agnes." The canvases were painterly and well executed. You couldn't take that away from her—but whether the public would respond was another story.

"Do you think so?" Her composure broke and she trembled. "It has to be."

"I do." A light smile crossed his lips.

"I'll think about what you said. I've come to think of you as my compass." She reached up and hugged him.

"Have a great Christmas," he said.

HE WALKED A few blocks uptown before hailing a cab back to the gallery. Lost in thought, he nearly bumped into a sad-looking Santa in a faded suit collecting coins for the Salvation Army. It was cool out. He felt a frost coming in. The stalls outside the greengrocer were piled with clementines, oranges, and grapefruit. He listened to cars stop and start and the sound of Christmas music coming from outside a shop. He walked slowly, pleased with himself. From time to time he looked at his BlackBerry and slowed to answer messages. Walking, he pictured the paintings in his mind. He'd given her just enough praise and encouragement to allow her to think about his few hesitations. And he had mostly kept his commercial concerns to himself. Never talk to an artist about what her paintings are worth. That's why she had Reynolds. If Agnes was willing to push the work a little further, it would come across as more agile and less lugubrious and break through the chains of influence to become fully her own. The work would be more difficult to get across than her last show. There was little zest for life in the paintings. They were made with precision and technique but the energy and continuity had been sucked out. How do you get the viewer to see that the darkness and seriousness of the composition, its ability to make the viewer uncomfortable, is its asset? That would be the gallery's job.

A painting was built up in layers. Start here, add this, subtract that, and so forth. It expanded and developed undertones and richness. Then the painter pulled back and added more texture, more shade and nuance. He knew what Agnes needed to do. In their next conversation he would articulate it for her more clearly. It was best that he hadn't overwhelmed her. If she wanted to use materials that mimicked the debris of 9/11 she needed to let the materials speak for themselves. He thought of a few collectors who would connect with the work and value it. He'd just begun a relationship with one in Stockholm and a hedge fund mogul in New York and he was sure both would be interested.

Back at the gallery he answered a few e-mails and returned some calls. He read over a contract and made notes for his assistant, trying to get work off his desk before the holiday. Then he went in to see May. "Agnes's work is good," he said. "It could be brilliant. But we have some hurdles to jump. It's painted with dark energy." "Not 9/11 again? Will it sell going into the trough twice?" "It better. It will take some engineering to make the public believe they're bettering themselves by viewing these paintings. And that what they need is art that conveys a deeper, more serious experience. We need to send out the message that the paintings are historic works. We should begin to get the word out soon. I'll have Cynthia drop a teaser to the *Observer*."

"You're happy that we've bet the farm on her, then?" May smiled wryly, in her way making sure that he knew (as if he could ever forget) that his ass was on the line.

"We've tripled our expectations on *Immortality*. I don't think we'll do better but I doubt we'll do worse. Every dealer in America wants to represent Agnes Murray. At the end of the day our job is to sell obsessions articulated as objects. Agnes's obsession is with mass annihilation and its historical significance. It's a big statement."

He returned to his office and prepared to shut down his computer and pack up for the night. He looked at his e-mails again and saw one from Agnes and clicked on it.

Dear Edward,

It was great to see you today and to finally show you my work. I was so frightened. I thought about what you said all day. I went back into the studio and thought again. I have to be honest. I'm completely freaked out. I can't make any mistakes with this show. It's my chance to make my mark. It can't be as good as "Immortality," it has to be a leap forward. You said it yourself. I'll do whatever you

say. I trust you completely. You're a wizard. A visionary. I
always knew that about you. Nobody gets the work like you
do. In the studio, I was defensive when you said the work
hadn't quite jelled and that I need to step back. But now I
see what you mean. You mentioned something about getting
a more emotional response from the work? Do you think
the work is not emotional enough? I read a biography of
Jasper Johns. I suppose you're right. He is an influence. He
said at the beginning of his career he didn't want to expose
himself through his art but eventually he realized that "one
must simply drop the reserve." That's it, right? I haven't
let go. When I was Nate's student, he observed my work
carefully. He told me what worked and what didn't work
by isolating certain areas. I can't ask that of Nate anymore.
He needs to see me as his equal. Will you come to the studio
again after Christmas? You're the only person who will tell
me the truth. I'm in your debt. Agnes.

He read the e-mail again. Agnes's e-mails were always polished
and professional. This was the first e-mail that hadn't been edited
and reedited, as if she were preparing it for posterity before she
sent it. He was glad she'd made herself vulnerable and was willing
to listen. There was nothing deeper than to work for years with the
same artist. He shot an e-mail back saying that he'd come to the
studio the first week after Christmas. He told her not to worry. The
work was there. It just needed to be tweaked. He told her he'd been
reading Jacques Derrida's monograph "On Touching," and he saw
her desire to disturb and pierce the viewer by deconstructing the
images of 9/11. She'd like the allusion. He told her to relax and, if

she could bear it, to take a break from the studio over the holidays, so that she could come back to the work with fresh eyes. He told her that the work would be a step forward. He wouldn't show it otherwise. She could trust him. He sent the e-mail before he left the office that evening.

THE DAY BEFORE Christmas he worked steadily all morning on e-mails, clearing the decks for the holiday. Three days had passed since the studio visit. He occasionally thought about Agnes and her e-mail and his response and figured she'd get back to him after Christmas. He felt relieved that she wanted to improve the paintings and better about preparing for the upcoming show in the spring. He looked at the clock. It was five thirty and eerily quiet. The gallery had closed for the holiday and only his assistant and a few other back office employees were in the building.

His assistant buzzed. Ryan Reynolds was on line two. "Ryan, The new work's a game-changer. It's almost there. Did Agnes fill you in?"

"Edward. Let me get to the point. Agnes called this morning. She's been thinking things over. She said you didn't get the work. That your comments were, how should I put it . . ." He hesitated. "I'll just come out with it. She said that your comments were stupid."

Edward stiffened. He told himself to take it easy. "I told her the work was brilliant. She agreed. We talked about what more could be done. She wrote me an e-mail. I'll forward it to you."

"She mentioned that. But over the next few days she thought about it again. She brought Nate back into the studio. He disagreed. He thinks she's nailed it. He says Agnes shouldn't change a thing. She said you mentioned critics. And you're worried about how long it's been between shows. She thinks she needs to be with someone new."

His heartbeat quickened. He was struggling to maintain a sense of calm and not give up his power. "That's absurd. Don't you find it all a little odd?"

"Are you saying her reaction is odd?"

"You warned me. You used the word 'dark,' when you told me about the paintings. You told me to be honest with her. You said my job is to be her worst critic and that's what I did. I was gentle. I love the work. She knows I do."

"She doesn't feel you do. She wants out. She says she needs to be with someone who's confident in what she's produced. Look, in the end, it's her work."

"I don't have to tell you the time and money this gallery has spent on marketing and promoting her work. And our production costs. We put her on a hefty salary all these years, sight unseen. That's what she asked for. Something isn't adding up. Has she been talking to other galleries?"

"She mentioned a dealer from Reinstein. Alex Savan."

"Savan? You've got to be kidding."

"I hear you, man," he said and then grew serious. "Listen, I can't control who she's drawn to. Nate invited him to her studio yesterday. They're friends. Savan didn't have any trouble with the work. I know you're shaken. I know what this feels like. I've been dumped before. You can't be in this business and not get dumped."

His heart thumped. "What?"

"She claims you said nothing about the work's intellectual drive."

"Oh for Christ sakes, Ryan, come on. You know the work needs tweaking."

"Let's sleep on it. Let her cool down. My guess is that she'll come to her senses. We'll be in touch after the holidays. We've got time."

"Let me talk to her. We've always had a good relationship. We're very close."

"I'm not sure she sees it that way."

He picked up the Mont Blanc pen she'd given to him and looked at the inscription again. *Together we have realized the essential rhythms of art.*

"Ryan, I know her sensibility and what she's capable of. Every artist needs a second pair of eyes. I worked with Leonard closely on her brand. Leonard and I talked sometimes three or four times a day. You have no idea what we've done for Agnes. How I've talked up her work and contextualized it. She knows. " He paused. The phone went quiet. "Are you saying you didn't back me?"

"She's sensitive. Everyone knows that about her. Call her if you want. We'll talk soon. Give her some time. Sorry to give you bad news the day before Christmas."

Edward bit his thumbnail and it cracked. He looked out the window at the congested city streets and buildings. He remembered that when he first moved to New York the Empire State Building had stood out among the other skyscrapers, with its steel antenna at the top pointed like a rocket ready for takeoff; it represented power and promise. He'd wanted a piece of it. He looked at his blank computer screen. It had shut down. He picked up the phone and called Agnes at home. No answer. He left a message. He called her mobile and left a message there, too. He rewound the phone call with Reynolds in his mind. After the success of *Immortality*, Savan had managed to bring Agnes up in nearly every conversation they'd had. That motherfucker. He couldn't move from his chair. A half hour later he rang both phones again and left messages. Fuck. Fuck. Fuck. He looked out the window. Between the buildings a mass of clouds rolled through. Inside hundreds of office deals and transactions were being made, an invisible human chain of commerce that made the city hum. He watched the sky of winter slowly closing in and then got up and kicked his wastebasket. Agnes's work was not quite there yet. Nate should have seen it.

He methodically packed up his briefcase to make the 7:05 train. Before leaving the gallery he stopped in to see May to tell her. By then everyone else had cleared out for the holiday. He walked into her private space. She faced the window, her back to him.

"May?"

She turned to look at him. "The city's all lit up," she said. She blinked her eyes closed.

"May, What is it?"

"The holidays. I always think of Charles this time of year. And Abigail. I thought she'd be home for Christmas."

"Have you talked to her?"

She shook her head. "I don't know where she is. I told my lawyer to put some money into her account. The only way I know she's alive is by monitoring her bank funds. She used to love Christmas. I can picture her face coming down the stairs and seeing all the presents."

"I'm sorry."

"Maybe she'll still call," she said, with a resigned smile.

He wanted to tell her about the phone call with Reynolds but he suddenly couldn't bring himself to do it. He told himself that

Agnes would change her mind and that there was no reason to worry May.

"Do you want to have Christmas with us," he asked instead. "Holly would love to have you." She thanked him and declined the invitation, saying she was having Christmas with friends.

COOL NIGHT AIR brought him out of himself. The avenue lay hushed under the first snow. A man in a Santa hat dragging a Christmas tree, his baby stowed in a pack on his back, came up the street leaving a trail of fresh needles in the white. In another mood it would have made him smile. On the train he sat next to the window. The rain blew softly against the pane. Stands of trees and ramshackle houses passed by in a furious blur. The seats rattled. He listened to the rumbling and heaviness filled his body.

T HE SMELL OF ginger, cinnamon, apples, and currants rippled throughout the house. Christmas was Holly's favorite holiday. She was baking pies, a dusting of flour in her hair, the kitchen table covered with bowls, sifter, jars of molasses, boxes of sugar and bags of flour, cans of pumpkin, spice bottles lined up in a row like competent little toy soldiers.

"Hi, Daddy." Annabel reached up to give her father a hug.

"I'm glad you're home. I finished the shopping. Will you bring up the card table and extra chairs from the cellar? And we need firewood from the shed." Holly wiped her hands on her apron and kissed his cheek. "Do you like these Santa salt and pepper shakers I picked for the table? They're a little kitschy but it's Christmas."

"Sure," he said, barely looking. He cracked open the window and breathed in the December air. He could scarcely focus or think. His eyes wandered around the room. He admired the long mahogany table and matching chairs in his dining room. He admired the Williams-Sonoma pots hanging in his kitchen and the original Steichen and Eggleston photographs in his living room, which he and Holly decided to buy shortly after some of the revenues had come in from *Immortality*. All of it they had bought little by little in the years he had worked at Mayweather and Darby. Was it possible that Agnes could undo everything he had built? He began to calculate how many millions the gallery would lose if she left. And not just money. The news would go viral. She had the power to scar his reputation. All because she was running scared.

He was going to the dark place. Clara had cautioned him against it. Her voice had become like a chip implanted in his brain. She was moving him toward experiencing the emotions that had been wound up tight ever since he was a young boy. "Take it one day at a time, hour by hour, don't get so far ahead of yourself," Clara had told him when he mentioned moments of panic.

"I'll bring up the card table. Going to change," he called to Holly.

"Annabel wants you to come to the stables on Saturday for the Christmas pageant. And the Waxmans invited us over for Friday night leftovers. Saturday we have cocktails at the Ackermans'. I know you're annoyed, but you could at least pretend to enjoy the holidays," she said playfully.

"I'll pretend," he said. "By the end of it we'll be pickled and preserved in alcohol. Should be good."

He climbed the stairs, which were carpeted with an antique rug he'd bought at an auction. It was a present to his family after he sold one of Agnes's paintings to LACMA. He went into the master bathroom and looked at his pale and oily face in the mirror. On top of the toilet tank was a basket that contained fragrant soaps in the shape of seashells. He looked at the rack. There were two soft bath towels lined up, one for him and one for Holly.

He took out his BlackBerry from the breast pocket of his jacket and called Leonard.

"She's unbelievable," Leonard groaned. "I'm sure everything you said was on the money."

"It all happened so fast. I'm not sure of anything anymore."

"It's a setup. You locked her into a deal and she wants more money."

"I don't know, Leonard. I think she's running scared. Do you think she'll come around? There's May to consider. And the gallery. She needs a firm hand."

"Be prepared, my friend. She's used to getting what she wants."

He took off his jacket. It was heavy in his hands. He went to his closet and gazed at the rows of shirts and suits, forgetting what he was doing. Then he slowly hung the jacket on an empty hanger and stood in the dressing room looking out at his vast lawn. Everything outside was darkening. Across the yard a family of deer scattered.

ON CHRISTMAS MORNING his job was to make the stuffing and prepare the turkey. He put the butter in the pan and melted it. He chopped onions and wiped away the sting of tears with his sleeve. He chopped up apples and pecans and then tore up crusts of whole wheat and corn bread and tossed it all in a pan and let it simmer. He began to attack the turkey with the same vigor. Annabel was upstairs in her room. Holly was ironing the tablecloths and napkins. It was ten in the morning. Edward had barely slept the night before, and when he did his dreams were dark and unsettling. He put in a CD of Benjamin Britten's *Peter Grimes*. It was one of his favorite operas. He stuck his hand into the cavity of the turkey and pulled out its neck and giblets. The turkey was cold and naked, and when he rubbed butter over it he felt the pimply nubs where the feathers had once protected it. Outside a cold rain lingered. He opened the window just a little to air out the warm kitchen and breathed in the hickory smell of rotting wet leaves. Thunder rumbled through the clouds. The temperature had dropped. Maybe it would snow.

He looked out the window at the branches of the cherry tree they had planted when they bought the house nearly fifteen years ago. Now they almost touched the side of the house, suffocating one of the windows. The leaves were nearly gone, a few holding on. The years were going by. Annabel was growing up so quickly. He could remember his early years of Christmas with her and how she used to pull up a chair beside him and watch him stuff the turkey. He could remember how she squealed the first time she saw him take out the giblets and how she had been a little sad when she put together the fact that the bare turkey, stripped of its black feathers and loose neck, was like the wild turkeys she sometimes saw in their yard. He remembered how Annabel had seemed to forget all about it later that day once the turkey was carved, and she took particular delight in breaking the wishbone.

When he thought about the years disappearing, the new crew of young assistants at the gallery, the crop of newly marrieds in their neighborhood, he felt that something was moving steadily away from him. He wondered if Holly felt the same. He observed her in the same gray sweatshirt and sweatpants with their faded Princeton emblem, still trim and fit, her hair loose at her shoulders. She was rigorously ironing, pressing down on the white linen tablecloth, no doubt thinking about how she would lay out the desserts and when she should make the salad instead of depressing thoughts about the passing of years. For a moment his body ached for her.

Christmas, the year ending, was a time at which he had always taken a few minutes after they had finished eating to look around at his family and take stock of how lucky he was. He supposed he wished Holly had taken more of an interest in his work and his artists. She'd gotten the receptionist position at the gallery because one of her father's clients had a connection, and she'd taken a few art history classes, but she'd never really understood his personal attachment and investment in art—it wasn't just a business for him—and he supposed that you either felt that way or not. Early in their years together it hadn't bothered him. But once he had made something of himself, Holly stopped keeping track, stopped brainstorming or daydreaming with him about how he could go to the next level, advising him about what he should or should not say when he wanted a raise or a promotion. She was good about thinking through that kind of thing—better than he'd ever been. Now she seemed to think little about what he did in the hours he was away from her, unaware of the daily stresses, the ups and downs he navigated, as if his pressures and worries didn't exist if she didn't recognize them. She didn't appear to want anything to change, whereas he was afraid of the stagnation. He recalled the dreams they used to share, the house they would buy, the family they would have, their furniture and trips and celebrations, and now that they had realized them, he wondered what was next. All of it felt empty. Annabel soon to be at college, solitary evenings alone with Holly, the house slowly rotting and falling apart—already they needed a new roof. What would they do together, or talk about, without Annabel? Was the next stage of his life about watching everything they had built fall away?

He wondered if he would feel better if he told Holly what had happened, that he'd potentially lost his prized artist. For the first time since it had happened he allowed himself to wonder if he had handled everything wrong. Why had he needed to be honest?

Hadn't he learned enough about handling artists and the delicacy of their egos? In the military there were certain rules that kept the institution running but always the powerful generals were the ones who broke rank. He had never broken rank. He should have told her the work was brilliant and left it at that. Maybe his flirtation with Julia had brought all this on, on some level. Maybe all this was payback, on some karmic scale, for his being infatuated with another woman. He couldn't bear to think of Agnes showing her work at another gallery.

He opened the turkey cavity and began spooning fistfuls of stuffing into it. Then he sewed the flaps and squeezed juice from an orange over the bird and put it in the oven. He washed his hands and moved into the dining room, where Holly was still ironing. Love, as he had understood it, involved dedication and commitment. It meant pushing past the things that annoyed him, the way Holly looked at him from the corner of her eye when she disapproved, learning when to reach for her and when to retreat. It involved beautiful days of harmony and then weeks of jagged disappointment. It wasn't about affairs in attractive cities. He thought of Picasso's *Woman Ironing* and Alice Neel's *Nancy and Olivia*, Jennifer Bartlett and her houses. Donald Judd and his tools. He thought about other painters documenting their domestic moments, and suddenly felt enlivened by the idea that he ought to curate such a show. He leaned over and kissed Holly's neck.

"Edward," she said and laughed.

He felt a rare need for reassurance from her. "Holly, has anything changed? Do you still love me?"

She looked up from the ironing board. He could hear the sizzle the water made when she lifted the iron from the cloth.

"Do you really need to ask me that?" she said, as if she expected that he understood that everything she did, all this, all they'd built and accumulated over the years, was for him, and wasn't that enough? Her face wore that slightly confused expression when he was looking for romance and titillation instead of the down-to-earth love she offered.

He watched her stretch the Christmas evergreen tablecloth over the long table and then remove the china from the cabinet. The porcelain dishes, thin, delicate, she took out carefully one at a time so they would not chip or break. It was the cream-colored wedding china, each plate trimmed with a gold rim to mark its significance. He looked underneath the tree where Holly had small gifts for their guests wrapped with cutouts from magazines. The night before, Edward came upon her on the bedroom floor going through stacks of magazines and snipping pictures to personalize each gift. Annabel's were wrapped with pictures of horses and dogs.

He decided not to tell Holly about what had happened with Agnes. Why burden her? Agnes would come around. Her work meant more to her than anything—possibly more than Nate and the twins—and she would consider what Edward had said about the work and see that he had been right. Edward was certain she needed him. In those early days of working together, writing copy, hanging the show, e-mailing every review or comment from the press back and forth, going over negotiations, an intimacy and understanding had developed between them. It wasn't just business. Beneath his anger was fear for her. Being a gallerist was a delicate dance, to know how much to push and hold back in service to the work, to find a shared sensibility that perfectly meshed.

Edward believed he and Agnes had achieved that balance. He felt a little better. She'd be lost without him.

He went back to the kitchen to baste the turkey and clean up the dishes he'd left in the sink. He needed to go down to the wine cellar and bring up the wine and went to find Holly to ask her which of the reds she wanted to serve. He looked in the living room and then the dining room and couldn't find her. He remembered he'd heard her go out the back door and assumed she was going to take out the trash. He looked out the window and saw her SUV in the driveway and Holly inside it. Her head was leaning against the steering wheel. He went outside and knocked on the window. When she looked up he saw she'd been crying. She unlocked the door and, cold, he slipped into the passenger seat next to her. "What is it, Holly?"

"I don't know exactly. It hit me, earlier, wrapping presents. Annabel is almost sixteen. And we never . . ."

"Never what?"

"You know. Had another child."

He thought of her full, swelling breasts and rounded abdomen when she was pregnant with Annabel and how he had placed his ear against her belly to hear her gurgle. It had excited him to feel that quick kick of life, that stronghold that held them close. He thought about the years in which they'd tried to get pregnant. He remembered how sometimes after Holly got her period he would find her despondent, curled into the couch after Annabel went to bed. In the middle of the night she washed their clothes, the swishing of the washer and the spinning of the dryer in his dreams. In the morning when he came down for coffee she was in sweatpants ironing, polishing their silver, or cleaning the refrigerator. Then one year, he didn't know why, she seemed to have turned the corner and stopped talking about having another baby. So as not to upset her, so did he.

He stroked her arm. "I'm sorry."

"It isn't anything either of us could control. I thought things would be different, that's all," Holly said. She dried her eyes with a Kleenex and gave him a kiss on the lips. "I'm okay. We have so much. Let's go in," she said.

He followed her inside wishing he knew how to comfort her.

BEFORE LONG IT was time to go upstairs and shower and then greet their guests. Holly's parents were staying in the city for Christmas this year. His own mother preferred not to leave the retirement home, as if life outside had lost its meaning or frightened her. Each passing year her world became smaller and more contained. He'd go to see her sometime over the weekend with Annabel and bring her gifts. He was grateful the holiday this year would be with friends. He wanted to sink into the wine and get lost in the company.

After he dressed he came downstairs and admired his living room and the sprays of winter-white flowers Holly had carefully composed for the table and mantel. He poured himself a glass of wine and focused on trying to have a good time. Before long the house was filled with the sounds of conversation. Yet when he caught himself alone, either carving the turkey or pouring the wine, a wave of dread washed over him.

Dinner was served. He looked across the table at Holly, her cheeks glowing from the wine, and then at Annabel laughing with the Lawson boys. "You hide yourself from me," Holly had told him once early in their marriage when she had found him in the third-floor study late at night working on a presentation for the board of a museum. She ran her fingers through his hair. "What keeps you so locked up?" she said, kissed his cheek, and then lay down on the couch and fell asleep so he would not be alone. He watched her passing the gravy for the turkey and talking about the fundraiser she was planning for the refuge, and admired how quickly she seemed to have pushed past her sadness from earlier in the afternoon.

After dessert around the fireplace, the Christmas tree lights on, he placed another log on the fire, but before he was able to join Ruth Atkinson and Holly chatting on the sofa, Chip Lawson approached him by the fireplace. Chip was a successful hedge fund manager; in a matter of a few years he'd amassed a shitload of money. He was handsome in a Kennedyesque way, dressed in corduroys and a sports coat. His on-top-of-the-world disposition reminded Edward of Holly's father. Chip's wife, Marilyn, was an ex-ballet dancer who Edward suspected drank too much in order to endure her husband's philandering. Chip flirted with Holly at cocktail parties. Observing the coy jostling that went on between them, he perversely wondered if Holly would have been happier with a man like him. He talked in gestures and grunts and could barely put together an articulate sentence, but Edward imagined he fucked like a racehorse, or was it piss like one, he couldn't remember.

Certainly Holly's father would have preferred him for a son-in-law. Edward knew that Frank Moore disapproved of him. He mostly spoke to him about making sure he had long-term health coverage and had already paid for family plots in an elite section of a cemetery in Westchester where four generations of the Moore family were buried.

At dinner Chip had hijacked the conversation by talking about the vacation he'd booked for the family in Anguilla. He boasted about the great year they'd had at the fund. Holly's cheeks flushed and she laughed, a little too robustly, at his jokes.

Chip patted him on the back. "Amazing dinner. Your wife outdid herself. She's one beautiful woman."

The cliché made him wince.

Chip generously refilled his wineglass from the bottle on the coffee table. As the night went on the guests were getting louder and drunker. "How's the art market?" he asked, as if it were regulated like stock. "Anyone we should know about?" But before Edward could answer, Chip leaned over. "I've had a boner for five days straight. Goddamn Viagra."

"Sounds rough," Edward said and excused himself to have a cigarette on the screened-in porch. *Viagra. Is this what it would all come down to?* He put out his cigarette in the ashtray and walked back into the party. He turned his head to look back at Chip and caught him nodding at Holly from across the room. He didn't like it.

Holly was standing with Ruth by the fire, its light wrapping them in a soft insulated cocoon. He was drawn into their glow. Ruth had studied art history in college and was an amateur collector, and one of the few neighborhood friends with whom he felt a connection. She liked to come into the city and visit one or two galleries, and they often discussed particular artists or shows they had seen. Edward advised her on art. The other guests still lingered in a half-comatose state from overeating, their faces rosy, sipping wine. The children had fled the adults for the den. He joined Holly and Ruth.

"Is there anyone new you've discovered?" Ruth asked.

He thought for a moment. The truth was that lately he hadn't taken on anyone new. Instead of telling her this, he heard himself say, "There's this sculptor whose work I like. Julia Rosenthal. Do you know her work? There's something utterly magical about it. The struggle for any artist is how to capture with materials exactly the way of feeling and seeing. With her work it seems effortless." His face warmed, recognizing he'd gone on. He'd had a little too much to drink.

"I've read about her. In *ArtForum* maybe?"

"Wasn't she that artist who won the Rome Prize?" Holly broke in. "Ages ago. When I was still at the gallery. We were at that reception right before we got engaged."

Heat rose to his face. He nodded.

"She's controversial. Now I remember. I saw a show of hers years ago. Are you taking her on?" Ruth asked.

"Thinking about it. We were in Berlin together. She was part of the group. Years ago she made a stir. Her work's moving in a new direction. It's softer now."

"Really," Holly said. "You didn't mention it." She looked at him, and unable to meet her eyes he looked at her forehead.

"Mention what?"

"That you were in Berlin together. If Ruth's interested in her, we'll have her for cocktails. And then we can invite you and Martın to join us," Holly said, without missing a beat.

"I'd like to learn more about her work," Ruth responded.

"Maybe it's the cure for restless husbands." Holly had had a few glasses of wine. "Inviting pretty artists to the house."

E mpty wineglasses and dessert plates still on the coffee table and scattered throughout the living room, cigarette butts in the ashtray on the porch, the cushions on the couch sunken, still holding the ghosts of their last inhabitants, the fire nearly extinguished. Edward went to the kitchen to start the dishes. Dirty plates crowded the sink. On the counter sat the picked-over turkey carcass and charred casserole dishes. The windowpanes above the sink were black. The house felt uncomfortably still.

Holly wrapped the leftovers, pulling out a sheet of plastic wrap and meticulously placing it over the bowl, stretching it so that it sealed the container without letting any air in. He thought of the way she had flirted with Chip at dinner. He slipped the sponge into a crystal goblet and the glass broke in his hands. "Goddamn it," he said.

"Are you okay? Did you get cut?"

"I'm fine." He shook his hand to stop the blood.

"You're not fine." She came over and wrapped his finger with a paper towel. Blood oozed into it.

"I'm sorry." He pressed his finger against the paper towel to stop the flow of warm blood.

"What's wrong?"

"Chip Lawson is a dick. He never stops talking about himself. He put me in a bad mood."

"He's Chip."

"He's an asshole." He turned to the sink and with his free hand picked out the broken glass. "Sorry. I'm not myself tonight."

"I'm not either." In the half-light of the kitchen, Holly kicked off her heels and appeared suddenly smaller, more diminished.

"Maybe it's the holidays? I always feel a little sad this time of year."

"Maybe."

He dried his free hand on a dishtowel and turned to Holly.

"That's not it," Holly said. "I've been thinking. You know, about what I said earlier to Ruth. About inviting that artist, Julia, to the house for cocktails. Why don't you ever bring your artists home? Or take me to one of your dinners?"

"I guess I didn't think you'd be interested."

"It's like you're ashamed of me," Holly said.

"I'm not ashamed of you. I thought you'd be bored. You know what it's like when you get a group of artists together. They only want to talk about themselves. Hol, you don't invite me out with your friends at the barn either."

"I guess," Holly said, drifting. "I've just been thinking. In taking care of everyone else—you, Annabel, Mother and Daddy, this house—I've lost a bit of myself."

"That's not true. We'd all be lost without you." He wondered about his own unhappiness but it upset him to think Holly was unhappy or disappointed or had lost faith in him. Was what Holly said true? Was he embarrassed by his wife? That wasn't it. He liked keeping her separate. Home was his refuge.

"I don't know," Holly said. "Nothing seems fun anymore with us."

She stretched out another piece of plastic wrap. His eyes moved down her body and stopped at her legs, covered in sheer nylons. On one leg her nylon had snagged, causing a rip up the seam. He leaned into her back and nuzzled her neck. A shimmer of desire went through him. As if sensing it, she moved away, picked up the plastic wrap, tore off a sheet, and placed it tightly over a plate of cookies. Why was she always moving away? If only she would come into his arms and kiss him—for so many years he lived for her to take him in like that. He wanted to be adored. Maybe all men—everyone—did.

"It seems as if you've lost interest."

"I've lost interest?" She turned to look at him. "You really are dumb. In the morning you don't look above your coffee cup to acknowledge I'm there."

His thoughts raced. He could not break through the layers to figure out how to reach her or what to say. Or how to get what they once had back. It seemed in that moment that if he went any further it all might fall apart. He looked at the copper teakettle on the burner next to the sink. It was a wedding present from one of Holly's cousins. It was discolored after years of tarnish; the bottom had corroded and puckered from built-up residue and the copper had pulled back to expose the raw metal underneath.

He wanted to say something more to her about their unhappiness, something simple that might fix it, but the words fought him. He considered telling her about Agnes and stopped himself. He didn't want to bring it up. Not then.

"My work seems to have lost its meaning."

"Until your next discovery. The way you spoke of Julia Rosenthal, it doesn't sound as if the magic is gone just yet."

The room seemed to go around him. His heart sped. He peered at his reflection in the dark pane, and farther back, the shadow of Holly. The grandfather clock in the hallway chimed.

They finished in the kitchen, unease lingering, abstract but all-inclusive. He turned off the lights, one after the other, darkness shadowing them, and followed Holly to the staircase.

PART TWO

1 LONDON

THE FAIR PRESENTED more than a hundred galleries of modern and contemporary international art. Julia gave a talk about her exhibited work in the crowded space of a new British gallery: "Sculpted figures that hang from the ceiling like naked mannequins in dancer-like poses," the catalogue read. *All Powerful Individuals Eventually Become Powerless*, the show was titled. In her talk she said she aimed to depict the unknown individuals in society. "At the end of the day, who are we really?" she said, then she quoted from Auden's "Musée des Beaux Arts": "About suffering they were never wrong, / The Old Masters: how well they understood / Its human position; how it takes place / while someone else is eating or opening a window or just walking dully along." She spoke about the strangeness of making something out of nothing and of how her dancers lifted themselves out of the iron in which they'd been molded and brought themselves to life. Her cheeks were pink as she turned to look anew at her sculptures projected on a screen behind her.

Edward waited for her in the back of the gallery. After Christmas, in clear moments, he had told himself to cancel their dinner plans, but from the moment he boarded the plane to London she was the only person he wanted to see.

"It was wonderful," he said to her, after the last of the crowd had drifted to the drinks buffet. "I'm spellbound." He kissed her on one cheek and then the other.

Julia's face was flushed, high from the talk. "I didn't embarrass myself?"

"No. You were terrific."

"I'm glad it's over."

"Charlotte invited us to her dinner. Do you want to join?"

"Charlotte knew we were getting together?"

"I ran into her at Saatchi this morning. She asked about you. She's been trying to get in touch."

"Will the others from Berlin be there too?"

He nodded. "Charlotte said if we don't attend her dinner she'll make sure we're the main topic of conversation. And people need to see you after your talk. It was brilliant."

"Well, then, we have to join," she said, a little reluctantly.

"We have time for a drink first," he said, walking her toward the door and then around the corner to a small, dark, and crowded pub. They sat in a back booth. He ordered a Guinness and she a glass of cabernet.

"I'm glad that's over. I have to admit, though, that it is exhilarating to speak about my work in front of others. It's like coming out of hiding."

"So then you want to go to the dinner?"

"To watch everyone impressing each other? Of course."

"Is that how it looks?"

"You're one of the gatekeepers. Don't you know when you're being impressed?"

He laughed. "I try to keep my head down. My job is to keep the stable filled."

"And you represent Agnes Murray."

"So Agnes makes me famous?" For a moment he considered telling Julia about the studio visit and what had happened, but he wasn't ready to articulate it. He still hoped Agnes would come around. He took it as a good sign that Reynolds had not been in touch. It meant Agnes was thinking things over. Or maybe it wasn't. He didn't want to think about it.

"No. You made her famous." Julia looked up and brushed back a lock of hair.

"Thank you."

"It's not an act, is it?"

He looked bewildered.

"You really don't see it, do you? That's your gift."

"My gift?"

"That you don't see it." She paused and looked at him with curiosity. "Who you are. You should have more confidence."

"When I walk through galleries and see what sells it can be humbling. I take on what moves me and then worry about whether it'll sell. People like Savan, he's smarter. He takes on what sells."

"Don't let them corrupt you. The Savans of the world."

"It works for him. Collectors respond to his energy. Artists, too. He's a terrific salesman."

He thought again about Savan going to Agnes's studio. It infuriated him all over again. He looked across the table and then past her out the window. The rush-hour crowd streamed past.

"Do you ever wake up and wonder how you got here? And what it all means?"

"Sometimes. I try not to think about it. When I think that way it's usually when I'm unhappy or doubting myself."

An idea possessed him. "Would you consider moving to Mayweather and Darby?" As soon as he said it, he wondered if he would regret it. It wasn't his style to poach from other galleries. If an artist was on the market for a new gallery, then he'd listen. But there was something about Julia that made him want to make an exception. And if Savan got away with it, why not he? He thought about her talk, her dancers and the idea of being powerless, and it made him think about the randomness of life and death. Why some are touched by tragedy early and others are spared, and what, if anything, it meant.

"That wouldn't be too weird?"

"Why, because we're friends?"

She nodded. "I don't know. I've been with Watkins from the beginning. He didn't come to the talk this afternoon. And he's been in London all week. I've been handed over to one of his underlings. And yet he understands what I do."

"I love your work. I knew I would that first night I met you when you got the Rome Prize."

"You remember that night?"

"Of course I do. You said you hadn't done anything remarkable yet. Now you have. What are you working on now?"

"I'm doing some commissioned work in Vienna and Amsterdam. Watkins got them for me. And a work of public art here in London. Tomorrow I have a meeting with the Arts Council. But what I'm most excited about is more personal. I'm working on a series of small stone pieces."

"I'd like to see them when we're back in New York. What you said in your talk about sculpture, about it being the poetry of shape?"

"Yeah."

"I liked that."

"When I make something I can hear my materials. They sometimes laugh at me," she said, and grinned. "But really, the stone pieces mean a lot to me. They're helping me. I told you. We lost a child."

"I know. I'm sorry."

She lowered her eyes. "I still see her face in my mind."

"I'd love to see the sculptures."

"I can't think of anyone I'd rather let see them."

"Two foreign cities," Edward said, suddenly brightening.

She waited for him to finish his thought.

"Berlin and London."

"Three cities," she corrected him. "Don't forget Hamburg."

"And your lost passport," he said.

"Lost among my possessions." Julia rolled her eyes.

"Aren't we all?"

"I don't feel lost tonight, do you?"

"No. I'm happy to be away from all the nonsense at the gallery. It's been tense."

"Who will be at the dinner?"

"Charlotte's arranged it. Everyone will be there."

CHARLOTTE'S DINNER WAS held in a trendy, too brightly lit restaurant. Though there were twenty or thirty people at the table, aside from the quick hellos and pecks on the cheek when they arrived, he barely spoke to anyone other than Julia.

"Your husband?" he said, after their starters. They were sitting next to each other on the banquette of a long booth.

"Roy."

"Yes. Remind me, what does Roy do?"

"He's an architect."

"Ah, yes."

"I tried living with an artist once. I told you. Frederick. Inevitably one or the other becomes more successful. Or is deemed such. It's dangerous."

"I suppose so." He thought about Agnes and Nate. "But maybe the competition is good for the work?"

"Maybe for some. Roy doesn't expect me to be brilliant. He wouldn't know how to judge what I do. He keeps me honest. It's better for the work."

"His name makes him sound like a cowboy," he said, and then regretted his pettiness.

"He's not a cowboy," she said, protectively. "He designs buildings. He's designing a library in the city and projects in Portugal and Spain. He's been working on one in Tokyo for years. Some eventually get made and some don't."

"Does he mind when *you* travel?"

"I suppose he does. Doesn't your wife mind?"

"Sometimes."

"And does it bother you? That she minds?"

"Yes." He looked at her and grinned. "What is it about marriage?"

She looked up from her wineglass and began to laugh.

"Is something funny?"

She touched his arm. "I'm not making fun. I understand what it's like. Being married. Roy and I built our careers side by side."

"Have you thought of me? Since our lunch at the oyster bar?"

She grew thoughtful. "Yes, of course I have."

He slid closer to her on the banquette they shared, and having made a decision, or having had the decision made for him, whispered in her ear, "I want to be with you." He breathed in to calm himself. He'd been thinking about it all through the talk she gave earlier in the day, and then at the bar, and throughout dinner. Here he was in London, far away from his life at home. It was improbable that they had met years ago when he was first starting out as a dealer, and then again in Berlin, and now here in London, and each time there had been a feeling in the air between them that seemed as if nothing was at a distance; it was not simply a matter of the way they looked at each other, or spoke to each other, but a sensation in the gut, and whatever it was it felt, in the state he was in, impossible to deny. The idea of it had already inhabited his consciousness.

"To go down on you," he added.

"What did you say?" The restaurant was noisy. She began to blush and moved uncomfortably so that she could see into his face.

"You heard me, Julia. I can't stop thinking about it. About you."

He'd been feeling unsure of himself since Christmas. Another week had passed and still no word from Agnes. He'd gone to London reluctantly, unsure of whether he should stay until things with her were sorted, but told himself he couldn't rush her. The not knowing was unbearable. He felt disconnected from Holly. And from himself, and something had been building inside since Berlin;

he felt reckless, impulsive, unable to control himself. And then here was Julia, having pressed up against his mind for months and now suddenly realized in the flesh before him. He couldn't stop thinking about it.

"Would you let me?"

She laughed and then she looked at him and her face flushed again. She nervously reached her hand into her marvelous stream of hair and sent it cascading from her fingers.

"You're serious, then."

"Yes."

She placed her napkin on the table. "What you're asking. That would be asking me to reveal everything."

"Yes."

"But why would you ask that of me? When there hasn't been anything . . . I mean, anything physical really between us," she said, her look at once provocative and unsure at the same time.

"Because I can't not ask it. But you don't want to."

"I didn't say that."

The room grew quiet. Charlotte stood up to give a toast. She was wearing a tight spandex dress and half her breasts were showing. She welcomed everyone and acknowledged the ones who had traveled from New York, Tokyo, San Francisco, Paris, and Amsterdam. He tried to catch Julia's eyes to read her gaze, but after the toast she started a conversation with the person on the other side of her. He glanced across from him at an odd character with a broad and deformed nose, beefy, wearing a hoop in his ear. He was giving a tarot reading to a woman next to him dressed in a pink leotard and ballet tutu. When he saw Edward staring he said, "They hired me for the after-party. To read cards."

"The after-party. It's going to be one of those circuses, then."
Edward sighed.

"Will you read hers?" He pointed to Julia, who had turned back
to look at him.

"Mine? Really?" Then she laughed. "Why not yours?"

"Because I know what I want," he said, staring at her as if he
had already undressed her. Who was he kidding? He wanted to do
everything to her, with her.

The card reader motioned for Julia to sit next to him. He shuffled the deck and turned up a card. "The Fool," he said, handing it
to her. "The Fool is the power behind all manifestations. He is the
spark that sets everything in motion."

The second course had been finished, coffees drunk, and talk
began about going to the after-party.

Edward leaned over to ask Julia if she was going, but before he
could get a response, Charlie high-fived him at the table. "Dude,"
Charlie said, and Edward stood up and they gave each other a hug.

"I didn't know you were coming, Charlie. When did you get in?"

"About an hour ago. I took a cab from the airport straight here."

Whenever Edward and Charlie were together a dangerous adolescent streak rose inside him. They'd had a lot of good times in
his early days in New York. Charlie married Cath, a tall, slender
museum director from Boston, shortly after Edward and Holly
got married. He moved to Boston with Cath and opened a gallery
there. They saw each other occasionally at art fairs and Charlie
always called when he was in New York.

"How's Holly?" Charlie asked.

Edward suspected Charlie still carried a torch for his wife.

"Holly's good. Her father isn't doing so well."

"That's too bad. Let's do dinner in New York. It'd be a kick to see her. Coming with us for a smoke?" Already stoked for a good night of it, Charlie's hair was out of place and his skin glistened. He'd put on weight.

Edward looked back at Julia, who was engaged in a conversation with the tarot reader and the woman in the tutu. There was a fuss about who was going to share a cab with whom, and he saw Julia pick up her coat and glance back at him anxiously to let him know she was leaving. He acknowledged that he'd follow, but once outside he watched her crowd into a cab with a group and take off.

Jimmy Oldman emerged from the restaurant with a young female art student on each side of him. "Hey, man, you'll see her at the party. Don't look so strung out," Jimmy said. Yes, he told himself, he'd see her at the party.

He smoked a cigarette on the curb with Charlie, Jimmy, and the two lanky grad students with jet-black hair and twiglike legs. The tarot reader joined their conversation.

"There's another side to the Fool. He represents unmolded potential, pure and innocent. He does not care what others think or say about him, because he knows that what he is doing is right for him."

Edward stood a foot taller than the card reader. He put his cigarette out on the ground, rubbed it with his foot, and urgently hailed a cab.

WHEN HE ARRIVED at the club it was jammed. Three or four hundred intoxicated and overheated art fanatics packed the room. The loud music thrummed through his body. He felt surprisingly alive. He craned his neck to see above the crowd. Where was Julia?

Was it possible that she'd gone back to her hotel without him? Maybe she was having second thoughts. He bumped into Charlotte and thanked her for dinner while anxiously peering over her head. A gallerist in New York, she was a tastemaker known for her expertise in the international art scene. Robust with stringy blond hair and needy blue eyes, she thrust out her breasts so that they bounced against his chest. He stepped back just a tad. Her energy repelled him.

"Charlotte, have you seen Julia?"

"I saw her come in." She gave him a peck on the cheek. "Don't look so desperate, darling," she whispered.

"It's an oven in here," he said, tugging at his collar, unable to think of anything but Julia.

He spotted her near the windows. He elbowed his way through a group of wilted and wrecked Spanish artists to reach her.

"I thought I'd lost you."

She looked up at him and smiled. "You haven't lost me."

Body girdled and spilling out of her spandex dress, Charlotte tagged behind. She leaned over and whispered in Julia's ear and then reached for her hand and lured her to the dance floor. Julia looked back reluctantly. The women swayed together, moving loosely to the rhythms of the music. Everything was moving slightly and his head felt heavy. He labored to keep focused. He sipped his warm beer, already wishing for another though the glass was not yet empty. He elbowed through a group of stylish Italians to the dance floor and dislodged Julia from Charlotte's arms. He took her by the hand, brought her close, and kissed her.

Afterward, she looked at him, stunned, and then her eyes broke into a smile. Relief flooded him. He tugged her by the hand and whisked her away from the mayhem of the dancing crowd and then through the packed club. They wound their way upstairs to the vestibule of the hotel. The lobby was overlit; he wished for darkness and beauty.

"Let's have a drink. Can we go to your hotel?"

He helped her into her coat and, night still holding, led her by the hand to the taxi stand. If they spoke it might not happen, so he refrained. In the cab, he kissed her again and reached for her hand in her lap. She seemed as bewildered as he by what had overtaken them.

"Did you really do that?" she said.

Her hotel room was very tiny. He felt as if he could not stand straight, that the ceiling would crush him. *Just one night. I'm allowed one night.* He was alone with her, helping her take off the thin slip of her coat. There had been some awkwardness in the hotel lobby when she went to claim her key, and then some fumbling to get the key into the lock. They had drunk an awful lot. He took off his coat. She looked at him and went into the bathroom. When she came out he smelled toothpaste in her mouth and kissed her mint-flavored lips.

"I've never done this before." She was trembling.

"Done what?"

"Invited a man to my hotel room."

They began kissing. He slowly moved her against the wall to press himself against her more fully. Her mouth was full and warm and penetrable. They were kissing standing up, she still in her tight skirt and sweater and tights, having taken off only her high boots. He pulled up her skirt to feel the shape of her. He drew her across the room and took off her sweater and her skirt and they fell onto the bed. Then he sat up and unbuttoned his shirt and took it off and unbuckled his belt and took off his pants and left them on the floor and for a moment stopped just to look at her. There was a tiny mole on her neck just beneath her ear. He'd never seen it before. He pulled her hair away from the nape of her neck and kissed it. Then he moved his lips to hers again. They were soft, wet petals. Her lithe body was hot to his touch. He slipped his hands underneath her bra—it was lacy and black—and he felt her breasts. He tried to slip a hand underneath her pantyhose and panties, but she stopped his hand with hers and looked up at him, uncertain for a moment.

"I want you, Julia," he said. He had to have her.

He slipped his hands back underneath her panties and she let him, *thank God*. He moved over her and felt himself gather more force and intensity, and they moved until they found their rhythm, until he felt as if he had explored every region of her body, her mouth now tasting of wine, her hair caught underneath him, her hands and mouth on him, until her breathing and motion quickened and she groaned, digging her fingernails into the back of his neck, and then he held himself there until he couldn't anymore and came into her. It was a relief beyond relief, as if all his mindfulness for those months had dissolved, and he was out of his head, free of his directive. He lay on his back and then turned to kiss her.

"Are you okay," he asked, pushing her hair back from her face, afraid for a moment.

"Yes, it's okay," she said, her breathing beginning to quiet.

"It was inevitable, wasn't it?" she said.

He thought about how little he knew about her. The abandonment of her father, her forays in art school, the pain of losing a child, it was all there underneath the flesh that he had touched and held and kissed. Somehow, in a manner of days, hours, she'd become utterly indispensable to him. He opened his arms to her and she fell into them. He closed his eyes. It had been twenty years since he had slept beside a woman other than his wife. It was at once extremely peaceful and nearly unbearable. He wished to stop the clock, to allow himself a few more luxurious hours in limbo before the night ran out. He sank further into the bedsheets and felt her stirring next to him.

"With you it's so different," she said.

He looked at the clock. It was five in the morning. He'd fallen asleep. He turned on his bedside lamp and looked at her asleep next to him. He viewed the room. Across from the bed was a small desk on which she had laid her accoutrements: a black Moleskine sketchbook and some drawing pencils, two books, a pot of tea, and a solitary cup. He thought of her alone in the room with her tea and her drawing pencils and pad. He imagined the two of them living together, both solitary figures sinking into their own inner reflections. He thought about what she'd said about him being different. He turned to her and she opened her eyes sleepily and he felt a sudden overpowering urge to escape. She was a dark pit he was falling into. He was deeply, completely in the thrall of her. He got out of the bed, found his clothes, and put them on while she watched. Like a fawn lying on her side, she was quiet and sullen, as if she, too, sensed his sudden desire to flee not from discontent or displeasure but from fear of where staying might take them.

"You're leaving?" she said.

"I have to."

He explained he had a breakfast meeting with an important British dealer in just a few hours. The dealer represented an artist whose work he had been following. He tucked Julia underneath the covers and then sat down next to her. Her eye makeup had smeared and in the bedside light he could make out small imperfect lines fanning around her eyes and forehead.

"I'm sorry. Should we not have? Is that what you're thinking?"

"No. I wish you didn't have to go."

"It was a wonderful evening."

"I can't believe you're here," she said, sleepily.

"I'm here." He moved the hair from her face. "What did you mean before? When you said I was different?"

"We have no history," she said with tears in her eyes.

He gazed at her and then they kissed and he was drawn back into her warmth, reluctant to break away.

"After my meeting today I leave for Houston. When do you leave?"

"Tonight."

"I'll call you when I'm back in New York. In three days."

"I don't want you to go."

"I don't either," he said, and they kissed again. And then he slipped out of her room like a thief. It was still dark outside when he hailed a cab.

THE PHONE RANG in his hotel room. After he left Julia and returned to his hotel, he had fallen back to sleep. He was disoriented. For a minute he didn't know if it was morning or night. He parted the curtains. Sunrise lightened the winter sky. He picked up the phone. It was May calling from New York. She apologized for calling so early but knew he was catching a flight later that day and would want to know immediately. She had just left a long dinner with Reynolds and waited up for a respectable hour to call him, not wanting to miss him before he left his hotel.

"Sorry to have handled this without you. The news isn't good. Agnes sent us a letter through Reynolds asking us to let her go."

"What? Why didn't she send it to me?" He paused. "She's gone over my head, then."

"He led me to believe you knew of her intentions, and yet you didn't tell me?" May said. He pictured her face, powerful as a building.

"I was handling it," he said. "I was hoping she'd come around. I didn't want to worry you unnecessarily."

"I told Reynolds under no circumstances are we letting Agnes leave the gallery—not with all we've advanced. So she's staying."

He breathed a sigh of relief.

"The bad news is that she's taking a larger percentage of the profits."

"What?"

"They renegotiated. Edward, you should have told me. I was blindsided at dinner and felt I had no other recourse. We couldn't let her walk away. It isn't just about Agnes. We have our other artists to think about. It won't look good if she walks."

"How big of a cut?"

"She wants sixty percent."

"That's outrageous."

"And she wants Alex Savan."

"Savan? What are you talking about?"

"We've talked about expanding. I made Savan an offer. It was the only way. Listen, Edward, it's not going to change anything. You're still the managing partner. Savan will answer to you."

"No," he said, firmly. "She's used us. She used *me* to get a larger cut. She agreed with me about the work. I have her e-mail. She's scared shitless and she let Nate run her over."

Neither spoke for a second. "Her motives were unclear. I'll give you that. You should have told me there was trouble with her. You brought her to the gallery. That's all that matters. Savan's a friend of Nate's. She trusts him. Alex likes you. He's thrilled he'll get a chance to work with you. Put your sore feelings aside. This is for the gallery. Nothing is going to change. You're the linchpin in all this. You have to see it this way. I trust you, Edward. This gallery would be nowhere without you. It's your vision. You have to step back from your hurt feelings and do what's best for the bottom line. Think about our other artists. And our employees. Look, it's her work. In the end, she makes the decisions."

His mouth tasted like chalk. He'd drunk too much the night before and was crashing. He brought his hand to his face. What had he done? He was dizzy when he stood up. He sat back down to steady himself and focus. Maybe it was best for the gallery, but the idea still fought against him.

"No," he said again. "It's about our integrity. It isn't right."

"You'll come to see it this way," she said, and the line went dead, the receiver silent in his hand.

2 CONNECTICUT

FROM LONDON HE flew to Houston and met with the museum director, putting himself on autopilot to get the deal done. Because of the success of Agnes Murray he had the cachet to set extraordinary prices for the newer work he represented and collectors bought into it, sometimes not knowing or even caring if the work they were buying had historic significance but because he had succeeded in making them believe the work was important. Did this make him any different from Savan? He wasn't sure. It still amazed him that people overpaid to be part of his world. He'd managed to make two half-million-dollar sales for a young abstract painter, Liam Wilson, and though he should have felt good about it, he didn't. He gazed at the wedding band on his hand and twirled it around on his finger and it almost flew off. He pushed it back in place and looked out at the blackness in the window.

Traveling through the hemisphere's netherworld, he had time to reflect that his life had changed dramatically within a matter of days. He tried to close his eyes but he couldn't sleep. He sipped his drink and raised the shade and peered again into the clouds. Thoughts flooded him. Agnes Murray was no longer his artist. Savan had joined the gallery. May had made an executive decision without consulting him. Gertrude cautioned him when he first joined her gallery never to get too attached, that the work finally always belonged to the artist. But he'd never been burned by an artist he represented before. Not getting too attached was easier said than done.

His mind jumped from the gallery to his last night in London. He'd broken his trust with his wife by sleeping with another woman. He thought about Jimmy and the other men he knew who had affairs and wondered why he should be left out of the club, and for a few moments he made himself feel better about what he'd done. But it didn't last very long.

He glanced at a young woman across the aisle, lip-synching words, head bobbing from side to side, lost in the dream induced by the music coming from her earbuds. He thought about Julia. He wondered what had happened to him to be in the thrall of another woman when he truly loved his wife. He couldn't blame Holly. Marriage was an amorphous brain with its own mysterious beliefs and myths, fueled and distorted by unconscious wishes and hopes. Perhaps because there were two different versions of the truth and the truth of these versions didn't always coalesce. Perhaps because one's spouse saw one in a particular way when in fact the spouse did not see him or herself in that way at all, because the self is always evolving, or so one hopes. It baffled him. He wondered how Julia was feeling and how it would be for her to return home. He wondered too if their versions of each other, the narratives they had shared of their lives, were authentic, or whether they had inflated their stories for their own purposes. He knew, he was sure, that Julia loved her husband. To some, is betrayal another form of intimacy? He had read that somewhere.

At Kennedy he got off the plane and sat in a seat by the gate. He dried his damp face with a paper towel he'd taken from the bathroom. He looked around at strangers peering into their laptops and thumbing their electronic devices, to the picture window watching the lights on the runway, and wished he could disappear. He wasn't like Jimmy, capable of juggling two women. He knew himself better. Or at least he thought he did. He'd supposed, until now, that it was not possible to love two women at once. But maybe it was? And then he thought about Holly. He couldn't do that to her. He couldn't hurt her.

Terrible thoughts about Savan usurping his position at the gallery filled him. It was May's way to take care of matters quickly, but this time she hadn't thought it through carefully enough. It was all falling apart. He began to panic again and his mind went to his father sitting in the darkness of their lonely house, his hands shaking from his meds.

For a moment he thought about where he might go. He could go back to Europe or to South America. With his credit card he could pay for a flight to anywhere. He took out his wallet and fumbled for the card Julia had given him. He could ask her to meet him. He'd take her to Italy, to Rome and Florence, and they would look at art and dine in cafés and drink wine and eat exquisite meals and travel further into the dark corridors of desire. Reality intervened. He should call her and apologize. He hoped he hadn't made a fool of himself. He wondered if she regretted it.

He punched her number into his BlackBerry. She picked up on the first ring. She was in her studio.

"Edward, is that you? I'm glad you called."

"I'm sorry for what I did. What we did. We got carried away. When I'm with you I can't think straight."

"Please don't apologize. It's okay. I feel the same way." She paused. "Where are you? You sound like you're in a wind tunnel."

"I'm at the airport. I just flew back from Houston."

"So you're not at home yet?"

"No. I'll be in touch soon."

"I'll be in Vienna at the end of the week. When I get back?"

"Yes, when you get back."

"What are we doing?" she said, just before they were about to hang up.

"I don't know. We'll figure it out," he said. The call was breaking up. "Julia?"

He sat back down and watched another airplane land. A new flock of passengers came through the doorway and into the terminal with their sleek rollaways and carry-ons, urgent to get home. Slowly he began to calm down. He watched passengers deplane, including the flight attendants and pilots, until he was alone at the gate, the only passenger among the rows of empty seats.

He reluctantly rose and saw the lit-up entryway to the duty-free shops where luxury items from Hermès, Cartier, Chanel, and Mont Blanc beckoned. He entered the small Cartier booth and looked at the watches and jewels. His eye caught hold of a sapphire ring and he thought about how it would look on Julia's slender finger. He studied the ring and the depth and sparkle of the stone set in a platinum crown, and before he could think he took out his credit card and purchased it and for a moment felt some relief. He put the box in his jacket pocket and occasionally put his hand in his pocket to hold it. He heard Clara's words. *Why do you buy things you love and then not enjoy them?*

He followed the signs to ground transportation, where the car he had hired was waiting to take him to Westport, lost in the flow of other passengers rushing to get home. Once in the car, on the freeway, rushing past dilapidated buildings and ugly blocks of identical row houses, where he imagined day and night their inhabitants listened to the endless flow of traffic, he put his hand in his pocket and felt the box that held the ring. What was he thinking?

HE THRUST OPEN the door to his home and sank into the house's familiar air. Annabel brushed past.

"Don't I get a hug?" He put down his luggage in the hallway.

"Oh, sorry, Daddy." She reached down, already on the stairs, and clasped her hands around his shoulders and gave him a squeeze, and then, before he could smell the top of her hair, a smell he'd loved since she was a baby, quickly let go.

"How was your trip?" she called back from the upstairs landing, not waiting for an answer.

He found Holly in the kitchen and kissed her. "Good to be home," he said. "It smells good in here." Seeing her in their cheery kitchen—painted soft yellow because Holly said it was a happy color—where he'd left her, unease cut through him. Holly gave him her happy-to-see-him-and-resentful-that-he'd-been-gone smile and they hugged awkwardly. He looked at the open shelves where they displayed their decorative dishes; they'd begun to sag and had a sad, failed look to them.

"How was the flight?"

"Not bad. Is Bell having dinner with us?"

"She's going to a party. Dan Wasserman is picking her up. You remember Dan? They went to camp together."

"Is he driving already?"

"He's a senior. Yes, our daughter is hanging out with seniors."
Holly smiled.

He'd hoped to begin his repentance by having a family dinner.
He would talk to Holly. He'd tell her that Agnes had fired him and
that May had sacrificed his integrity for the sake of the gallery.
Holly always had sound advice. Maybe it was time for him to give
up his position at the gallery and do something completely different. He could direct a foundation or a museum, or perhaps teach.
Holly wanted him to stop traveling. She complained that he was
away too much. She'd help him formulate a plan. It was wrong for
him to mix art with commerce. Art, in essence, was priceless. Once
seen, it distilled itself into a memory, an image in the mind. At that
moment it seemed absurd that he had devoted his life to putting a
price on something so intangible. Artists, the whole bunch of them,
self-absorbed narcissists. He told himself to calm down.

On the way upstairs he stopped to look through the mail on
the counter in the foyer. Among the magazines was the new *Vanity
Fair*. He looked at the cover and quickly scanned the bylines.
Among them, "Nate Fisher and His Multi-Million Dollar Splash."
He flipped through the article and remembered how Nate had told
Agnes not to do the profile. That motherfucker. He'd usurped her
spot. He shook his head, disgusted.

Upstairs he looked out the bay window in their bedroom. Dusk
would fall in an hour. A rangy squirrel raced up the tree and back
down. A deer lingered in the backyard near the bed of ruined pines
and then, hearing the sound of a car racing down the block, fled
for the woods. A police car blasted its siren chasing the speeding
car. Everything seemed in a state of chaos. He willed himself to
forget all of it, Agnes, Nate, Julia, and London, and fall into the

gentle domesticity of evening. His eye caught the small orchid on the windowsill. He hadn't noticed it before. Its leaves were rubbery and green, and from its crown had thrust a lone stem with purple flowers papery and thin. It moved him that Holly had cared for it so tenderly.

AFTER HIS SHOWER he went down to the cellar for the wine and came into the kitchen. Annabel emerged from the cave of her bedroom in a loose top that slipped off one shoulder and a miniskirt. A pink streak trailed down her dirty-blonde hair. She was suddenly tall and willowy. She took his breath away. He remembered how fine and soft her blonde hair had been when she was a child. He remembered her chubby legs, her pink pajamas with horses and lassos. He remembered watching her in her bedroom with her toy horses and jumps and riders spread out on the rug and how she could spend hours dressing up the little doll in her riding clothes and putting the saddle on the little toy horse. Now boys were on her mind. Her face was soft and pale with beautiful cheekbones like her mother's.

"Be careful," he called, and then heard the door shut behind her and the screen door bang closed.

Holly had made one of his favorite dinners, chicken cutlets with olives and almonds and tiny red potatoes. He opened the wine and they sat down together with their full and splendid plates. When their daughter was absent he and Holly sat awkwardly together, trying too hard for conversation. They were in love with her. He wondered in his darkest moment if their great love for her would somehow harm her; how could that love be trumped? They could not part with even the white gliding rocker that once was in her nursery. It had been reinstalled in their bedroom and sometimes Edward caught himself looking at it with longing and suffered the deep pangs a parent feels when his child is growing away from him. When Annabel left for college it would be terrible for them. He knew it and even though she was only fifteen, he was already trying to get used to the idea.

"Annabel's different," Holly said at dinner. "She's secretive. I don't even know her anymore."

"She's a teenager." When Holly played bad cop, he played good cop. And vice versa.

"She hasn't been going to the stables after school." Holly sipped her wine.

"Where does she go?"

"I don't know where she goes." Holly sighed.

"She's a teenager," he repeated.

"That's what I'm afraid of."

Exchanging their private worries and anxieties about Annabel had the effect of making him more anxious rather than less. "We have to let her go a little," he asserted.

"She's lost interest in riding." Holly added. "All that time and money."

"Did you expect it would get her somewhere?" He glanced at Annabel's empty chair and then at Holly.

"Just through high school. To keep her out of trouble."

"It could be worse. She's a good kid."

"I know she's good." Holly pressed her lips tightly in thought. A pulsing vein of tension appeared on her pale forehead. "I miss her."

She cut a piece of chicken and pushed it to the side of her plate. She looked up and her eyes landed on the drapes in the dining room.

"I'd like to change the window treatments. Look how they've faded. And we still haven't done anything about those trees," she said, in a tired voice. "Look. Out the window." Scrawny pines framed the garden bed in front of the house. The needles at the bottom were eaten away by deer and Holly had been on him to take them down. "I can't stand to see them like that," she added, and lowered her eyes. Then, perking up slightly, she said, "How was London?"

He wished he could turn back the clock and erase it all. What if Holly found out? He couldn't decide which bothered him more: the idea that she'd find out he'd been with Julia, or that she'd find out he'd lost Agnes.

"The usual carnival. Meetings with artists and curators. At one of the presentations, a performance poet wound through the audience unraveling a piece of yarn. Something about lost connection," he moaned.

He stood and offered to clean up the dishes. He reassured her about their daughter. "Don't worry about Annabel. She'll come back to us."

He kissed her on the forehead and told her he had missed her and was glad to be home. "I'm just not the same man without you two."

She raised her head and glanced at him.

"Maybe you could come with me on my next trip to Europe. We could take Annabel too."

"Really?" Holly softened and slipped her hand underneath his sweater and hugged him and he took her in. "That would be fun. I missed you, too."

He wanted to bury his head in her shoulder and hold her, but instead she broke away and moved into the kitchen.

"Why do you do that?" he asked.

"Do what?"

"Move away."

"I'm putting the dishes in the sink," she said and went to the sink and turned on the faucet.

"No, really," he said.

"Every time you want to be close you assume I do. It doesn't work that way."

"You never want to be close," Edward said.

"It's you that's always running away," Holly said, sharply.

He stopped to think about she said, watching as she loaded the dishwasher. He started to say something and stopped himself. "I'll do the dishes," he offered again, not wanting to start something. "You look tired."

He motioned her into the den. The temperature had dropped. The moon cast a shadow on the lawn. Snow started falling, millions of snowflakes like a swirl of fallen stars in the dark. Heat rose in a blast from the furnace. He listened to the little pings of the radiator and the moans and creaks in the wood. Holly was the heart of their house, like the blue pilot light in the furnace providing warmth and sustenance, but he felt her fading away from him. He made out the snowflakes still falling steadily onto a tree limb and felt a weight in his chest. And then he heard the limb bend and crack. He turned away.

Before the dishes, he went out to the garage—Holly would think he was taking out the trash—and lit a cigarette and took into his lungs the harsh, punishing smoke. The cool air overtook him for a moment. He thought of Julia, her image already drifting into memory so that he could not make out her features, only the vague outlines of her. He pictured her turned on her side in her hotel bed among the soft blankets and pillows where he had last seen her and unease filled him again.

THE HAND ON their bedroom clock swept slowly past midnight. Annabel missed curfew.

"Where is she?" Edward said. He got up and paced, looking out the window every time he saw headlights brighten the road. He feared an accident, or something else. He pictured Dan Wasserman. "Why did you say she could ride with that Wasserman kid? He's two years older than her."

"Because she wanted to. Are you blaming me for the fact that she isn't home?"

"I just wondered why you let her."

"So you are blaming me," Holly said.

The key turned in the lock at two in the morning. Holly reached for the remote and muted the sound of the TV. Edward closed his eyes with relief. Annabel stumbled up the stairs.

"Let me see you?" Holly trailed her into her bedroom and Edward followed. "Annabel, You've been drinking." Holly touched her shoulder.

"Hey. What the hell, Mom."

"Let me see you," Edward said. Annabel's face was pale and sweaty and the pupils in her eyes were big and unable to focus. Her shirt had crept up, exposing a sliver of her waist, and slipped off her shoulder to reveal a pink bra strap. He thought about Dan Wasserman again.

"Your mother's right. You're drunk."

"I'm not, Daddy."

"Edward," Holly said. "Calm down."

"You're telling me to calm down? Look at her." His heart was racing.

"Daddy, I wasn't drinking," Annabel slurred.

"The hell you weren't. Look at you. You can't stand up straight."

Annabel stumbled and reached for the bedpost. She faltered again.

He imagined his daughter in a dark basement or the backseat of a car, Dan Wasserman on top of her. "Stop lying." He instinctively reached out his hand and then he raised it in midair.

"Edward!" Holly exclaimed and pulled him back. "Don't."

Annabel burst into tears and fell into her mother's arms.

"Annabel. At the party—did anyone hurt you?"

"No one hurt me, Dad." She stared through him as if he were transparent. Then she turned to her mother. "I . . . only . . . had . . . a . . . few beers . . . And then we did some shots of tequila. All my friends drink. Everyone does." She wiped her tears with her sleeve. "What am I supposed to do? Not go out with my friends? Stay at home every night with you two?" Her makeup smeared, leaving black marks around her eyes.

"You're only fifteen," Holly said. "And what's wrong with staying home with us?"

"Are you joking? I'm always disappointing you."

"Disappointing us?" Holly said.

"I don't even want to be here. Dad sleeps upstairs. I know what's going on." Tears streamed down her cheeks. She rubbed them with the bottom of her shirt.

Heat rose into his face. He was trembling.

"I'm sorry, Annabel."

Annabel broke out of Holly's arms. "I feel dizzy. I don't feel so good." She ran to the toilet and vomited.

"Are you okay?" Holly followed. Edward sat on Annabel 's bed, still trembling.

Annabel skulked back into the room, wiping her face with a damp washcloth. "I don't feel so good."

"Come here." Edward patted the bed next to him. He put his arm around her. "Your mother and I are fine," he said, into her hair. "I have trouble sleeping sometimes, that's all."

"I'm sorry. I don't know why I said that. It's just, you know, I'm out with my friends. It's fun. Don't you remember when you were my age?"

Of course he remembered. He'd spent most of his senior year getting high and trying to feel up Karen Fairmont. His daughter was changing. The thrill of life was inside her. Things were different now. His daughter could see things in him he might not be aware of. He couldn't expect the same kind of affection or adoration from her that she'd given freely when she was little. He couldn't hide from her. Or expect her to be different than other teenagers. He took her in his arms again.

"We don't want you to come home in this condition." He brushed the hair away from her forehead. "We worry about you. You have to make good decisions."

"I will, Daddy. I promise." She looked up at her mother. "Mom, will you take me to the stables tomorrow?" she said in her little-girl voice. "I want to see Rocket."

"I'll take you tomorrow." Holly said. "Do you need a glass of water? I'll get some Tylenol."

Annabel nodded. She took off her boots and, still in her clothes, crawled underneath the covers. "I'm sorry," she said again, when Holly came back into the room with the water and Tylenol. She sat up to take the tablets and then lay back down.

"Love you guys," Annabel whispered.

"Love you too," they both said.

"What was that all about?" Holly said, once they were alone in their bedroom. "You can't lose control like that. No matter what she does."

"I know," he said, shaking his head. "Seeing her that way . . . I don't know what happened."

"I don't know what's wrong with you."

"I'm just tired from all the traveling."

"Can you take some time away?"

"Maybe. Soon," he said.

"I'm afraid for her sometimes too," Holly said, touching his shoulder. "Something isn't right."

"Remember when you were her age? We have to steel ourselves and ride it out. It's called being a teenager."

"That's not what I meant." Holly looked at the clock. She turned on her side, her cold toes grazing his leg, and within minutes she seemed to be asleep.

Uncomfortable, he lay on his back and stared at the ceiling, listening to the rain tap on the roof. Had Annabel intuited something different about him? Did Holly know? He thought about his own parents and their troubled marriage, and how he had often felt that his role was to make them happy to compensate. The thought made him want to protect his daughter. He'd been absorbed in the gallery, in Agnes, and Julia. His dishonor was spilling into all of them.

He looked at the clock again. Three in the morning. After an hour or two he crawled out of bed and tiptoed upstairs to his study. As he fell asleep the sun was rising.

Annabel came downstairs close to noon, her hair pulled back in a ponytail, wearing a long nightshirt. She looked pale. Holly and Edward were reading the paper and drinking coffee in the kitchen, waiting for her to get up before starting their ritual of Sunday brunch.

"Can I get you a margarita?" Edward said.

"Thanks, Dad." Annabel rolled her eyes and then slumped down in a chair.

He rose to make them eggs. He turned on the grill and put in a slab of butter and the skillet sizzled and then he cracked open the eggs and watched them spread into the pan. He turned his head around to look at his wife and daughter.

AFTER BRUNCH HE went upstairs to shower and change. One of his artists, Jake Carter, was in town. He dreaded setting foot in the gallery now that Agnes had left him and Savan had stepped in. He'd have to keep his head down, grin and bear it, and avoid Savan at all costs. After his shower, he dressed and grabbed his briefcase and reluctantly proceeded outside to his car. Holly was in the garden with a large shovel in her hand. She'd hacked down the half-eaten dried-out pine trees; they were stacked in a pile like a heap of dead bodies. She wore a blue bandanna tied around her head, gardening gloves, and jeans, her cheeks and the tip of her nose red from the cold.

"Jesus, Holly. What are you doing?"

"I couldn't bear seeing them anymore. We didn't take care of them. We should have . . ." Her face looked tense.

"Holly, it's the deer." The early afternoon sun flooded the frozen lawn and then a cloud passed over the sun and the garden darkened. "I'll see you tonight. I'm late for the train." He kissed her on
the cheek. "Annabel's fine. Everything will be," he said, his betrayal
lurking like an outsider at the edge of the lawn. The pebbles from
the driveway shifted underneath his feet as he walked to his car.

"Edward," Holly called out.

He peered back.

"I don't want you sleeping in your study anymore. We have to
be different." She gazed toward the empty spokes of the hydran-
geas in the garden, bare and exposed, and then back at him with a
look that made his heart catch.

3 NEW YORK

H E SAT UNCOMFORTABLY in the leather chair across from Clara, unable to meet her eyes. Three weeks had passed since London. He hadn't spoken to Julia since the airport, after he landed in New York. He didn't know what he wanted or didn't want to happen between them and was relieved that Julia was in Vienna working on a commission. His mind darted like a skee ball from Julia, to Agnes, and then to his wife and daughter.

"What is it?" Clara said. "Where are you?"

He looked into Clara's clear eyes behind wire rims and told her about Tess.

He felt as if he couldn't breathe and loosened his collar and broke down. He wasn't a man who cried often.

"Do you think your wife would love you any less if you told her what you've suffered?"

"I'm not sure. We were young. Tess and me."

"Of course you were," Clara said.

He broke again. Clara leaned in closer. He looked down at the kilim rug.

"You're not responsible for Tess's death," she said, her glasses slipping to the end of her nose. "You don't have that power. No one does. If anyone is at fault it was the driver."

"You say that. And of course it's the rational thing to say. But if things had been different between us she wouldn't have gone home to Michigan."

"So you can control how you're supposed to feel toward someone? Not possible. Let me ask you." She stared at him without shifting her eyes. "Are you doing something now that you don't want Holly to know about?"

He wanted to tell her about Julia. He thought about it for a few moments, but he didn't know what to say or how to put it into words. He'd already said too much. He scanned the faded spines of books by philosophers and psychoanalysts on the bookshelf and wondered what they thought about patients who hid from even their therapists. He was a coward. Maybe all men at the heart were cowards.

He observed other couples they knew in the neighborhood and wondered how much they shared with each other. He preferred keeping certain things about himself private. He couldn't tell Holly everything about himself. He had to keep his equilibrium, to not appear weak in her eyes.

"My parents kept things from each other," he said, looking at the hanging spider plant on her window, its long, spearlike leaves dangling over the pot.

"Tell me about it," Clara offered.

"It's not something I can put words to."

"Do you know you're angry? I'm telling you this because I think it might help you. Not to scare you. To recognize that your suffering is real."

"Did you think I didn't know it was real?" He tempered an urge to get up from his chair and pull the dead tendrils from the spider plant's head of sprawling hair.

"Let's think about that for our next session," Clara said, looking at the clock placed strategically on a shelf above his head.

HE WALKED FROM Clara's office back to the gallery and told himself to end things with Julia. His family was too precious to risk. Remarkably, when he opened the door to the gallery she was there, sitting in the reception area waiting for him.

"I hope this is okay," she said, rising, when he greeted her. "I was in the neighborhood. I just got back."

"It's fine," he said and led her into his office and closed the door and then turned the blinds. They stood close, looking for a moment long and deep. Julia moved toward him.

"Your tie's crooked," she said, and adjusted it for him. Tears were in her eyes.

"What's wrong? What's happened?"

She looked shaken and began to talk, something about needing to see him to see whether what actually happened, happened, and whether she had imagined the feeling because she wanted to feel that way again, to feel, and yes, in seeing him she knew it had happened and she apologized for coming without calling because if she called she wondered if she would come at all.

He gazed at her and she leaned forward and suddenly they were kissing. He could not trust his emotions from one moment to the next. It scared him to lose sight of himself. They remained close, their breaths mingled, hardly any room between their bodies.

"Since London I can't stop thinking about you. I know it's wrong, but I thought if we saw each other maybe it would stop. Maybe I wouldn't feel it so intensely."

He kissed her again, pressing her against the door of his office, wanting her to feel his excitement. The tension of the weeks since he'd been back seemed to fall off of him. They clung to each other and kissed again, his hand on the bare skin between her skirt and blouse, her hands reaching to touch his back and buttocks, her body pressing against him.

His intercom buzzed and, out of breath, they came apart. Georgia said his four o'clock was here. He gazed at Julia, her face flushed, hair out of place, and clothes ruffled and a little undone. *It's all almost like the first time, the very first time, and I'm a man in my forties.* He watched her pulling her blouse down where it had crept up, exposing the full shape of her breasts, and walked toward her again and put his face in her neck.

"I shouldn't have come?" Julia said, in a question. "Is that what you're thinking?"

"No, I'm glad you did."

"I came to say we shouldn't see each other. That was in my head."

"We'll figure it out," he said, because he couldn't lose her.

"I should go now. I need to get back to the studio."

"We'll talk when our heads are clear," he said and then took a drink of water from the glass on his desk. He offered the glass to her and she drank a long sip and he watched the way the water drops remained on her lips. She moved toward him and straightened his tie again and before he took her to the reception area, he kissed the drops from her mouth.

4 CONNECTICUT

SLOWLY SHE CAME into focus. In the dream he sank into deep pleasure as if it were a warm pool. It had been twenty years since he'd come home to Tess sitting at the breakfast table with her tort law book and notes spread out on the table. She looked bright and beautiful with that glint of irony in her eye and a ponytail on top of her head, wearing her short nylon running shorts and Amherst T-shirt. Just as he relaxed into the pleasure and anticipation of seeing her—it occurred in slow motion, the two of them locking eyes and being slowly drawn together—she faded into the distance.

A shiver went through him. His body was weighted to the bed. He didn't want to get up because if he got up he would lose the chance of finding her. His head was heavy, and his body twisted in a strange paralysis. He tried to lift his head from the pillow, then, slowly, his arms and his legs.

When he awoke again he heard the sound of wheels spinning in the gravel of the driveway. He looked at the clock on his night table. It was ten twenty, Saturday. All quiet. Holly must have let him sleep in and was with Annabel at the barn for her lesson. Once again he tried to raise his head, but it was like lead. Throughout the hours of the morning it was as if he were living inside his deepest and most fearful thoughts, filled with dread and guilt, afraid Holly would find out his secrets. He wondered whether in waking life he was responsible for his dreams. For months after Tess died he'd reenacted in his mind the weeks before she'd left him, stopping at the point at which she'd gotten angry, holding out some strange hope that he could reverse what had happened and be released from his torment. On the subway he stared incredulously at other commuters who were laughing, or smiling into their newspapers and books. At work he watched his colleagues engaged, Savan making deal after deal, resentful that they could go about their day effortlessly while his life had ended. His world had reordered into a shape and structure that was completely foreign.

At noon, exhausted by his thoughts and memories, he forced himself to get up. He felt sluggish and disoriented. He lifted his upper body and sat up. He brushed the sleep from his eyes and dragged himself to the bathroom. He splashed water on his face and trudged downstairs for coffee. Drinking it, he forgot about his toast, blackened in the toaster. He threw it into the garbage bin and walked slowly through the rooms of his house. He absorbed the auras of Holly and Annabel and the feeling of the three of them together, the way in which when he was a boy he had absorbed the atmosphere of his own family. The house was unbearably quiet.

He climbed upstairs to his study to work, but before he got settled he heard Holly's car come up the driveway, the storm door slam shut, and the sound of her footsteps climbing the stairs. By the time she reached the third floor she was out of breath. The frosty air of winter rose from her down jacket when she entered. He looked at her chapped hands without gloves holding her keys and her hair tucked into her winter hat. There was something about seeing her that way that made him feel he could confide in her and finally free himself of his terror. *Let yourself be known*, he heard Clara say.

But Holly looked ashen.

"What's wrong?" Edward asked.

"It's Daddy. They've put him back in intensive care. I'm going in to see them."

"Let me get dressed. I'll come with you."

"It's better if you stay with Annabel. Marly's dropping her off at four. I'll call from the hospital."

He couldn't stop himself. He felt he could tell her, that he needed to tell her, that now was the moment. It was as if he thought he was doing her a favor by suddenly coming clean.

"Before you go. Will you sit down for a minute?"

"I don't need to sit. Tell me."

"I should have told you a long time ago."

"What is it? You're scaring me." She leaned against the bookcase with the car keys in her hands.

"Remember my college girlfriend. Tess, from Michigan."

"Yeah."

"She and I were married."

"Married?" She shook her head, confused. "This is some kind of joke, right?"

He bowed his head and then looked up. "It's not. I wish it were."

"What happened?"

"She got sideswiped by a truck when she was jogging. She was killed. We were twenty-two."

"I don't understand."

"We were living in New York. We weren't getting along and she packed up her stuff and went back home to Michigan. The accident happened three days later."

"I'm sorry. Oh, I'm so sorry." She reached toward him and touched his arm and tears filled his eyes and she leaned in and hugged him, as if his grief for Tess could be absorbed in her grief for her father, as if his guilt for sleeping with Julia could be absolved, as if all could, somehow, be well. He held her tighter.

"I wanted to tell you," he said into her hair.

She moved away and narrowed her eyes. Her face changed from compassion to confusion, as if she'd then taken in the full meaning of what he'd said.

"Why are you telling me this now? I don't get it. Why couldn't you tell me?"

"I couldn't tell anyone."

"Anyone? Is that who I am?"

"Holly, it was like all the lights went out. I felt so ashamed."

"For what?"

"I don't know. It wasn't rational."

"I feel sorry for you. And her. And her poor family. But I can't hear this now. How can you tell me this now? When my father . . ."

She looked at him and shook her head. She started for the stairs, then hesitated for a moment. "Edward. What other secrets are you keeping from me?" Before he could answer she turned away.

On the surface it didn't make sense—that he hadn't told her before, that he did tell her, now, in this moment, when her father was dying. Why hadn't he told her? Because in him he held Tess's memories and if he revealed them they would not be as precious. Because if he talked about it, it might justify the pain and he did not want the pain to lift and be relieved of his guilt, which, in turn, would relieve his grief. His father used to say that what you couldn't control, you had to identify before it broke you to pieces. He didn't know why he hadn't told her. It wasn't out of malice or mistrust. It was a way of punishing himself. Or because after all these years—was Clara right?—he still couldn't face that Tess was really gone.

He watched from his window as Holly climbed into her SUV. She swiftly pulled out of the driveway. He got up and, unsure of what to do, took from the desk drawer a pack of cigarettes. He opened the window and blew out the smoke, aware that with each exhale he was infesting his family's home with its fumes, that his daughter would be home soon and he didn't want her smoking. His BlackBerry trembled in his pocket. He took it out and watched it vibrate in his hand.

"Hey," he said. "Jimmy?"

"I'm in trouble, man."

"What is it? What's happened?"

"Lucinda. She found out about Melody. She called me at home."

"Shit, Jimmy."

"Lucinda threw me out of my own house."

"You sound bad. Have you been drinking?"

"Of course I'm fucking drinking. My marriage is over."

"Jimmy, what can I do?"

"I'll call you tomorrow. Belinda's back."

"Who the fuck is Belinda? Jimmy?"

The phone went dead.

HE LISTENED TO the start, stop, and hum of the refrigerator as he waited for Holly to come home. After dinner and homework,

Annabel had gone to bed. He nursed a thumb of scotch in a coffee cup. He looked up at the big orb of the kitchen clock. It was like an eye watching him. He would stop the thing with Julia. They had found themselves together in a foreign country when they were both vulnerable. He hadn't meant for it to go anywhere. Something about her had taken away his reason and clouded his vision. He had to get hold of himself. He was a faithful man. He loved his wife and their life together. He wasn't like Jimmy. He looked again at the clock ticking the minutes off as if in agreement with his reasoning. Minutes before midnight Holly's car came up the drive.

She walked in looking a few years older than when she'd left, unbuttoned her coat and left it in a heap on the kitchen stool, and began walking toward the stairs.

"How's your father? I've been calling the hospital to check in."

"He's in intensive care. We'll know more in the morning."

"Did you eat? Can I make you a sandwich or some eggs?"

"I ate with Mom at the hospital. How's Annabel?"

"Fine. Sleeping. About this morning. I'm sorry," he started.

She looked through him coldly. "I need to focus on Daddy."

Her bitterness took him by surprise, as if having hoped for it and reasoned against it during the hours she was away he imagined she'd already forgiven him. After she left the kitchen it felt cold and drafty. He poured himself a glass of water. His head ached. He reached for the Advil in the cabinet above the sink and downed three. A rancid odor came from the trash can when he opened it to toss the paper cup. The bag was full; he'd forgotten to take it out. He tied the bag up to tamp down the smell, then opened the back door and walked outside into the rash of wind and cold. The wet leaves seeped into his socks. He came back into the house and washed the smell of rot off his hands and took off his socks. He put on the teakettle. He'd make Holly a cup of milky tea, which she liked before bed. He waited for the kettle to whistle and then he poured the boiling water over a bag of Earl Grey and added just the amount of milk that she liked. He still thought that maybe he could make up for what he'd done. He slowly walked upstairs. Outside the door of their bedroom Holly had piled blankets and a pillow. He poked his head into their bedroom. The room smelled of the lavender lotion she rubbed on her arms before bed. The cozy room with its thick carpet and creamy drapes drew him. Though many nights, restless and uncomfortable, he had preferred to sleep alone, he felt suddenly shut out and longed to be near her. She came out of the bathroom, and then walked into the bedroom and he handed her the cup of tea like an offering.

"I shouldn't have unloaded on you like that. Not when you're worried about your father."

She looked at him and placed the mug on the nightstand. "Thank you for the tea. But I can't do this now. I can't even think about it."

She climbed into bed and then she shook her head, as if to say no, and motioned with her hand for him to go. He closed the door and picked up the pillow and blankets from the floor.

5 CONNECTICUT

I T WAS THE middle of March. The clouds huddled in, dark and brooding, ready to take everything into their devouring shapeshifting form and break open. He waited for the storm. The air turned moist and cool. It pimpled his skin. He took in the darkness and then slowly the air warmed, the clouds broke apart, and the storm did not come, which was almost worse than if it had.

A month passed. Holly's father was still in intensive care. Holly received a call about a stray litter of newborn kittens found in a field. The mother cat had been killed by a fox. She fetched the kittens, and instead of taking them to the refuge brought them home to care for them until they were big enough to be adopted out. She kept them in a basket lined with a blanket in their heated garage. After a long day at the gallery, eager for her company, maybe a glass of wine together, he found her in the garage feeding the baby kittens milk from a baby bottle. She barely looked up at him. She stroked the kitten, not yet the size of her hand, and pressed her lips to its fur.

Retreating to his study, he opened an e-mail from Julia. She'd read a piece about Swartzman, one of his artists, in *Bomb* and was curious about his upcoming new work. He wrote back that he'd read a short piece about her commission in Vienna in *Art News*. She said she'd been reading "Ode on Melancholy." It was inspiring her new work.

He took down his copy of Keats and read the ode. "But when the melancholy fit shall fall / Sudden from heaven like a weeping cloud." He smiled. It made him feel connected to her. It was enough. He told himself that they could still be close friends and not jeopardize each other's lives. He told himself a lot of things.

6 CONNECTICUT

HOME WAS NOW a foreign country. Annabel, suddenly a full-blown teenager, secretive and private, an earbud in one ear, the other dangling, a strange, dazed, love-induced look to her face. When her friends were over the room crackled with their energy. Holly barely acknowledged him. She waltzed through the sunroom and kitchen, touching the soil in her pots of ferns and jade to see if they needed watering. At breakfast she executed the crossword puzzle with concentration and intensity, as if she were amending the Constitution. Annabel slumped in the kitchen chair next to her, spoon-feeding cereal into her mouth, buried mercurially behind her laptop. His back was to them as he took the last sip of his coffee at the sink before heading for the train, the glare of morning sun showing cracks in the thinning plaster and the indentations of its inevitable ruin. Though he felt at the core that he was responsible for his sudden alienation, he was at a loss how to win them back.

"How about we barbecue when I get home tonight?" he suggested. The estrangement was unbearable. Neither of them spoke for a moment.

"Mom?" Annabel said, annoyed.

"What is it, honey?"

"Dad's talking to you."

"Oh, I didn't hear," Holly said, putting down her pencil.

"He wants to know if you want to barbecue tonight." Annabel looked up from her screen—the paradox of puberty, one minute his little girl and the next a teenager with a chip on her shoulder— and said, "Jesus. You guys are freaks."

"Sure," Holly said, not raising her eyes from the puzzle. "If that's what you want to do. Edward, what time will you be home tonight?"

"Around seven."

"See you then," Holly said, and put down the crossword puzzle and went upstairs. He followed her, opening the bedroom door to find her in front of the oval mirror combing her hair. He stopped to look at the strands of gold in her locks and the gentle slope of her nose, and her dark eyes in the mirror. Aging had made her beauty more substantial. She looked back at him coolly.

"Holly," he began.

"No, Edward," she said, brushing her hair in fierce strokes. Her voice trembled. "You can't tell me something like that and expect it to be all okay."

"It's been weeks now. We have to talk about it. We have to talk."

"No." She continued to brush her hair. "It's amazing how we sleep side by side, eat our meals together, and I didn't know maybe the most significant thing about you aside from your father's death. I've thought about it a hundred times. It feels like a betrayal."

He felt as if the lid of a rusty, stubborn can had been pried open. He held up his hands as if to say something, but he didn't know what to say. How could she not understand how painful it had been for him to keep it from her all these years?

He had forgotten a proposal he was working on for an exhibit, so before he left for the train he went back upstairs to his study. He found the proposal and put it in his bag. Next to it was his father's copy of Keats's poems on the desk where he had left it. He thought about Julia. She would understand. He felt like one of those dogs he saw every morning when he passed the neighbors' yard, locked up in a pen, roused, wanting to burst out. What had he been telling himself? Holly had shut him out or he had shut her out and it was too complicated to put back together. He could give up his will and let it happen and see what this new life might bring him. Maybe he'd been wrong to be protective of his family and private life. He wanted to bust out of himself. He wanted to see her pale arms and long throat and beautiful breasts that he'd glimpsed once or twice in the twilight of a hotel room but had reviewed and rewound in his mind more times than he could count. He could almost taste her. Why always this need to protect himself? The desire was unbearable. He felt in that moment that he might break if he did not see her. He wrote a note and put it inside the copy of Keats. *Meet me at the Peninsula this afternoon at three*, the note said. He would have his assistant messenger it to her studio as soon as he arrived at the gallery. It was simple. He could be a man who'd send a note to a woman that he was completely and utterly in the thrall of and not hold back or look the other way. He witnessed uncompromising passion all around him. It was the inspiration behind the art he saw and loved, the books he read, and the music he listened to. He'd read once that an artist must commit himself to his project as if he were committing himself to love. Why shouldn't he too surrender? By saying no, wasn't it inflating the importance of the thing itself? He had to know if it was real. He felt certain that his ache was the same as that which had inspired the look he saw of the girl in the Vermeer painting, the one with the pearl earring. All through the train ride into the city he held the book in his hand and looked out the window and envisioned her face and nothing else. Nothing but a face and a mouth and a hand and he could have everything.

SHE ENTERED THE hotel room. He saw her dark hair with light streaks and full body and tender eyes and wanted her more than he'd ever wanted anything.

"I am glad you sent the book," she said with a smile, her hair unhinged from a barrette she held in her hand. "I feel lost without you."

There was no time to pull back the sheets or dim the lights, or undress. It was three in the afternoon and the little light from the afternoon pushed its way through the curtains the way he pushed his way into her. The minute he saw her they were all over each other, both having given up the idea that they should not.

Afterward they made plans about how it would be and where they would go and how they would abandon everything just so that they might be able to be wrapped in the darkness of a hotel in the middle of an afternoon where no one knew where they were or how they could be reached, where for maybe one or two hours no one, *no one* expected anything from either of them. Of course they were young again, no more brainpower than teenagers, because no one expects much of you then. You can be reckless and get away with it. Dim the light. Arrive. Stay with it. For isn't one day a series of commitments? What if there were none? What if the commitment was just to show up for the only thing that mattered, which was to be true to oneself? His head was filled with all of this and he knew without question that he did what he needed to do. *Yes, darling*, he said. *Darling, yes.*

DAYS LATER HE traveled to Florence to meet with a museum director, and after his meeting he wandered the streets adrift and disoriented, stopping at the Uffizi and the Accademia, everywhere art and crumbling beauty and austere Renaissance palaces. On his last morning in Florence he walked the cobbled and uncertain roads, looking up at the blackening soot on the corroding and silvery buildings. He visited the church of Ognissanti where there was a Botticelli fresco of Saint Augustine in meditation in his study. Augustine was a sinner, but he had absolved himself through faith and his writings. He looked into Saint Augustine's face, wanting like Augustine to be clean and pure and free. He stopped for an espresso in an outdoor café. Everywhere, in the faces of young lovers, in the men and women sitting alone in cafés, in old fat women and decrepit men reading Italian newspapers, he searched for signs of what he should do but found only the faces of strangers. He carried a book with him when he traveled. At the airport he had picked up a copy of *Death in Venice*; he was going to Italy after all. But as of late he couldn't read things properly anymore. He started a novel and then read one quarter and then went to the last quarter and then needed to go back to where he'd left off before he could figure it out and he found he liked this way of reading, as if it seemed to mimic that nothing was quite right. Life was messy and filled with loss and pain and disappointment and he had thought for some reason that it didn't have to be that way and he had tried too hard and had failed at it and from now on he would prize the way in which he succeeded because he could not know what might happen and he had to let go. He had to let it unwind.

WHEN HE RETURNED, exhausted and now in exile in his own home (Annabel had gone out with a friend), he tried to explain things to Holly. He apologized for keeping his marriage to Tess a secret. Agnes had unhinged him. He explained that she'd threatened to leave the gallery and how things had changed with Savan joining as a partner, and that his work life suddenly eluded him and he hadn't been himself, but all through his soliloquy she remained unmoved.

"I see," she repeated. "I see." She stood up to put on the kettle. When she returned he hoped from her a solution to their misery. She always knew how to put things into perspective. He looked into her face expecting compassion. But all he saw was a mask made of an intransigent metal. He'd done things he shouldn't have done, but if they'd been happy, if things had been different, he wasn't sure he would have been attracted to Julia. He was tired of hiding. And Agnes? Holly knew how much he'd invested in her. Or maybe she hadn't quite, seeing as Agnes was to her simply an artist whose work he had taken on and in turn had prospered by. Holly couldn't understand the intangible intricacies—who could, really?—the meetings and phone calls and conversations, the planning and strategizing that had gone into the success of their campaign. How much he believed in the work.

He looked across the table at her tight mouth and furrowed eyebrows, waiting for a response. She looked like a different woman. He waited some more and as he waited he grew angrier.

"You've changed," he finally said.

The kettle screamed. She got up and turned it off and poured hot water into her cup. For a second she blinked her eyes closed, the steam from the hot water clouding her face. She sat back down. He couldn't stand her at that moment.

"Nothing I say matters? You're impenetrable," he said.

"Me?" she said, bobbing the tea bag up and down in her mug.

"I don't know that you see me. I'm not sure you ever have."

He looked at her hard eyes and tight throat and held his breath. What was he doing?

"If I'd told you, would you have stayed with me?" he asked.

"I'm not sure I'm going to."

"Holly."

"No," she said, cutting him off. Her voice broke. "You've always kept yourself away from me. I never understood it until now. I'm not one of your works of art," Holly said. She got up from the chair and pushed it back. "I'm going back to the barn."

"I need you," he said, foolishly holding her eyes in the reflection of the kitchen window before she turned away.

HE WAITED UP for her to come back that night, looking at the screen of the television, his mind drifting. It was after midnight—what was she doing at the barn until midnight? She came in flushed and said she had gone out for a drink with Tom and some others and then she walked through the den and into the dining room and went upstairs. Would she leave him? He thought about what it would be like to return to his house without her, and then realized that if they were to separate he would be the one who would have to leave their home. He saw in a flash the many things that kept him grounded and gave him pleasure: returning to sit on the couch at night with a glass in his hand, knowing Holly was upstairs or in the kitchen; the sound of Annabel clamoring down the stairs; the times when they were all together. The days they liked to sit on the porch to watch the sun settle in the trees.

GOING FROM ONE gallery party to another knowing that he no longer represented Agnes Murray was unpleasant. He typically loved the Armory show, where he had the opportunity to meet with his international colleagues and show off his artists. Part of the Armory Show was to goose expectations. This year the gallery was not showing Agnes's work—they'd wait until next, after her new show, though of course her name was the lead on the roster that showcased the gallery's stable of artists and seeing it there made him feel like a fraud or a failure, or both, he wasn't exactly sure. Thankfully, Savan was in Europe for the week. At his booth, which like all the booths was the size of a stockyard stall, they featured the nude ensembles of Christy Craig, a Scottish artist whose work was about subversion of the female form. Every booth was a different experience: one exhibited bold paintings in psychedelic colors, another prints on vinyl, a Danish dealer showcased a grid of glowing digital light boxes, in one stall birds were chirping. A gallery from Brussels, "Sorry We're Closed," called itself a project room.

Christy Craig's charcoal drawings created enough of a stir to bring hundreds to the booth and Christy was thrilled with the attention. Days before, at the preview for VIPs, Edward had made three lucrative deals, one with a trustee of the Art Institute of Chicago and two with a Latin American collector, and there wasn't much left for sale. The two days of the fair, where two hundred of the world's premier galleries exhibited, were more like museum face time.

Amid the din, Nate and Agnes—the beautiful couple, as Cynthia, their publicist, remarked—strolled down the aisle toward his booth. Agnes's red curls unwound from the headband she typically wore to hold it in place and cascaded down her back. In black tights, a black mini, and a clingy top, her arm tucked into Nate's, every eye focused on her. An aura of unattainability lit up her face like a torchlight signaling to come close and stay away. Nate had work at the Gagosian stand, some prints from a new exhibition that while provocative had irritated the critics. Notwithstanding, the public flocked around the booth, which was kitty-corner to Mayweather and Darby's.

Agnes raised her chin, a tight smirk on her face to acknowledge him, or maybe she hadn't, and then slowly the crowd engulfed the two like a swarm of gulls preying on a scrap of bread. The woman who had once regarded his every word suddenly felt herself superior. He hadn't expected to see Agnes, and seeing her brought back all his complicated feelings. It was interesting to him that she did not stop by to say hello to the colleagues at their booth. He was hot with shame, and it burned through him. It was shame for not having stood up for himself or shame because he wasn't good enough. Or shame because maybe somewhere in his core he felt she'd been right. Maybe the work was good and his comments were, as she said, stupid. Maybe he hadn't understood what she was after. Or was it shame that she could reinvent history and somehow he'd missed that about her—that she actually believed he had nothing to do with who she had become? Or maybe shame was easier for him to bear than being wounded.

He was in conversation with Christy about an Italian collector interested in her work. Christy sensed his preoccupation and subverted the conversation to ask about Agnes Murray and when the gallery was mounting her new show. Early in his career he had learned never to talk about one of his artists when in the company of another one (egos too frail) and so as not to get into too much detail he answered as if he still were her dealer at the gallery, rather than Savan. After the exchange, on his way to meet a collector at another booth, he ran into Julia—all throughout the day he'd hoped he would. Seeing her, her wide smile and her fantastic eyes, his mood brightened significantly. He remembered what Julia had said in London, that he'd had it wrong, that he'd made Agnes famous. They spoke for a few minutes in between appointments.

During the fair he stayed in the city for the weekend, as it would be two late nights and early mornings. Julia mentioned that she was having dinner with Watkins and others from her gallery. Still reeling from seeing Agnes, he asked if she wanted to meet him later for a drink and she nodded and suddenly it was wonderful. Everything was wonderful.

After dining with Christy, his sales staff, and two associates, and dropping Christy off at her hotel, he arrived at the Peninsula's grand staircase a little after midnight. He climbed the shiny marble stairs and waited for Julia at the bar as they had planned.

People in his world didn't frequent the Peninsula, enjoying instead the hipper downtown hotels like the Standard or the W. But he liked its illusion of grandeur, its gold railings and subdued turquoise pool, as he sprawled on a lounge chair after a sauna and a dip overlooking the New York skyline. There he could remind himself that he was a player.

As he waited for Julia he thought about Agnes and wondered how the critics and influential figures would react to the new work. It was as if, having seen the work, he carried within him an explosive that could or could not be detonated depending on how he played it. It was up to him whether he would choose to reveal outside the gallery the truth of what had transpired and his own misgivings about the work and whether his reputation would trump hers. The way in which art was viewed and responded to was unpredictable. It involved intangibles: the particular political climate in which it was made, how critics and curators reacted, whether the culture had been saturated by a particular style or technique and was in need of a correction, public recognition. He thought about the pleasure aroused in him by looking into the eyes of a Rembrandt painting or a Vermeer, when he could see the soul of the individual locked in that gaze and the brilliance with which it was accomplished. He'd seen that gaze in Agnes's original work. He wanted in her new work the very thing that was missing: that indescribable spark of life and energy that brought to the viewer a surge of feeling and challenged both senses and intellect.

He looked for Julia and canvassed the bar to make sure he didn't see anyone he knew. He swished the ice in his glass, impatient until he saw her walk in.

He ordered her a cabernet. They rattled on about the usual— whom they'd seen and art that was causing a stir, and their dinners. All the while she didn't take off her coat. She faced the mirrored bar, arms crossed over her chest, protective, sipping her wine. It struck him that she was a woman who hadn't had many men in her life. She was too serious to open herself casually.

"You seem tense," he remarked, looking at her white knuckles as she clenched the globe of her wineglass.

"It's Roy. It's hard."

"Is he suspicious?"

"Of what?"

"You know."

"I really don't. You've been hard to read."

He leaned back and contemplated what she'd said. Strands of hair had slipped loose from her barrette and hung over her eye and she brushed them away.

"I'm sorry. Have I made you unhappy?"

"It's not that simple." She gazed openly into his eyes. "Everything's changed."

He looked at her and smiled. "I know."

"What are we doing?" she said.

He was reluctant to answer. He had no idea, but it seemed important somehow to him that he answer with integrity. "We're both married. We have to do the right thing."

"And what's that?" she asked, with a catch in her voice.

"To be friends." He didn't know why he'd said it.

"Well, we are friends," she agreed, looking at him deeply. "I suppose what we are most is friends."

She thrust her hand into her hair and it fell back on her shoulder. She glanced around the room and then down at the temple of prayer she'd made with her hands. Then she looked up and with sudden angry brightness, she said, "At my dinner tonight everyone was talking about Fisher's new work. Did you hear that a reviewer mistook one of his figures for a penis?"

"Really." Edward laughed and she laughed too. "I'm sure it was intentional. The subtext of all Nate's work is sex."

She slipped off her coat and hung it behind her chair, more relaxed, as if she'd made some decision.

"Didn't Freud say sex is the subtext for everything?"

He wished to be alone with her instead of in a populated bar. "How are you? I've missed you," he said, straining, though it was difficult, to remain unmoved.

"I'm feeling a little down. Watkins has taken on Mira Auchincloss. We went to grad school together. Do you like her work? She's making him a fortune."

"I can see what Watkins sees in the work. She's doing something different."

"Do you think so? I don't know. She's too curated for my taste. Everything she does is about making a statement."

"Listen, you have nothing to worry about. Your work, what I've seen, it's completely different."

"Did I sound competitive?" she asked.

"I have something to tell you too. It's about Agnes Murray." He didn't know why he hadn't told her before. It hadn't been the right time, or he was reluctant to talk about it, thinking, hoping perhaps, that Agnes would come back to him, but after seeing her waltz into the fair with Nate, he knew he'd been fooling himself. He kept his own face blank. Never let them see you bleed, his father had told him. He had to show backbone. All men did. He quickly told her the story.

"She's unbelievable." Then after a long pause she said, "Look, you're better off without her."

"Am I?"

"I *think* so."

Meanwhile, a look that said *you poor thing* passed across her face. He couldn't take being pitied.

"It sounds like she was defensive. I'm sure you were right, about the work. I've heard you speak. I've seen the work you show. You did your job. You have to let it go."

He swiveled his stool. Her eyes blazed with feeling. She understood.

As if she'd intuited his thoughts, she said, "What I said . . . in London. About Roy not being involved in my work. He doesn't understand my world. Or what I do. Or the emotional risks involved. It's lonely."

"Holly isn't interested in mine," he said, though once he said it he wasn't sure if he believed it or if by keeping his work life to himself he had shut her out. It didn't matter. What mattered was that he was completely alone in the new turn it had taken, or felt he was. He thought about what Holly had said. She wasn't one of his pieces of art. Shame filled him. Had he always kept her at a slight remove?

"Things have been tense at home for me too. I told Holly about Tess."

"How did she take it?"

"Not well."

"I'm sorry. At least you told her. You had to get it out there. It was killing you." Suddenly uncomfortable, she looked at her watch.

"What is it?" he said.

"Over there. I thought I knew them. I should go. It's late. Roy will be home." She got up quickly and excused herself for the ladies' room.

A man walked over from the other end of the bar. "She's beautiful," the man said as he passed by. Pleasure and then shame quickly
swept over him.

He paid the bill and they walked toward the lobby to say good
night. It seemed that he'd only begun to relax into the pleasure of
her. He didn't want her to go just yet. "Do you want to come up?
Just for a little?"

She peered around quickly.

"Just for a few minutes. I can't think here."

"For a few minutes," she agreed.

Once they'd gotten past the awkward moment in the elevator,
both wanting to be alone and regretting their want, and then the
long walk down the hallway to find his room, he fumbled with
the card key until she took it in her hand and slipped it in and
opened the door. Once in the room, he flipped out his BlackBerry
and looked to see if he had any messages from Holly. None. He
excused himself. In the bathroom he splashed water on his face and
returned to find Julia sitting at the little café table by the window.

She turned back to him. "What's wrong? You look uncomfortable."

"I wouldn't want Holly to know, that's all."

"Don't you trust me?"

"No, that's not what I meant."

"I have my marriage to protect too."

He sat down on the chair next to hers. "Of course you do."

"Maybe we're both doing this, whatever we're doing, so we
don't have to face our lives." She lowered her eyes. "That's what
I've been thinking, sitting here." She folded her hands together. "I
don't want to live with the thought that you might call or e-mail or

we'll bump into each other like we did today, or last time, and suddenly ask me to meet you. Or that you won't. I'm not cut out for it. Some people are. I mean, for what we're doing."

Exasperated by the complexity of his feelings, he took her hand and clasped it. "I don't know if I am either. Can't we lie together? And maybe not talk. It would be nice to just hold you for a few minutes," he said, leading her toward the bed.

They lay down and began to kiss. He tasted wine on her lips and rubbed his hands along her thighs and she kissed him back. Within minutes they were both feverish. He turned off the light by the nightstand.

In the dark, she twisted out from underneath him and sat up. "I'm sorry. I can't do this. Not here. Not now. I keep thinking about Roy. No, I can't."

She leaned against the pillows propped on the bed. Her face looked different. He noticed a ridge above her eye and furrows around her mouth.

"I said I wanted us to be friends only because it is the right thing to do, to be friends, not because I want to." He moved a piece of hair that had fallen into her face behind her ear.

"I know," she said, resigned.

"Let's go downstairs. I need a drink," he said, tucking in his shirt and slipping into his shoes.

She straightened her hair with her fingers and smoothed her skirt and put her heels back on and then looked at him. Tears filled her eyes.

Neither spoke as the elevator descended, the air thick with what was unsaid. He walked her up the staircase to the bar, where he ordered them a drink and they sat on a couch and sipped from their glasses slowly and she began to talk again. He listened to the light and sexy sound of her voice and looked into her softening eyes. She apologized. All of this, new to her. Something like that. Maybe they could take a trip together, figure it out. Maybe he could meet her in Vienna; she had to go back to do some publicity.

When they finished their drink he walked her out to get a cab and they told each other they'd meet tomorrow at the Armory. Back in his room he couldn't remember what they had talked about. He lay on the bed where she had been, smelled her in the pillow, and put his face in it—his mind swimming—and eventually in the velvet black behind his eyes, where a whole theatre unfolded, he slept.

THE NEXT MORNING he did his time at the booth and spotted Julia across an aisle. She had work on display at Watkins's booth. He saw her dressed fashionably, as if she'd put time into it, and she saw him and for a moment their eyes locked and she smiled upon seeing him, even in her own unease. Instead of smiling back, he glanced over her head as if he were looking for someone else. Seeing her in broad daylight amid all his colleagues and the anonymous passersby, he couldn't acknowledge her. He saw a break in her face and he turned and walked back into his booth and did not go after her. He didn't know why he'd refused to acknowledge her. It was like when he was a kid and didn't want to face his father after his father found out he'd been getting high at Bennett's house when he was supposed to be at soccer practice. He'd thought if he did not acknowledge his father that somehow his father would not be disappointed in him, or that he could distance himself from it and pretend he didn't care, when what he cared about most was not disappointing his father. Almost immediately after, he hated himself for it, and a few times during the afternoon he dodged through the cattle call pushing through the aisles and tried to find her to apologize.

In the afternoon, at the crowded canteen where stylish men and women sat on stools and drank champagne, some dealers and gallerists and others there to see the ebb and flow of new work or to encounter new galleries, grabbing bottled water, parched from the lack of natural air pumping through the large cavernous pier, she came toward him, arms swinging beside her and her eyebrows pointed downward and her mouth twisted in a hardened scowl. He was glad to see her. She pulled him aside to the end of one of the aisles with a nod of her head. Throughout the day he had chided himself for giving in to his passion, for asking her to meet him the night before and for the uncomfortable situation they were both in, for having lost Agnes and his fear of the repercussions and his inability to move past it, and vowed to himself that he had to earn back his integrity. He wondered if he had a right, if anyone had a right, to personal happiness if it meant hurting others in the process.

"I've been looking for you to apologize. Will you forgive me, Julia?"

"You can't do that." Her voice quivered to restrain her emotions. "We have to stop this. It isn't good for either one of us."

She turned, threaded through the aisles, and dissolved into the crowd before he had a chance to explain himself. Once or twice when he took a tour of the booths he spotted her again, deep in conversation with another artist or dealer, and though their eyes met she did not acknowledge him.

A PRESS ANNOUNCEMENT WAS released. Savan gave a state-ment: "Agnes Murray is the master painter of her generation. These new works dare the viewer to look away." To escape the pandemonium the media attention was spilling into the day-to-day activities at the gallery, Edward took long lunches, going to his club and swimming laps as if he were training for a race. Back at his desk, his eyes blurry and stinging in a chlorine haze, nothing looked exactly right. He could side with the gallery and swallow his pride, or he could maintain his integrity and publicly denounce the new work and Agnes's behavior. It occurred to him that he did not have to be a passive party in the center of his own theatre.

Meanwhile, Savan had ordered ostentatious, slick, shiny black Italian furniture for his new office and was in high-octane mode—*fantastic, brilliant, a masterpiece*—his Bluetooth in his ear, fin-gers hammering away furiously on his keyboard when Edward walked by. More than a few times he observed May and Savan huddled in council together in her private space. Savan was May's new confidant. He knew the common sense of attaching himself to those on the rise and befriending his enemies, but he couldn't quite make himself heed it when it came to Savan. In their weekly meetings Savan brought up new artists he wanted to sign, woo-ing Fay Reinhart, and River, an up-and-coming video artist, from

Gertrude's shop. The *Observer* dubbed him "the Poacher." The more he was denigrated by the press, the higher his standing went.

May didn't seem to mind Savan's lack of modesty; rather, she watched with what seemed like proud fascination. Occasionally Edward objected to an artist Savan wanted to take on, claiming that the work wasn't up to the gallery's standards. He thought May would support him. Lionel Wood used dog hair as a medium, and in one of their weekly meetings Edward suggested that he feared the work would alienate a portion of their clientele. May said, excusing the pun, that she was going to give Savan a long leash. The work made a fortune for the gallery. *I'll give him a long leash too,* Edward thought to himself. Let him self-destruct on his own.

At their marketing meetings Savan name-dropped, one time about Ian Pearlman. "Edward knows him. Edward knows everyone that matters," he obsequiously said through his smile. "He writes about art for the *New York Review.*"

"Everyone knows Ian Pearlman, Alex," Edward chided.

"He's writing a long piece on one of my young artists, Milo Sorrento. I sent him images of the work and he flipped over it," Savan said.

May beamed. Edward left the meeting. No wonder Savan was successful. He'd befriend a serial killer if he thought it would get him somewhere.

Savan peeked his head into Edward's office afterward. "Sorrento's on the rise. I just landed him a huge commission."

"Good for you," Edward acknowledged. *Slick. Mediocre. Smug,* he thought to himself.

And yes, he could admit, he was ever so slightly jealous.

AFTER HIS LUNCH-HOUR swim he holed up in his office and privately tended to the other artists he represented. He wondered if, once word leaked out that he was no longer working with Agnes, his other artists would leave him, or think less of him, and in his worst moments he imagined a sudden and prolonged exodus that led to him being finished. Remarkably, it seemed as if Agnes wanted to keep it quiet too, and the press hadn't yet picked up on it. He asked May about it. She said that Agnes didn't want negative publicity before her show opened. Defeated, his confidence shaken, he wondered if he'd lost his competitive edge, perhaps even his judgment about what qualified as art, or as art that would sell. He wondered once again how Agnes's new work would be perceived and whether he'd been too critical.

WEEKS LATER, HE turned away from a contract he was drafting and faced the window in his office. The sun traveled behind the building across from him and covered his desk in a swath of shadow. He thought of Julia again and though he shouldn't be expecting her to contact him, he checked e-mails throughout the day at the gallery and later at home to see if she'd written. Days passed. A week. At every event or function he went to he looked for her. Another few days passed. He was alone in his office when the receptionist buzzed to say he had a package. He opened the brown wrapping paper. It was his father's copy of Keats he had given Julia. There was a note inside. *I thought you should have this back*, it said.

AFTER A LONG day at the gallery and a tedious dinner with a collector, he arrived home near midnight and labored up the stairs to their bedroom. His feet ached in his heavy shoes. He sank onto the bottom of the bed and loosened his tie and bent down to untie his shoelaces. Holly was absorbed in an obscure journal on animal habitats, reading glasses at the end of her nose, her hair pulled back. Desire threaded through his core. She looked at him with a half smile and continued reading.

He took it as a sign that maybe he could resume sleeping in their bed. He changed into his pajama bottoms and T-shirt and crawled into his side. He smelled her familiar odor and longed to put his face in her neck. She closed the journal, turned off the bedside lamp, and curled into her side of the bed. "Night, Holly," he said, and reached over and kissed the top of her head, waiting for her to say something, but she didn't and he turned into his own corner and though he was uncomfortable, he forced himself to sleep in the bed beside her.

In the morning the blasting sound of the vacuum cleaner greeted him downstairs. He leashed the dogs for a walk. Tracing his familiar trail through their neighborhood, he stopped by the pond. The swans hungrily ducked their heads into the cold water and a chill went through him. Trudy reached up and yelped and he calmed her down and gave her a treat from his pocket. Simon did the same, both desiring and commanding his attention. He found a soft, dry spot on a bench near the pond to sit and watched the water slipping over the rocks at the very edge. The air was cold down his back.

He entered the house and unleashed the dogs. Holly was in the dim breakfast nook, her knees drawn up against her. It took him a few moments to recognize the anguished sounds. She was crying. A piece of hair fell into her eyes.

"It's Daddy. He's gone." She examined him carefully as he entered the room.

"When?"

"This morning." Her eyes filled again.

"Holly, I'm sorry," he said, and wrapped his arms around her.

"I'm just so mad at you," she said. She pulled away for a moment and then leaned her shoulders back into him. He held her tight and kissed the top of her hair. Over her head he watched the bright light press into the blinds, illuminating the hues on the floor and brightening the walls until it hurt to see. Her tears seeped into his shirt. She clung to him tightly. The funeral was Friday. Her mother had made all the arrangements months ago.

She slowly lifted her face from his chest and stood up. "Annabel will be home soon." She wiped her wet face with her sleeve. "I knew it was coming," she said.

"I know. You don't have to explain."

He watched her open the refrigerator and take out vegetables to start a salad, and though he wanted to say more he sat on the breakfast nook bench. He sat there for a long time as if he were keeping vigil as she chopped the carrots and then the radishes, not wanting to leave her, and she seemed neither to mind his presence nor to want his help.

The dogs followed Holly, sensing her grief. They rubbed against her legs and looked up at her with their noses in the air and let out little sounds, not quite cries or whines but something in between. Holly reached down to shush them and they licked her face. "Good dog, good boy," she whispered, breaking up again and putting her head in Simon's fur.

"I'll finish here," Edward said. "Go upstairs. Get some rest." She moved slowly and without apparent consciousness, as if in a dream.

THE STEREO WAS turned on loudly. Mahler. He followed its sound to the bedroom. All the windows were open. He found Holly cross-legged in the middle of the bed wearing only a long T-shirt and panties. Her lips were blue. She did this occasionally. She'd turn on the music loudly and get into some kind of zone. He closed the windows and wrapped a blanket around her.

"All these years I blamed Daddy for Lizzie's death. It just hit me. And now it's too late to tell him."

"I'm sorry, Holly." He scooted next to her on the bed and cupped his hand around her shoulder. "Your father knew how much you loved him."

"I don't know. I don't know about anything anymore." She gazed up, teary. "Why, Edward?" Tears flooded her eyes. She rubbed her nose with the back of her hand.

"I don't know. I didn't mean to hurt you."

"Something's happened to us." Her face hardened. She looked into the air rather than at him as she spoke.

The room darkened in shadow. They both rose and descended the stairs. He followed Holly into the cool and drafty garage. She kneeled on the cement floor in the half dark, near the litter of kittens, with the little runt cupped in her palm.

"Did you know that the mother cat won't care for the runt? She knows instinctively if something is wrong and won't waste her time when she has healthy kittens to attend to." She pressed her lips into the kitten's matted head. "Poor, precious thing. Can you imagine?" Holly sighed as they saw through the garage window the lights go on, one after another, in the house next door.

AT THE FUNERAL, the pews of Saint Patrick's Cathedral were filled with mourners, others standing in the outer aisles. After the service Edward embraced Holly and his own eyes filled. She broke away, dried her eyes with her handkerchief, and put her arm in her mother's to greet their guests. At her mother's apartment afterward he observed her warmly receive her parents' friends and relatives, all dressed respectfully in black dresses and dark suits. He awkwardly took the coats and carried them into the master bedroom.

He wandered into the dining room and found the painting of Holly and her twin, Lizzie, on the wall in the dining room above the credenza. Though it had faded, the image of the two girls in their white knee socks, Mary Janes, and matching collared dresses still asserted its poignant authority. Tom Drury arrived with flowers. Holly led him through the back hall into her old bedroom. From the hallway he observed the two of them huddled together in conversation on Holly's canopy bed. Holly leaned over and Tom held her. His gut clenched watching another man hold his wife.

THE OPENING OF Agnes Murray's show arrived the first Thursday in May. Fortunately someone had persuaded her to change the name to *Grand Illusions*. Edward's revenues were still down—lower than ever—and he still hadn't signed anyone new. He'd curated a show of anatomical drawings by Miles McDermott, an artist he'd signed in his early days at the gallery, and though he liked the work and liked Miles, his heart wasn't in it. He found less in the art world that he cared about. He feared he'd not only lost his edge, but perhaps worse, the ability to be truly moved. He remembered the first show he curated and the sense of his connection to the motion and beauty of a particular moment in time as expressed through objects and felt by the way in which he helped to conceptualize the show as if he were a conduit for preserving history. He hadn't felt that way in a while.

The morning of Agnes's opening, May peered her head into his office and explained that she thought it would be best for the gallery if he did not attend. He hadn't been planning on it, but it insulted him that May asked.

Later that evening, he retreated upstairs to the eerie darkness of his study and turned on a small desk light. Outside the windows were shadows of trees and the faraway roofs of other houses. He nursed a scotch and reluctantly turned on his computer to see the press. Page six of the *Observer* reported that the gallery was packed. Every critic, important art figure, and gallery owner attended. When asked in a profile in *Vogue* about why she became a painter, Agnes said, "I've been chosen by painting to work in its service."

He found himself avoiding the papers. Avoiding everyone. He entered the gallery every morning and swiftly walked past her paintings mounted on the walls—seeing them up for view, and still not quite buying into their vision, disturbed him. He didn't like the way the paintings were hung. Agnes and Savan had chosen large frames and lots of wall space, as if to emphasize the sense of drama in the work, but instead they made the work look flat. No one had thought to ask his opinion. Agnes hardly came to the gallery. Once he thought he heard her voice and ducked into the showroom to see, and he saw her quickly turn her head. So as not to make her uncomfortable, he retreated to his office and then regretted it. Why should he be the one hiding? What had he done? Hearing her name, seeing it in print, catching anyone speaking of her brought all the humiliation back.

The reviews began to trickle in. The *New York Times* said there was a lack of continuity to the paintings. The *New Yorker* wondered if Agnes was cashing in on 9/11 and found the work overly determined and grim. There was a long retrospective piece in the *New York Review*. The reviewer suggested that the work, though powerful, hadn't quite jelled and was a disappointment. Edward thought he'd feel vindicated, but instead the coverage angered him. Agnes had settled for putting a filter between her hand and the work, when what the canvas needed was conflict and intensity and challenging eye movement. The gallery was going to have a rough go of it.

No longer exuding his usual bravado, Savan looked tense, and for a few luxurious moments Edward was glad not to have to deal with Agnes. She was probably fit to be tied. And then he wished, somehow, that he was still her dealer. He'd stand by her during the rough times. That is what dealers did if they believed in the artist and the long haul involved in nurturing talent.

Initial sales were low and it took effort on Savan's part to get collectors to pay attention. After six weeks, the show had brought in not even a third of the profits of her first show. May was surprisingly quiet about the situation, but he could hear that when Agnes's name came up she no longer gushed the way she had in the past.

"There's still Europe," Savan soft-pedaled in one of their weekly meetings. "We may be able to recoup our investment over time." He reported that Agnes had complained that the gallery hadn't advertised enough or marketed the show to the right clientele. May refused to pour any more of the gallery's money into advertising and marketing. To distance himself from disappointment, Savan rolled his eyes when Agnes complained, as if he'd forgotten that he'd brought this on himself.

EDWARD ATTENDED THE opening of a retrospective at Dia of the conceptual artist Jenny Holzer, known for her displays of words and ideas, like billboard advertisements, in public spaces. The last time she'd shown at Dia was in 1989. If he was honest with himself, he would admit that part of the reason he'd gone to the opening was that he hoped to find Julia. It had been two months since the weekend of the Armory Show. Once Agnes's show was mounted, Julia was the person he'd itched to discuss it with. To his amazement, he found her standing in a corner of the cavernous space chatting with two other women. A quick rush of adrenaline swept over him. Her attractiveness struck him anew, as it always did when he first saw her. She raised her chin to acknowledge him, and motioned with her head for him to come. He quickly strolled over.

She introduced him to her companions, two artists with studios in Bushwick: Simone Klein and Nancy someone, he didn't catch the last name. After a round of small talk, he pointed to a piece he wanted to show her against the opposite wall of the open space and they excused themselves, stopping only to say hello or nodding to colleagues he knew, champagne in hand, as they negotiated their way through the crowd.

"It's good to see you," he said, once they were alone. Up close he noticed beneath her glasses dark circles under her eyes, making her blue irises appear more luminescent. It gave her a penetrating and unassuming presence.

"What happened?" she finally asked.

"I don't know. I saw you across the hall at the Armory looking at me and I couldn't bring myself to face you. I'm sorry."

Her face looked sullen. Something in it was different.

"Look, can we sit down?"

He wanted to take her to a secluded place, but where? It was impossible. There were people everywhere. He saw a door to the back and motioned for her to follow, and they sat on a bench in the courtyard decked with ornamental trees, still surrounded by people socializing in their own insular pods. Once they sat down, he quickly took her hand and squeezed it before letting it go.

The crowd had grown larger and he could barely hear her over the din. Distracted, she peered into the throng.

"We better go back in. My friends are waiting."

She wandered back to the group and before he could follow Sam Marcus, a dealer from another gallery, tapped him on the back and Edward spoke to him for a few moments, distracted. His eyes followed Julia over the tops of other heads. He shifted so as not to lose her and watched as she drifted slowly toward the back of the gallery. She still possessed him. It was agony. After Sam peeled off and he spoke to two or three other people he knew, he found her again.

"What is it?" she leaned in and whispered.

"I'm just happy to see you."

"I'm glad to see you too."

The tension evaporated and they quickly eased into their easy intimacy. They moved into a quieter corner of the space.

"Did you see Agnes's show?"

Like other prominent artists living in New York, Julia had an ear for gossip. If you lived in Chelsea or Tribeca, and now Bushwick, Dumbo, and Williamsburg, it was impossible to get a cup of coffee without running into another artist or dealer, and he wondered what the perception of Agnes's show was on the streets, what she thought of it.

"I'm afraid it didn't seem to make a loud splash. Is the gallery disappointed?"

"I can't say that we're happy about it. It didn't live up to its promise. And May doesn't like to lose money." He stopped. "It's been grim."

"Well, maybe it will save her marriage."

"Agnes's?"

"I heard they were in trouble. Apparently Nate didn't come to the opening?"

"He never comes to her shows. She doesn't want anyone to associate the two of them together. That's where she draws the line." He was oddly protective of Agnes. He had possessed—still possessed—such intimate knowledge of her.

"The word is that Agnes is going to be up for the Tanning Prize. My friends, Simone and Nancy, were just talking about it."

"Really?"

"Simone said Frederick Jackson is one of the judges—I think he's the chair actually—and of course he and Nate are pals."

"The Tanning prize. You're kidding," he said again.

They walked over to a piece from Holzer's *The Living* Series.
"I like this one," Julia acknowledged. It was enamel on metal with
black type. The inscription read:

SOMETIMES YOU HAVE NO OTHER CHOICE BUT TO WATCH
SOMETHING GRUESOME OCCUR. YOU DON'T HAVE THE
OPTION OF CLOSING YOUR EYES BECAUSE IT HAPPENS FAST
AND ENTERS YOUR MEMORY.

They turned to each other in mutual acknowledgment. Julia's
fingers reached into her hair. She scooped it back.

"I'm sorry about Agnes. It must have disappointed you. You've
put so much into her career," she offered.

"The paintings weren't quite there yet. I tried to tell her."

"She should have listened."

"Enough about Agnes." He'd thought he'd gotten through
the worst part of it, but the long runup to the prize ceremony—if
indeed she was up for the prize—would keep Agnes front and center. It would be agony.

"How's your own work?"

"It's going well. Do you still want to come to my studio?
Since London I've wanted to show you what I've been up to. I've
switched mediums. I'm painting, which is crazy. I haven't painted
since graduate school."

He stood close enough to feel her breath on his neck and heat
rise from her thin sweater.

"Yes, I want to see it."

In London he'd said he was interested in representing her, but he
wondered whether it would be a good idea. She seemed to register

his concern. "Don't worry. I want you to see my work, but I don't want you to represent me. That would be career suicide."

"Would it?"

"You know it would. Wasn't it you who said an artist should never mix business with friendship?"

She motioned to where her two friends were standing. "I should get back," she said, uncomfortable, but unable to quite leave. Her face was in a knot. She looked at him as if there was more she wanted to say and then shook her head, resigned to their circumstances. A wisp of her soft hair caught on his face as he leaned in to say good-bye.

13 CONNECTICUT

H E ENTERED HIS quiet house. He saw Holly's sweatshirt draped on a chair in the kitchen and picked it up and brought it to his lips. He looked out their bedroom window at the cherry tree Holly had planted. Each spring, the tree would begin to blossom, and every year the tree grew more robust. The extreme beauty of the thick, rich pink and magenta flowers in bloom and quick death once all the blossoms had dropped always caught him short. He withdrew upstairs to his study.

He reclined on the sofa facing the wall where he had mounted his father's landscapes and attempted to read a draft of a catalogue. He couldn't concentrate. He couldn't get Julia's changed look at the Holzer exhibition the evening before out of his mind. He remembered her warm disposition in Berlin and the aggrieved look he observed at the gallery.

He turned another page and tried to concentrate, and then raised his eyes from the catalogue and gazed at his father's paintings. He had spent days at the university teaching and evenings locked in his study. But once he became ill, the stream of his thoughts ran dry. In their sunroom he painted the same landscape outside their window, obsessively attempting to pin down something that eluded him. On the horizon of each painting was a cloudlike face and in the foreground a stand of spindled trees. After he died, Edward's mother aired the sunroom, gathered the paint supplies in a box for the trash. She donated his clothes to Goodwill, packed up his papers in a trunk, and boxed his books. Edward was appointed the literary executor of his estate. The drafty room, emptied of personality, felt as if it belonged to strangers.

He picked up his father's edition of Keats's poems and opened it. Inside the front flap his father had made notes to himself in pen. *Where are you? Why are you hiding? Who are you?* He'd circled key words in the poems, written along the margins, underlined passages. Through his work he constructed a system of hiding and subterfuge. *We must be broken in order to heal.*

As a kid he occasionally heard his father cursing in his study. He'd come out after a weekend when he'd retreated, emerging only to make coffee, moody, exhausted, grumbling that he didn't know whether he'd made his manuscript better or worse. He explained how his ideas felt simplistic the minute he tried to pin them down and was frustrated that they did not live up to the originality and brilliance he imagined. He accompanied his father on long walks in the woods behind their backyard with their dog, Beckett. Sometimes his father walked in silence, and other times, consumed by problems with his work, he obsessed. One of his obsessions was with the notion of character. His first major academic work was on Keats; it received numerous academic prizes and had secured his tenure at Yale. Keats described poetic character as having no self but only serving the imagination, as if the poetic self were a mirror to reflect back to readers their own inner lives. Keats strove in his work not to reconcile contradictory aspects of character by fitting them into closed systems. "Human character is essentially unknowable," his father once said, stripping bark from a branch as he walked. The deeper he delved inside his own intellectual thought, the harder it was for him to be in the world of the day-to-day. "You keep me whole, son," he confided after they had spent the morning fishing in the stream. His father was fit and handsome, with a square chin and sensitive smile. He always looked better in the outdoors, when color came into his pale face. Years before he became ill he'd been collaborating on a book in private with John Kincaid, a Wordsworth scholar in the department. While Keats believed that immortality could be sought in art, Wordsworth sought it in nature. His father was excited about their partnership, more than he'd been about any project in a long while. Though they argued heatedly at times, his close intellectual bond with Kincaid fueled his work and gave him renewed faith in it. Once when Edward returned from school he heard the two men speaking with raised voices behind the study door. After Kincaid left, his mother confronted him.

"What do the two of you do in there for hours? Don't you see enough of him at the university?"

His father retreated back inside his study, as he always did when she was critical. His mother returned to the kitchen where she'd been preparing dinner, with tears in her eyes.

"It's me she's disappointed in, son, not you," he said to Edward later that night. Edward didn't know which was worse: to be ordinary like his mother, or to strive for the perfection that had taken his father away from her.

EDWARD LOOKED OUT the window. It was getting dark and the woods behind his yard vanished in blackness. He turned on the light in the study. The frenzied layers in the paintings disturbed him. In the gnarled trees in the foreground he made out a soft etching of black. He stood up and moved closer. A pair of initials, J and K, was painted into a crook in the branches. He looked closely at the other paintings and discovered in each one the same initials obscured in the crooks and crannies of a branch.

The trunks in the closet held his father's private manuscripts and papers. After his death Edward found it too painful to read through them. He put off the Yale library's requests to purchase the papers, not yet willing to let them go. Edward pulled out one of the heavy trunks from the closet. It was coated with dust and its casing was brittle. He opened the latch. Inside were stacks of letters in rubber bands and sheaves of papers and manuscripts with smeared and fading type. He read through some letters. The paper had turned yellow and brittle, crumpling around the edges. The letters were from colleagues and students. He'd been a beloved teacher. He opened another manuscript box slightly dampened by mildew. *The Unrealized Self*, the last, unpublished book his father had been working on before he grew ill. He began to read. *Art is the window to the interior.*

The first chapter opened with Blake, whose visionary narratives were idea-driven. Using his own mythological characters, Blake portrayed the imaginative artist as the hero of society and suggested the possibility of redemption from a fallen state through art. In the second chapter he wrote about Wordsworth. *The Prelude,* the most significant English expression of the Romantic discovery of the self, was dedicated to his friend Coleridge. Edward's father had written that it was Wordsworth who proclaimed the self as a topic for art and literature. In his "Ode: Intimations of Immortality from Recollections of Early Childhood," Wordsworth contemplated the pathos and potentialities of ordinary lives. As Edward read on, his father's sentences became more long-winded and convoluted; he intuited his father struggling for coherence. He wrote about how the Romantic poets coming off the Age of Reason—the eighteenth-century poets believed it wasn't man's business to seek divine Truth—divine truth was accessible in God's creations—particularly nature—and that "chosen" people—poets (artists)—had the capability of discovering divine truth if they kept at it, were pure in their artistic pursuits of it, and believed in the possibilities of what their poetic search could yield. He wrote about the suffering that resulted from man's lack of self-expression and not being true to himself. Edward slid the manuscript back into its box. The work had become too insular. A note on Yale letterhead slipped out from the bottom of the manuscript.

> *Dear Harry,*
> *This has to stop. Nothing good can come of it.*
>
> *The heavens laugh with you in your jubilee;*
> *My heart is at your festival,*
> *My head hath its coronal,*
> *The fulness of your bliss, I feel—I feel it all.*
>
> *Yours as ever, John*

The lines of poetry in the letter were from Wordsworth's "Intimations of Immortality." Was Kincaid speaking about their professional collaboration? Or was there something more between them? Edward scanned his bookshelves. Along with inheriting his paintings and papers, he had acquired his father's library, including his collection of first editions. He pulled off the shelf Wordsworth's *Lyrical Ballads,* a poetic collaboration with Coleridge. The two poets were intimate friends. The book was a gift from Kincaid. Scrawled on the title page was an inscription: *Your comrade, lovingly, John.*

He looked at the letter from Kincaid again. It was dated a few months before his father was hospitalized. He returned the papers to the trunk, closed its latch, and pushed it back into the closet, thrusting the weight of his body against the trunk to move it. He looked out the window; it was completely black. Hours had passed.

Not wanting to think about it anymore, he retreated downstairs to find his wife and daughter in the den curled up on the couch watching a movie, their empty plates from dinner spread on the coffee table.

"Why didn't you call me to come down?"

"I did, Daddy. You didn't answer," Annabel said.

"We figured you were working and didn't want to disturb you," Holly added, barely raising her eyes to look at him. "We left a plate for you in the kitchen."

He wandered into the kitchen, poured himself a glass of wine, heated the plate of chicken, rice, and broccoli in the microwave, ate it quickly standing up by the kitchen window, and then wandered back into the den. He looked at the sheer curtain they had hung years ago to frame the window. It was slowly unraveling from its rod. He looked at Holly and Annabel absorbed in the drama on the television, unaware he was in the room. He walked through the dining room and into the living room, examining the empty wooden table shining with wax and the stiff-backed chairs, and then climbed back upstairs to the third floor. He passed the rest of the evening looking at his father's paintings and then out at the cluster of trees lit freakishly by the moon.

THE RAIN STOPPED. Reflections dissolved in the windows of the train. He climbed up from the depths of the damp Spring Street subway into the brightness of the afternoon. Bundles of pink peonies shimmered in buckets under the awning of a Korean market. He recalled that peonies made her happy and picked a bouquet and let the clerk roll it in paper.

Across the street from her building, anchored between Prince and Broadway, construction workers tore down an older structure. The crane screeched, a grating sound like chalk on a board.

Julia took his coat and led him into an airy space with creaky floors and a tin ceiling. She smelled the flowers. He took in her tender throat, warm bright eyes, and expressive hands as she arranged the peonies in a vase. He felt already as he looked at her that he was imprinting her image in memory.

He examined the studio. Coils of wire and stretched canvases were piled in a corner. Chips and wood shavings and a few oily rags collected on the floor. The room smelled of turpentine. Woodcarving tools were assembled on a butcher block. On another table, paint tubes, palette, brushes and palette knives, turpentine, and jars of varnish and oil. The cement floor was painted gray, chipped and spattered with paint.

On another table she displayed her figures made of marble and wood. The sculptures were in the shapes of an infant's curled body, each in a slightly different pose. The spare forms were sanded and shellacked. In their Zen-like simplicity they emanated an ethereal glow. She said the inspiration came from that temple in Tokyo dedicated to infants lost through miscarriage or stillbirth she had told him about when she came back from Tokyo. She led him to the back wall of the studio to show him some new paintings. She'd begun them when she returned from Japan.

One painting depicted a woman alone on a bench in a temple court-yard, her gaze impenetrable. In another, a naked pregnant woman draped only in a blanket appeared at the forefront of the canvas, her abdomen translucent, and inside her the curved body of a baby. In another painting impressions of mother and baby were drawn, erased, and superimposed to make shadings and shadowing so that it was difficult to see where one shape began and another ended.

She opened a large sketchbook and showed him the earlier stages of the project. At the temple in Japan worshipers pay a fee to adopt a figurine and inscribe their names on it. They sometimes come weekly or daily. The statuettes represent their own lost baby. Some dress up the figures like newborns, with bibs and hand-knit sweaters and booties and hats.

"A few weeks after our baby died I was on the bus and I still looked pregnant and I talked to the woman next to me about my baby as if she were still alive," she said. "I wasn't myself. I think I went a little mad."

"They're beautiful."

He turned from the sketches to study her. She brought a small lock of hair close to her face and twirled it around her finger. With his gaze he traced the river of veins running up the underside of her arm. In her studio she struck him as more viscerally real, a woman with a husband and a child they had lost, a life separate from his. He wondered about her husband and what more about her he didn't know.

They sat down at the end of a velvet sofa. Above them was a wall of lights. Once seated, she too observed him carefully. She gently rested her hand on his arm.

"How are you?"

"Not great." He shifted uncomfortably.

"How are things at the gallery?"

"Agnes's show has taken a toll. I've given it a lot of thought. I think she was afraid. Of going back into the studio and finding her way through it."

"Maybe it was Nate that put her up to it."

"Leonard thinks the same. He said that when he represented Agnes, Nate was driving every deal, constantly pressing to get more money. And shortly after May closed the new deal, he read in the papers that they bought a huge warehouse in Bushwick for Nate to start production. He's hiring a fleet of new assistants."

"That says it all. It must have cost them a fortune. She's allowed commerce into the studio. Or Nate. Either one won't work for her," Julia concluded.

"You make her sound calculating. I never saw her that way. Or maybe I didn't want to."

"There's another way of looking at it. Maybe Nate was sabotaging her. You made Agnes successful. The way you got the critics to notice and the right collectors to be interested. At some level, maybe not even conscious, Nate knows that."

"So what are you saying? That Nate didn't want the show to be a success?"

"Maybe. His ego is huge. I know something about this."

"Frederick?"

She nodded. "It's complicated," she said.

"All will be unveiled shortly. If she wins the Tanning Prize everything will change."

He picked up one of her stone pieces and examined it. "How do you remain untouched?"

She wasn't sure if she was, she said. What mattered to her was the work. One of her mentors lived for years in Westbeth. To him, the idea that art should make someone wealthy was obscene. Making art was a reaction against consumerism. There are the artists who always think someone else can do more for them. They leave one gallery to go to a better-known one. Or pin one gallery up against the other to squeeze out more money. Or their spouses support their art and they drift into feelings of unworthiness. "I'd rather make art and hope that it will be recognized and that I'll be paid market value. Art can't be a substitute for living. At least for me it can't," she said.

"It is for Agnes."

"Maybe. But she'll never be happy if she's looking for someone to place a value on her work. The prize is the creation. It's all that matters."

She thought for a moment more. "You're not powerless," she said. "You could forget the gallery and let it all go."

Everything he had he'd invested in the gallery. He crossed and uncrossed his legs uncomfortably. "It isn't that. No, that's not what I want."

He was silent for a moment and then gazed back at her. "The painful part is that I still care."

"I know you do. That's because you're decent."

She touched his arm gently and he felt a pleasant sensation travel through his body. It was quiet. No one in the studio, no one but the two of them.

"I'm not sure the way I feel about you makes me decent," he finally said. "I don't like myself very much right now."

"What are you saying?"

He looked at her pale throat and grave eyes. "I don't think we should be doing this anymore. Not because I don't want to. We're married. We'll destroy each other."

Darkness crossed her face. She was quiet for a moment, pondering what he'd said, and then, more subdued, she raised her head and spoke. "Since we lost the baby I've been dead. You brought me back. I don't understand how it all happened."

"I don't either."

She'd thought she was through with all of it—the wish for connection and intimacy. She thought she had that with Frederick and it was a disaster. With Roy it was less complicated. Easier. It was why they got married. She wanted to get on with it—to get on with life.

"I don't want this." Tears rolled down her cheeks. "This isn't what I want."

The last thing he wanted was to hurt her, he said.

She released her hand and brushed away a swath of hair that had fallen over her face, and her eyes welled again. "I know," she said.

He pulled her close and she pressed her face into his shoulder and held him tightly. All was quiet, like being in a snow-filled forest

of pine trees when dusk descends and you don't mind that you've
lost your way. She lifted her face to him.

"Roy's not like you. He's guarded. He has to be. It's the way
he functions. Sometimes when I look at him I see what we lost in
his eyes and what I'm unable to give him. It's incredibly painful."

"I don't like when you talk about him. I'm sorry. I can't hear his
name. I know it's selfish."

"Why?"

"Because then he's imprinted in my brain."

From the window a construction vehicle keened back and forth
until the blaring sound slowly blurred into an echo. "They're tear-
ing down the building across the street. The noise is driving me
crazy. It's like they're taking part of history away."

She stood up and looked out the window. "My view has
changed," she said, overcome by the realization. The sun shifted
and the room darkened. He looked at his watch. Hours had passed.
It was nearly four. He observed her work mounted on the walls
and propped on her worktable and she caught him looking and
she said, "I'm not interested in artifice anymore. It's fake. I want
the work, at least now, to mirror life. Not to mock it or to be in
opposition to it."

He smiled. It was what he liked about her most, her lack of artifice. You couldn't separate the work from the individual who made
it. They were one and the same.

"So you approve?"

"Yes, I approve," he laughed. He stood up and reached for his
jacket. Suddenly it was cold in the room—unbearably so.

"Please don't go." She reached for his arm. "Not yet."

Tacked on the wall above a small wooden desk were photographs and a typed copy of "Ode on a Grecian Urn." He glanced at one of the sculptures of a baby curled in its stone womb and then at the paintings.

"You've immortalized what you lost, you know," he said. He looked again at her painting on the studio wall and studied it. He noticed a black form at the edge of the canvas. "It's almost like a silhouette," he added.

"He's watching her but he can't help her. It's the nature of grief, isn't it?"

He wondered, thinking about Julia and himself, but also his father, whether in its suffering longing brings us closer to truth. And then, just as he thought it, he dismissed it. What difference did it make? No one wants to suffer.

"I don't want you to go," she said.

"You'll be glad when I'm gone. You love Roy. He's a good man." His throat closed up. "What will I do without you," he said, suddenly bereft. He put on his jacket and then kissed her cheek quickly before departing.

Once outside, debris hit the pavement. The sound vibrated through the ground underneath him, across the street from her studio. The wrecking ball hurled against the building. He turned to look. Glass smashed. Part of a wall crumbled. He looked up at the window of her studio and in the pinking ash saw her figure behind the curtain, her hand cupped against the sash, and felt another tremor in the seam of where the building once stood.

15 CONNECTICUT

THE FINALISTS FOR the Tanning Prize were to be announced, as they were every year, in the morning paper on June 1st and posted online before that, at midnight. Against his better judgment he logged onto the *Times* website before bed and read the post. Agnes Murray was one of four finalists. Though he'd expected it, he felt as if he were swimming away from himself.

Winning the prize would reconfirm, after a swath of lukewarm reviews, her status in the art world. Were she to win, it would not only ensure her own future but it would elevate Edward's as well, were he still her gallerist. He found himself wondering again whether his instincts had been wrong. Like many artists at her level, their egos inflated by praise, fame, and the sudden escalation of their work's monetary value, she might not have wanted a realistic appraisal of the work. He should have lied; he felt it in his gut.

And then he felt, just as viscerally, that he shouldn't have: that he had been right to tell Agnes—whom he cared for, who relied on his judgment and, in her own way, cared for him too. These were the values he held most sacred; this was what made him different—he hoped—from someone like Savan. With Savan now a partner, the dynamic and energy of the gallery had changed. Savan had tainted what the gallery had meant to him. He couldn't let Savan bring down the quality of what he'd built. He'd have to walk away.

Agnes's photo took up half the cover page of the arts section. She was dressed in a white shirt and a man's suit jacket, no doubt to distance herself from her femininity. She told him once that she did not want to paint subject matter a woman would paint because then she'd never be considered successful. He looked at the photo again. The affect, posed in front of the steps of the Metropolitan Museum of Art, looked calculated to elicit an impression.

He continued reading the article. Agnes Murray was the favorite to win. When asked if she was surprised by the nomination, she said, "My art is a mirror of the viewer's own projection. I'm very pleased that the judges saw themselves or their own experiences in my work." He turned away from the paper and looked out the window and sipped his bitter scotch.

He looked back to the computer and continued reading the article. Along with Agnes, a young performance artist called Hugo London was a contender for the prize. He remembered reading about one performance when he pulled a giant boulder with some kind of pulley and walked through Central Park, a modern-day Sisyphus. The *Times* quoted him as saying that he was a successor to the extraordinary performance art of Marina Abramović, known as the grandmother of performance art. "Although art-world insiders swear that the artwork takes precedence over its maker, it is really a double act. After all, artists are the people who have the authority to deem something as 'art.' They have all the energy, intention, discipline, and willpower that an inanimate canvas does not." A third finalist was Maxwell Flower. His technique was to fill a dark room with rays of fluorescent light. The viewer was meant to be a participant in the work; when the viewer entered the gallery he or she was given a light saber. Edward had been dismissive. The fourth finalist was April Stillman, an abstract outsider artist, relatively new on the scene. Leonard worked with her. Edward smiled, happy for Leonard. She was the least known of the four and apparently the long shot. He poured himself another inch of scotch and sprawled on the sofa and fell asleep.

HE AWOKE THE next morning stiff and groggy and went downstairs to make coffee. Holly and Annabel had already left. He'd overslept. If he still represented Agnes, the day would have been his. Gallery owners, dealers, collectors, and artists live for prizes. He couldn't bear to see Savan taking credit for it and endure the high-fives and pats on the back that would be going around the gallery. He called his assistant and said he was working from home. His BlackBerry vibrated in his breast pocket. He looked at the caller ID.

"Leonard. I know. Fucking unbelievable."

"Did you see who else is up for it? April Stillman."

"Congratulations. It's the only thing good about today."

"I want her to win," Leonard said.

"Of course you do."

"Do you think she has a shot?"

"A quarter of a chance."

"I don't know. You saw who's chairing the panel? Frederick Jackson. I'm sure Nate persuaded Frederick to put her up for the prize. If only to get Agnes off his back. She's the favorite, my friend. Can you imagine what it must be like to be married to her these last few months after those reviews? I don't know how he stays."

"She *is* beautiful," Edward said, looking at her photo again. "I'll give her that. And talented."

"That she's a finalist is Nate's doing," Leonard insisted. "She needs this."

"I don't know, Leonard." He stopped and looked out the window. "Fisher has his own reputation to think about."

"Don't be such a purist. This has nothing to do with making art. This has to do with who you know and who scratches your back."

"She's still a damn good painter. We can't take that away from her."

"Think about it. In her high-mindedness she thinks she's done it on her own. She'd still be sitting up in that ivory tower if it weren't for me. And you. I brought Aaron Moss to her studio. He was the first critic to write about her work in the *Times*. The first painting she sold was bought by a Guggenheim heir. You did a brilliant job with *Immortality*. The show you mounted knocked it out of the park. What goes around comes around. You'll see."

"Maybe."

"Where are you? Are those birds I hear?"

"I'm still at home."

"Stop hibernating. Walk into the gallery like you own it. You need to get out there again. I have three new artists whose work I want you to see. And there's April Stillman. I may be looking for a new home for her. You're on our dance card."

"You're an animal."

"So are you, my friend."

HE SLOWLY CLIMBED his study stairs. Leonard was right. There were other artists to consider. He logged into his computer and a mountain of e-mails lit up the screen. He couldn't focus. His eyes were blurry and his head groggy from oversleeping. Holly never let him oversleep on a workday. She barely seemed to think of him now. Anxious, he rose and paced, unable to sit at his desk. His gaze landed on the thick, agonizing swirls of his father's paintings and to the crook of the tree where embedded in a branch were the initials.

He lifted one of them off the wall, showered, dressed, gathered his things into his briefcase, and got in the car. With the painting on the seat next to him, he began to drive. Through the open window he inhaled the fresh air. It was unusual for him to be in Connecticut on a weekday, and as he wound through the small towns, he was surprised by the full and busy street life.

He hadn't been to Yale since he was a teenager visiting his father. He entered through the gates of the university and approached the gothic building where his father's office once was. As a boy it reminded him of a castle. He remembered climbing the winding stairs to his father's office and wondering as he saw students clustered in study groups in the lounge whether he would feel passionate enough about anything to want to dedicate his life to it. In a lecture hall, he sought out the original Tiffany stained-glass window, titled *Education*, that his father had once shown him. It showcased a panorama of allegorical figures signifying aspects of art, music, science, and religion. Looking at it as an adolescent had made him restless with want.

His father's office now belonged to Professor Margery Greer. He saw her plaque on the door. He continued down the dark hallway reading the plaques until he found Kincaid's office. He adjusted the painting underneath his arm and knocked on the door. Through the slight opening he saw Kincaid leaning over a manuscript, his cluttered desk lit by a green lawyer's lamp.

Kincaid looked up and motioned for Edward to come in. When Edward was a boy, Kincaid had been tall and distinguished. Now his shoulders were painfully hunched and his face craggy. His gray hair was combed back from his forehead. He wore a tie and sweater underneath a tweed blazer. He had been strikingly hand-some with eyes the color of turquoise. Now those eyes were rheumy and clouded. Kincaid peered up through his bifocals.

"Professor Kincaid. It's Edward Darby."

Kincaid came around his desk and reached out to shake Edward's hand. His nails were yellow and pointed like talons. He patted Edward a little too forcefully on the back, as if he had lost sight of his own strength. He must be in his late seventies, Edward thought.

"Of course it is. Sit down, dear boy. How's your mother?" He offered Edward the wooden chair across from his desk.

"Well. She lives in a retirement community in New Canaan. And Mrs. Kincaid and Violet?"

"Violet married a young professor from the department. He got a tenured position at Stanford. They live in San Francisco."

"And Mrs. Kincaid?"

"She followed Violet to California. She was tired of being the widow of a living corpse. Her words, not mine."

His clothes were old, the collar of his shirt frayed and a moth hole in the rib of his sweater. His cheeks were blotchy and freckled with brown spots.

"She never understood ambition."

Edward's attention was drawn to the books on the shelf behind the desk. Facing out and displayed on a stand was a large vol-ume called *The Unrealized Self: How the Romantics Invented the*

Modern Age. Below the title in large gold foil was stamped the author's name: John Kincaid.

"And you, Edward?"

For a moment he couldn't answer; he was still taking in the title of the book.

"I'm in the art business. A principal at Mayweather and Darby."

"Well done. Your father would have been proud." He picked up his unlit pipe from the ashtray and brought it to his lips. "They won't let us smoke here or in any of the buildings or classrooms. Harry would have hated it."

"I suppose he would have."

"I'm sorry I didn't keep in touch. I'm not much good at it."

"You weren't alone. It wasn't easy for people to see him like that."

Kincaid's eyes clouded. "No, it wasn't."

"I wanted to give this to you. For years the painting hung on my wall and I never noticed. Look, here in the crook of the tree. The initials." He held out the painting on his lap.

Kincaid's face lost its color. He was speechless and then struggled for words. "Your father . . . Harry . . . We were close. I never had a better friend." His knotty fingers nervously fondled his pipe in the ashtray.

"That book." Edward pointed to the shelf. "Wasn't it the collaboration you and my father were working on together?"

"It grew out of our conversations about the Romantic poets. But after Harry became ill, I reconceived it. It went through hundreds of revisions. Years of research and contemplation."

"I saw pages of the manuscript among his things." Once when Kincaid and his father were arguing in the study his mother told him that she thought Kincaid was jealous of his father because he was the faculty star, the one who received all the honors and prizes in the department.

Kincaid took the book off the stand and handed it to him. "I gave up everything for this bloody book. It took everything out of me."

Edward read the back copy. It had won several prizes. He read the inside flaps and turned to the acknowledgments page to see if his father was credited. He wasn't mentioned. He recalled a line from the manuscript he had uncovered among his father's papers. *Each choice the author makes more clearly reveals his character.* The office smelled old and destitute. African masks, sculptures from India, paintings, books, stacks of old and yellowed manuscripts on the radiator—they had been put there years, maybe even decades before and had not been updated or replaced.

"He trusted you. Your friendship meant everything to him."

"It meant too much to him." He cleared his throat.

Edward turned toward the window. He couldn't quite find the words. Students meandered down the path. Another group talking loudly burst out the door of a hall across the courtyard after class. All the trees were gloriously in bloom.

Kincaid stood up and moved toward the window and looked out. "Your father's gone."

Edward picked up the book again. "He was in pain."

Kincaid took the volume from Edward's hand and placed it back on its stand.

"Don't look for things you won't understand . . . Manic depression. It's a disease." He picked up his pipe and put it down again and banged out the tobacco onto his desk. "Feelings torture us but for God's sake they don't kill us." He stroked the stubble on his chin and picked up the pipe again and brought it to his lips. "Your father had furious amounts of energy. He propelled everything into his work because somewhere inside him he felt inert. That's not something medication can control. It was part of his brilliance. And his darkness."

He raised his eyes to the clock on the wall and stood up. "May I take you to lunch? I'd like that. I don't have much company these days." He motioned with the tilt of his head to the manuscript sitting on his desk. "Except this." He sucked on the pipe again.

Edward couldn't swallow. He looked at his watch and moved toward the doorway. "I'm afraid I have an appointment in the city. Another time. I'm sorry to have come unannounced."

"I'm glad you did. You were just a boy," he said, unable to finish his sentence. "It's remarkable how the years fall away."

He dusted the shoulders of Edward's jacket. "I'm glad to see you looking so well," he said, and held out his hand. Edward noticed his tremor before he took it.

He walked through the doorway, stopped, and turned around. "I'm selling my father's manuscripts and papers to Yale. One of his former graduate students is working on his biography. Readers will decide about your book, Professor Kincaid. About whether my father should have been credited."

He paced swiftly down the winding stairs of the hall and out the doors. The smell of the cool wind reminded him of his father. He walked through the college green until he found the memorial bench donated in his father's honor by his last class of students. Engraved on a brass plaque on the bench was a quote from Keats's "Ode to a Nightingale":

Away! away! for I will fly to thee,
Not charioted by Bacchus and his pards,
But on the viewless wings of Poesy . . .

He sat on the bench. The sun pressed into him and he closed his eyes. *What if your heart is so big it can't contain itself?* It came to him from memory. It was something his father once said. He opened his eyes to find a small blue bird perched at the far end of the bench. The bird pecked at a crumb and then lifted its wings into the breeze.

Slowly he walked back to his car. He looked out the window as he backed away from the campus. The gothic buildings, robust trees, and blankets of lawn receded. He had idealized the institution until his father was destroyed by it: he had seen it as a place removed from the world, where art and study existed apart from commerce. He thought about the ways in which some people strive to get ahead, throwing others under the bus in the process, and wondered how he had managed to achieve his small stake in the pond.

There was something else he needed to do. He hadn't spoken to Agnes since he left her studio over a year ago that day before Christmas.

He began the long drive into the city. He found a parking spot on Beach Street in Tribeca, and sat in his car in front of the trendy coffeehouse with hard wooden benches and steel industrial tables where he had met Agnes before. It was a few blocks from the building on Hudson Street. In the afternoon, after lunch, there was a lull downtown as if its inhabitants had all vacated the streets to go to their shops, studios, and offices.

From around the corner a couple holding hands strolled together toward the coffee shop. At a distance they looked like two teenagers. As they drew nearer, he saw that the woman was in her mid-twenties, thin and tall with long, graceful arms, straight spine and shoulders, long neck stretched and head held high. She walked with her legs turned out slightly, a ballet dancer, dressed in black leggings and tight, stylish black boots that went over her knee. A long robin's-egg-blue cashmere sweater—it looked expensive, maybe Italian—flapped open as she walked. Her hair was pulled up on top of her head into the shape of a tight little doorknob, and she wore huge black sunglasses like someone famous who did not want to be seen yet nevertheless called attention to herself. Beside her was a man twice or three times her age, hovering over her with a scarf draped around his neck, in black jeans and a sports coat. As the couple moved closer to the car Edward saw the walk he remembered, and the paunch. It was Nate, and the pair, the way they gestured as they walked, were unmistakably in a state of mutual rapture. Edward turned his head to the side so as not to be noticed and let them pass. Amazing how Tribeca could feel like a small town if you frequented it enough. He stayed parked in his car for a few more minutes, pondering what to do, as the two ducked into a dark basement pub.

He felt surprising compassion for Agnes, seeing Nate nearly falling all over a young ballerina who wouldn't have given him the time of day had he not been a famous artist. He wondered whether narcissists like Nate could ever really fall in love. Women were chosen merely to project his own ambitions. Perhaps he had married Agnes to ensure he would never lose his edge as an artist as long as he had her talent to push up against. He imagined Agnes

holed up in her studio uncomfortably fielding calls from the press,
alone in the temple she had erected around herself, every action
she made guided by Nate, whom she trusted to protect and counsel
her. He felt sorry for her. He recognized that whatever was done
had already been put in motion and that he was helpless to stop it.

He started up the car and drove away. He had no taste for
the theatrics of brutal ambition manifested in the sleekly designed
buildings that marked the skyline receding in his rearview mirror.

H E STOPPED AT the barn on his way home. The sky had darkened and the wind picked up. It was going to pour. Two golden horses with white markings on their fetlocks and their muzzles reared up in the open corral, riled by the approaching storm. They sniffed the dirt, pawing it with their hooves, and then one nuzzled the other's backside and then returned to smelling the ground.

He walked along the gravel driveway between the two big barns toward the stable where the girls had their lessons. Holly was leaning over the rail talking with Tom Drury. Their easy banter always made Edward feel excluded.

He observed Holly in shadow, her hair flowing loose down her back like a teenager's. In the dim light it looked lighter again, blonder. He hadn't noticed before. He admired her long legs and buttocks in her tight riding pants and her square chin and perfect nose. Tom was wearing dark blue jeans and boots. He was taller than Holly, muscular and broad and clean-cut. Holly touched Tom's arm as she leaned to speak and her eyes smiled at him. He saw a flash of something between them. Tom touched her back and rubbed the upper portion of her arm with his hand. He'd long noticed Holly's flirtation with their neighbor Chip, but now he saw it was Tom with whom she was truly intimate—not physically, he didn't think, or hoped, but emotionally. Maybe Holly confided in Tom about their troubles at home and their marriage as he had to Julia. He watched them and then he couldn't watch anymore and walked away.

He got back in his car and gripped the steering wheel to steady himself. It was over between him and Holly. He was surer about it than anything.

He drove, letting cars zoom past, his mind full of elaborate fantasies of Holly and Tom. He pulled into his driveway many minutes later. The wood shingles on the house had darkened and splintered. The heavy leaves drooped from the boughs of trees. The night began to fall, the sky turning from lavender to indigo when the last of the sun was nearly gone. He looked at it all from a far distance, as if it were no longer his. In the air the moisture began to build.

Under the darkened and peppered clouds he sat down on one of the two Adirondack chairs he and Holly had bought when they first moved into the house, drew his coat around him, and waited. A shiver went down his back. He remembered how sometimes just before dusk he and Holly would take their glasses of wine out to the backyard and sit on the chairs and watch the sun cast a shadow over the lawn as it went down and they could see the lights turn on in their neighbor's houses.

He got up and walked along the garden. The slender irises had sprung up and the green heads of the hostas poked through the ground. At the end of the season what remained would be half-chewed leaves. No matter how much they sprayed the hostas, by late August the deer would eat anything. He recalled their slender, long purple flowers and their rubbery green leaves and the sheen when the sun fell on them. What was the point of all the care and

cultivation? He circled back to the chair, sat down, and waited for
Holly. He pictured Tom touching his wife. He rose and walked
back through the garden and kicked the gate.

Holly's SUV pulled into the driveway. Annabel sat next to her in
the passenger seat. She got out of the car and walked toward him.
"Hi, Daddy." She took out one of the earbuds from her ears
and left it hanging. "Dad, what's wrong? You look sad."

"I'm not, love."

"Don't go away from us, Daddy," she said, and sauntered
toward the house. His heart sank.

He waited for Holly. Her hair was pulled back in a loose ponytail. She must have fixed it that way when she left the barn. Her
cheeks were red and wisps of loose hair framed her face. He walked
toward her. He smelled the horses and the sandy dust from the barn
in her hair and clothes. It was something, he thought, to look at her
and not know a single thing that went on in her thoughts all day.

"I'm not used to seeing you home this early." She reached down
and rubbed her inner thigh. "Edward, I wanted to tell you. Tom offered
me a position at the barn. I'm going to train the girls. I need more."

He flinched. "I know you do."

"When I'm at the barn everything is different. I'm completely
engaged. The horses. The girls. Everything else slips away. I suppose all these years I've been jealous."

"Of what?"

"Of you and your work. How much it fills you. How sometimes
you barely need anything else." She moved her key chain from one
hand to the other and it fell to the ground making a clanging, shat-
tering sound.

"That's not true. I've always needed you."

She bent down for her keys and started walking toward the house. "Holly, wait."

She studied him as if for a second seeing in him something she'd forgotten, and for a half a second her face relaxed and she stopped. She looked him up and down the way she did when she caught his eye across a room, or when she saw him coming toward her from a distance, and he felt a pull in his gut. It was still there, that thing between them. A bird chirped and another answered. A squirrel scurried through the garden. Then just as quickly, she moved toward one of her newly planted spruce trees and picked off the dead brown sprigs. He followed her.

"What is it, Edward?"

"Do you think your father would have let you marry me if he knew I'd been married before?"

"Is that what you thought?"

"It wasn't a conscious decision. We were kids."

She cocked her head, interest piqued, and then turned back to the spruce tree, as if to contemplate further what he'd said.

"Is there something going on? Between you and Tom?"

"Tom?" She laughed wistfully. "Everything in training is about getting the rhythm right. Without rhythm and relaxation a horse and rider can't get their communication in synch. You have to time your movement to the horse's feet at the trot. Tom knows the same language. You know what it's like, when someone speaks your language."

She turned away from the tree to meet his look.

"Holly," he started.

"No, Edward. Let's not." She tossed her bag over her shoulder and walked toward the house.

THE AFFAIR WAS held in two tents in the Botanical Gardens. A floating chalkboard invited guests to jot down what they'd like to do someday. *Get the fuck out of here*, Edward thought, looking at the circus of art enthusiasts wearing designer dresses and fashionable tuxes already gathering in clusters near the cocktail bar, feeling uncomfortable in his. He yanked at his collar. It was the last place he wanted to be. At one time the exoticism of the extremely rich had fascinated him; now it bored him. Weeks before the event, though every person of distinction in the art world would be present, he'd preempted the awkwardness and told May he wouldn't be attending the awards dinner. He couldn't imagine sitting with all of them—May, Savan, Reynolds, the gallery's senior publicist, and a few of their younger associates, all flocked around Agnes and Nate.

When Edward mentioned that he wasn't going, Leonard insisted Edward join him at his table. At first Edward had refused but Leonard wouldn't let it go. "I want you to get to know April. Now is as good a time as any to put the two of you together. You're sitting at our table," Leonard said. "I'd love to see the look on Agnes's face, seeing you sitting beside the next winner of the Tanning Prize. Wouldn't it be unbelievable if April gets it?"

Edward had allowed his friend's confidence and enthusiasm to persuade him, though all he could think about was Holly. Was she going to leave him? He didn't know.

The cocktail party was elbow to elbow. Edward was thankful that he did not bump into his colleagues from the gallery. He wondered how many people in the art world knew that he was no longer representing Agnes. A few of his friends greeted him—directors, traders, collectors—clapping him on the back and congratulating him, and Edward nodded. "All good for the gallery." It was the phrase he had chosen to keep anyone from asking or prying any further, and it worked.

Over the top of several heads he made out Savan, dressed to the nines, tapping people on the back as he worked his way through the crowd. For a moment Edward found himself face to face with him and greeted him with a nod. Savan patted him on the back. Edward pushed past.

The centerpieces were beautiful floral arrangements. At each place setting was a meticulously folded napkin. Projections in the front room switched between live video of the red carpet, a 3D "fly-through" video of the new museum, and images of the work of the four finalists. A tall woman in black stockings and black satin short shorts and platform shoes passed by. She looked as if her legs began at her shoulders.

Edward found Leonard's table and the card with his name on it, placed next to April's. On the other side of her sat Leonard, and April's husband, a polite academic, who nodded rather than spoke. Someone said he was a philosopher. April was great company, from a small town in Texas, and, in her own words, feeling like a fish out of water in New York. She preferred working in Texas, where no one knew her. Edward asked her how she got started.

"I don't know why I was driven to paint. I grew up in a trailer park. I sort of felt like the images and colors ran away from me if I didn't try and capture them." Edward liked her immediately.

The screen flashed to one of her pieces. "Incredible," Edward said. "Congratulations."

"Hey, thanks," April twanged.

They stood in front of their chairs, waiting for the guests still staggering in from cocktail hour. A woman draped in Ferragamo brushed past their table. A stream of women dressed in ballgowns crowned with ornamental glitter, with plunging necklines and feather boas, traipsed past. A group of Japanese investment bankers congregated at the bar. An artist couple bent on making a statement, he in long dreadlocks and she in a snakeskin dress so tight it looked painted on, took their seats at a table next to them. An artist who showed in a trendy new gallery in Bushwick (Edward had read about her) tried to insert herself into their conversation by asking Edward if he ever made studio visits. Each finger on her hand had nail polish in a different primary color.

"It's quite a scene, isn't it," Edward said to April, after he managed to dodge the conversation with the artist from Bushwick.

April was dressed in a simple black frock with a red rose tucked into the braid of her blonde hair. "It sure is," she said. "I'm ready to head back to the sticks. I could never make art here." She spoke loud enough for Leonard to hear her. "That's why I have Leonard."

"You're in good hands."

"That's what Leonard says about your artists."

He glanced over at the Mayweather and Darby group, two or three tables away. There they were—the great and famous art couple. Agnes looked radiantly understated, not too beautiful or overly glamorous. She was dressed in tailored slacks and a sleek satin jacket with a soft camisole underneath, her red hair pushed back with a velvet headband. On one side of her was Nate—she clutched his arm. He looked slightly beleaguered, unshaven, perhaps having partied all night, the old guard still trying to hold onto the fort. Planted on the other side of her, Savan leaned back in his seat wearing a broad grin. Nate leaned in to whisper in Agnes's ear. She laughed and kissed him openly on the mouth. Nate rose, loosened a cigarette from the pack he took from his breast pocket, and wandered outside the tent.

Edward's eye caught May's. A yellow and pink diamond necklace circled her neck. She was dressed handsomely in one of her pastel Chanel suits. Her knuckly fingers slipped over her champagne flute and she carefully brought it to her lips. She received his look with an awkward nod and turned to chat with Cynthia, their publicist, who sat beside her. Edward noticed some people at another table look at him and titter behind their wineglasses. Maybe wondering why he wasn't at May's table.

He heard voices coming from the area of the mostly vacant catering tent—the waiters were on the floor briskly serving the entrees. Two men in tuxes were engaged in animated conversation. One leaned over a tray and, using a rolled-up dollar bill, sniffed back a line and then passed the bill to the other. It was Nate, husband of the favorite, and Frederick, chair of the prize committee, and protégé and ass-kisser of the great artist. Edward shook his head. What was to come was inevitable.

He stepped outside the tent, lit up a cigarette, and took it in. Waiters moved in and out. Dishes clashed. Edward looked back and caught Nate's eye. Nate gave him a provocative smile. Edward nodded, turned, stamped his cigarette butt on the ground, and walked away.

He wandered back inside the main tent and sat back down at Leonard's table. Flipped through the program. Sipped his wine. Nate in his ridiculous white scarf and slight paunch strolled back in and made his way through the narrow aisles between the tables with just enough bravado to make sure he was noticed. He took his seat next to Agnes, pinched his nostril, and then slid his hand down Agnes's back and under her jacket, claiming her like a possession before kissing her neck. She smiled at him nervously in return.

Edward glanced back toward the wing of the tent and watched Frederick Jackson lean against a pillar in an attempt to compose himself. He took the speech out of his jacket pocket and approached the podium.

Edward sat back in his chair and prepared himself. He took a deep breath and awaited the performance.

Across the room he spotted Julia. She looked elegant in a spring silk dress, her hair styled in waves around her open and radiant face. Next to her was a man with a firm chin and wide forehead. He watched Julia touch the man's arm and a wave of emotion swept over him. The lights dimmed; everything was becoming clear.

Fredrick announced the prize recipient and the audience gasped. Still caught up thinking of Julia, he looked around to see April push herself up from the table. He was stunned. The first person whose glance he found was Julia, and she looked back at him and grinned.

Applause filled the room. April kissed her husband, gave Leonard a hug, and threaded her way to the podium.

"Holy crap," she boomed, and the audience broke out in laughter. Edward glanced over at Leonard. He nodded approvingly. His eyes skated toward the Mayweather and Darby table. Savan's face had fallen. Edward peered at Agnes—he couldn't help himself— and amid the applauding and cheer and commotion, for the first time since that day at her studio he caught her eye. Really caught her. She was clearly shaken. And in that one moment he saw in her the fear and desperation he remembered from when he first signed her. Then, aware she was being observed, she masked her hurt feelings. Edward looked away. He was not one to gloat. He saw Agnes get up, say a few words to May and Savan, her hand clutched in Nate's. Standing, she looked gaunt and thin, as if she might break.

During the champagne reception, the guests spilling against one another, he felt a tap on his shoulder. It was Julia.

"It looks like it turned out to be a good night for you after all."

He nodded. In her glow he saw that something was different. She seemed complete to him.

Frederick Jackson, with the right amount of scruffy stubble to project a faux-manly look, came by and grabbed Julia by the arm and kissed her on each cheek.

"It's been an age. We have to correct that." He smiled and his big teeth gleamed like a horse's.

"You know Edward, don't you?"

Edward nodded and the two shook hands.

"April Stillman," Julia said. "Why April? I mean, I love her work, but—"

"You know I can't say," Frederick said, taking Julia's hand to his lips to kiss it. "The judges' discussions are privileged. But I'll give you this," he said, raising his head. "You know what Abramović said in her manifesto. You said it yourself, you know, back when we were together." He took a sip of his champagne. "An artist should not fall in love with another artist." He slipped his hand from hers and winked. "April Stillman. She's fantastic. She's a game-changer. Even Nate thinks so," Frederick said, before walking away.

"What did he mean about Abramović?" Edward said, after he left.

"It's what I thought. Nate couldn't stand it if Agnes won the prize."

He searched for Agnes and Nate in the crowd. Nate was leading her by the hand as they walked briskly away from the festivities and toward the runway to exit the tent. Had Nate turned Agnes against him because he feared her work might flower under Edward's direction? Or was it for the money? By making the deal to stay, she'd managed to squeeze them for a larger percentage. Or was it her fear that had undone her? What difference did it make? He shook his head and sighed.

"You're with Roy tonight, aren't you?"

Julia nodded her head in agreement. "He's over there waiting. He hates these affairs, but every once in a while he tolerates them for me. We're doing better."

"Then we haven't really hurt anyone, have we?"

"Haven't we?" Her eyes filled and some unsaid thought passed between them. He watched as she stepped away.

H E'D HAD ENOUGH of the art world, but once alone after the awards ceremony and a nightcap with Leonard and April, melancholy descended as he walked through the cool and deserted streets, the lights turned off in the restaurants, gates pulled down over the shops, to the hotel he'd booked earlier—this time a small boutique hotel—knowing he'd miss the last train. He struggled with the room key and pushed open the heavy door to where the king-size bed with its arranged stiff pillows greeted him. He sank into its sterile comfort.

Throughout the long night he barely slept. His mind flashed intermittently to Holly and Tom at the barn and to other occasions when the two of them had been together, looking for some trace of the intimacy he now believed they shared—he hated the way Tom always cupped Holly's face when he greeted her, calling her "hon." He would have to ride it out, the way he believed Holly had—he was almost sure she suspected something—hoping she'd come back to him. He thought about their marriage. For twenty years he had lived with a woman and he'd never thought his love for her would change and then they had a child and their love deepened and they wanted for this child everything they imagined they should want for a child, when in fact their own childhoods had been imperfect. He thought that all the long years of Annabel's childhood they had set a path to make sure her life was not like either of theirs and in doing so they had lost a certain thread with each other, and then everything fell apart and he'd betrayed her. It gutted him. What it meant and how deeply he would be punished for it he was unsure, because in fact he was certain he would and certain too of how little he knew of Holly just then and he hoped that if their marriage was strong, they might endure this bump in the road, because it occurred to him that though it was a horrific time when everything had slipped and morphed into a shape and form he was unfamiliar with, it was over—everything as he knew it had changed and not changed. It was uncanny. He hoped he wasn't deluding himself. He didn't know anymore. He would dig his heels in. He would not let go of his end. He would be better.

The last time he looked at the clock it was five in the morning. His alarm blared at seven, after he'd finally fallen into a deep sleep, and he could barely drag himself from bed. The room service tray with its picked-over burger and oil-drenched fries, ketchup jelled on the plate, and two empty miniatures of vodka from the minibar greeted him. The state of the room, in its bleak, trashed beauty, brought him back to the present. The entire bloody year he'd been in some kind of demented fog.

He walked briskly to the gallery hoping the fresh air would revive him. He kept his door half shut, closed his blinds, not wanting to greet or see any of his colleagues. He took out the morning paper from his bag and looked in the arts section. There was a photo of April Stillman on the front page. "Outsider Artist Takes The Prize." He read the piece.

> Stillman's visuals, made out of R&W hamburger wrappers, bottle caps, soda cups, and motel signs, combine elements

of assemblage and construction and straddle figuration and abstraction. It isn't postmodern. It is of the moment. She is best known for her large, clumsy-looking sculptures made out of materials found in junkyards. "Going into a junkyard is like entering an art store filled with hundreds of different kinds of paint. It offers endless possibilities. I want to make shapes that can't be described." The images Stillman evokes, defined by her Southern background, are often banal, but unlike the splashy work of Nate Fisher, which also draws upon popular culture, April Stillman's work gets under the skin. You walk around her pieces and you can't get away from them. They don't exist simply as snapshots in the mind; they fill you. "People see what they must see," she said of her work. "Nothing can ever be fully known or held. It's all fluid."

The work melded beauty and ugliness into its own form of authenticity. It was completely its own and could have been made by no other. He must have it for the gallery, he thought. He put the paper down and began doing numbers. May peered in past his half-open door and he motioned for her to enter. She looked at him uncomfortably and then, to clear the tension, she began to laugh. A smile sprang to his lips and he laughed too.

"I owe you an apology," she offered with genuine warmth after the laughter stopped. She was dressed in a knit dress that clung to her bony frame, a string of gray pearls dangling from her neck, with matching oversized earrings and gold bangles clanging on her thin wrists. Wealth could mask disappointment, but not completely.

"I appreciate that. This year hasn't been pleasant."

"I know it hasn't. I should have listened to you."

"Tell me. Last night—how did Agnes take it?"

"Not well. She told Alex she felt let down and quickly left the table. First thing this morning Reynolds called to say they're leaving the gallery."

He shook his head. "It doesn't surprise me."

"She blamed us for not getting the prize. Something about us not doing enough publicity to curry the judges' favor. Savan having neglected her."

"Of course she did," Edward said.

"Even faux marble eventually loses its shimmer. She dumped Savan, too. He's clearing out. He's not the type who stays around to clean up the damage. It's not his style." She remained quiet for a moment and then leaned toward the spreadsheet sprawled over his desk.

"What's this?"

He handed it to her. "I've been going over the numbers. Calculating what we've lost. April Stillman. She has something. I think she's worth our investment."

"Really?" A smile spread across her closed lips. "She's quite a pistol, isn't she?" Her eyes lingered on the paperweight globe of Venice he had bought when he was there for the Biennale. She picked it up and shook it. The snow swirled among the buildings of the miniature city trapped under a dome of glass. They both admired it silently for a moment.

They heard a ruckus outside on the avenue, people shouting and chanting. They moved toward the window to look. Beneath them crowds had gathered.

"Look, it's a parade." May squinted to look past the sun's glare. Together they watched the decorative floats move past. "It's all a bit of performance, isn't it?" May said.

HE TOOK THE earlier train home. He pulled up to the weathered house. Holly's SUV was already there. He sat in his car for a moment watching the clouds break apart and the purple sky slowly darken, and turned off the engine. When Annabel was little, she and Holly would wait for him to come home. The minute they heard the car engine shut off, Annabel would run down the driveway to greet him and Holly followed behind, grinning.

He went inside to find her. He wanted to explain himself but wasn't sure how or if words were what was required. Maybe divine truth was love in the most down-to-earth, mundane form, like moments in which he felt at peace with himself, grilling steaks for his family, or watching the light in Annabel's eyes when she rode.

The house was eerily quiet.

"Holly?"

He walked through the living room, then the kitchen and the den. He went upstairs and pushed open their bedroom door, then Annabel's. Upstairs was completely dark. The floors creaked under his feet.

"Holly," he called again.

A vision of himself as a lonely man adrift and without purpose, busily trying to fill his days, flashed before him. Fear flooded him. He ran down the stairs.

"Holly. Where are you?"

He sat on the sofa to collect himself. He thought of Holly and Tom again and the look that passed between them. He told himself that what he saw was the familiar intimacy between two old friends. It had to be. A flapping sound coming from the screened porch drew him out. A bird was caught there. The glass door must have been left open and the wind slammed it shut, trapping the bird between the glass and the screen. It thrashed its body against the glass, then quieted for a moment and started again. It would kill itself. He fled through the back door and around the house and opened the screen and the bird flew out, its wings nicking the top of his head as it made its escape.

The sky darkened rapidly and the wind rustled the trees in the yard. The rain came down like sharp pins. It smelled of moss and dew and huge puddles quickly pooled in the yard. The white wings of moths seeking shelter zigzagged in the porch light. He felt something papery and thin fall on his arm and swatted it, a dead moth, withered and brown. Maybe Holly was in the garden or the basement and he had missed her.

"Holly," he called, walking around the house, his soft leather loafers sinking into the muddy earth. He pushed back a lock of thinning hair from his head. He was into the heart of his life, past the point of reinvention, a man who would have to accept who he was and what he had accomplished. But without Holly to share his life with it would be unbearable.

"Holly."

The rain subsided to a drizzle and then burst into a sudden, angry downpour all at once, all over again. In a matter of minutes he was completely soaked. He went back inside dripping wet.

The silence and stillness in the house made his blood run cold. The screen door blew open again; weightless and untethered, it banged back and forth.

"Holly," he called again. "Holly, where are you?"

He went down to the basement. He couldn't find her and came back up through the kitchen.

"I'm here," she said, wearing a dripping yellow slicker, one of the kittens in her hands. "I was in the garage. I wanted to make sure the kittens were okay once the storm began. What's wrong? You're soaked. You look like you saw a ghost."

She took a hand towel draped over the oven handle and handed it to him. "Look, she's going to make it," Holly said, holding up the black runt. She'd filled out and her coat had grown soft and full.

He looked into the smooth margin of Holly's forehead and into her open, youthful eyes and absorbed the steadiness of her being as if he were coming out of a long and fractured dream. He saw love in her eyes. It wasn't something that could be mistaken. He remembered when he was a boy and his father took him to a cornfield maze in autumn before Halloween. He had walked through the maze's twists and turns with his father and told him he'd race him to the end, and slowly released his hold on his father's coarse and gentle hand. His father went one way and he went the other, running as fast as he could. The cornstalks were above his head and when he looked up all he could see was the sky and around him the cornstalk walls. He took a turn and then another; everything looked the same. He didn't know which way to go. He ran breathlessly down the rows, making one turn after another, and found himself back where he started. He began to panic and breathed heavily, and then, just when he thought he would never find his way, he saw a cone of light and followed it and there was his father, waiting for him at the end of the maze. He remembered thinking no one would ever love him as his father had.

ACKNOWLEDGMENTS

E VERY WRITER NEEDS a second (or third, or fourth) pair of eyes. Thank you generous readers, Rebecca Schultz, Deidre O'Dwyer, Helen Schulman, Lelia Ruckenstein, Diane Goodman and Bill Clegg. Thank you Howard Norman, especially. Thank you Sanda Bragman Lewis for your support. Thank you Sarah Chalfant and Jin Auh for your steadfast belief and good council. Thank you Dan Smetanka for your passion, dedication, and keen editorial eye. We should all be so lucky. Thank you to my copyeditor, Allegra Huston. Thank you team Counterpoint: Charlie Winton, Kelly Winton, Rolph Blythe, Claire Shalinsky, Megan Fishmann. Thank you, husband and son, always.